Acclaim for Pet

The SECOND COMING
of MAVALA SHIKONGO

"Mavala Shikongo is one of the most deftly rendered and unforgettable characters in recent fiction. The men of Goas fall in love with her and the reader is helpless, too — she is a revolution unto herself. Orner's book is always elegant and always true, and its wistful and even hallucinatory mood haunts the mind for months after finishing it."
— Dave Eggers

"Orner writes with confident economy, evoking and peopling his parched, lonely world with patient detail. . . . His thrift only heightens the longing that vibrates throughout *The Second Coming of Mavala Shikongo*. Orner has written a starvation diary about desire, with as much sexual tension as a bodice buster."
— Mark Schone, *New York Times Book Review*

"As a work of African provenance, *The Second Coming of Mavala Shikongo* will take its place alongside Saul Bellow's *Henderson the Rain King* and Graham Greene's *The Heart of the Matter*. But it is a book unlike any I have ever read, a miraculous feat of empathy that manages to unearth — in the unlikeliest of spots — the infinite possibilities of the human heart. . . . Orner is incapable of dishonoring his characters. He treats all of them — even the minor figures — with a fierce humanity." — Steve Almond, *Boston Globe*

"It is rare that you come across a talent as singular as Orner's. Here, in his first novel, is a story never heard before, told in language no one else could write. It is a magnificent creation."
— Andrew Sean Greer

"Beautiful. . . . Orner is a miraculous writer with a stunning ability to compel the reader softly by ever-increasing increments. . . . This novel so evokes the place and its people that, by the end of the book, readers will find themselves reluctantly brushing the sandy loam of Goas off their feet to the reverberating voices of its inhabitants."

— *Library Journal*

"In chapters wrought with imagination and heart, at once talismanic and heartbreaking, dark and yet riddled with iridescence, *The Second Coming of Mavala Shikongo* is both a revelation and a joy — a stunning debut novel."

— Chris Abani

"Orner writes with such beauty that the reader cannot help but be carried along."

— Robin Vidimos, *Denver Post*

"Exquisite. . . . By presenting this tale in so many broken but beautiful shards, Orner has done the seemingly impossible: His novel becomes a kind of living village."

— John Freeman, *San Francisco Chronicle*

"It is a work on Africa that belongs in Africa. . . . Though it is universal, it is grounded in Namibian realities, including the guerrilla war, its accomplishments and abuses, and even the German genocide in 1904. . . . Unforgettable characters."

— Sheridan Griswold, *Namibian Weekender*

"Required reading because it is a book of such enviable brilliance that it is, I think, the standard by which all writing of this southern African region should be set. . . . Orner has a poet's generous soul and he somehow frees us from our skins (black or white), from our genders, our wars, our hunger. . . . Heady, exultant stuff."

— Alexandra Fuller, *Salon*

"The lyricism of Orner's staccato style reaches symphonic heights."
— Annie Tomlin, *Time Out Chicago*

"Brings close those far from the centers of power. . . . The weight of the brutal colonial and apartheid past is always there, but the freedom story is never reverential, and the taut vignettes, anguished and sometimes hilarious, are about ordinary people now. There are scenes that will stay with you forever."
— Hazel Rochman, *Booklist*

"Peter Orner's novel is insightful, believable, unbelievable, funny, and not funny at all. . . . Whether readers know his amazing *Esther Stories* or not, they should run right out and buy *The Second Coming of Mavala Shikongo*."
— Ann Beattie

"Quirky, lyrical, comical, full-blown. . . . A gifted short-story writer gives us his first book-length work of fiction, and does so with flair and panache. Let's give thanks that God wasn't so angry with Namibia that he didn't cut away the tongues of its tough inhabitants, or the good ear of the American fiction writer who fell in love with the land."
— Alan Cheuse, *Chicago Tribune*

"I read *The Second Coming of Mavala Shikongo* this week and it's amazing. . . . Great novels can be hard to find and sometimes we have to read a lot of good novels to find one. I thought I would save you the time."
— Stephen Elliott, author of *Happy Baby*, in the *Huffington Post*

"The sweeping power of storytelling lies at the heart of this transcendent debut, an insightful and revelatory novel told with authority, historical practicality, and a palpable sense of wonder."
— Connie Ogle, *Miami Herald*

ALSO BY PETER ORNER

Esther Stories

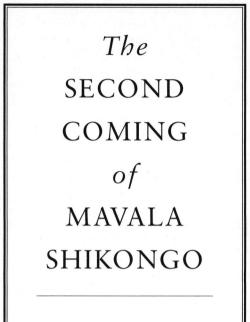

The

SECOND

COMING

of

MAVALA

SHIKONGO

A NOVEL

Peter Orner

BACK BAY BOOKS
Little, Brown and Company
New York   Boston   London

Back Bay Books / Little, Brown and Company
Hachette Book Group USA
237 Park Avenue, New York, NY 10169
Visit our Web site at www.HachetteBookGroupUSA.com

Originally published in hardcover by Little, Brown and Company, April 2006
First Back Bay paperback edition, May 2007

The characters and events in this book are fictitious.
Any similarity to real persons, living or dead, is coincidental
and not intended by the author.

Drawings by Eric Orner

Grateful acknowledgment is made to *Epoch,* the *Paris Review,* and *Ploughshares,*
where portions of this novel appeared in earlier form.

The lines of verse quoted on page 111 are from "Hosties Noires" by L. S. Senghor
(1948). The description of the plant *Wunderbusch* on page 275 is from
The Central Namib Desert, South West Africa by Richard F. Logan,
published by the National Academy of Sciences (1960).

Library of Congress Cataloging-in-Publication Data

Orner, Peter.
    The second coming of Mavala Shikongo : a novel / Peter Orner — 1st ed.
      p.   cm.
    HC ISBN 978-0-316-73580-3
    PB ISBN 978-0-316-06633-4
    1. Americans — Namibia — Fiction.   2. Boys — Education — Fiction.
3. Catholic schools — Fiction.   4. Women teachers — Fiction.
5. Single mothers — Fiction.   6. Namibia — Fiction. I. Title.

PS3615.R58S43   2006
813'.6 — dc22   2005024473

10 9 8 7 6 5 4 3 2 1

Q-FF

Book designed by JoAnne Metsch

Printed in the United States of America

FOR

Dantia Maur

We cannot speak with one voice, as we are scattered.

—HOSEA KUTAKO (1870–1970)

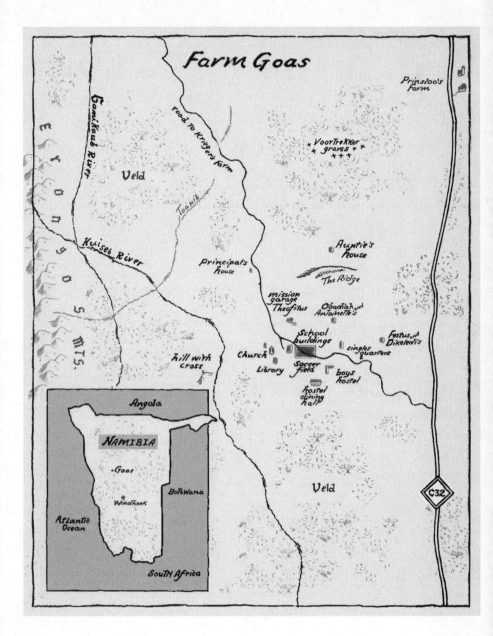

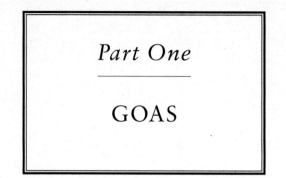

Part One

GOAS

1

THE TAR ROAD

Boys stand with road-sore feet holding cardboard suitcases. They stand clustered, but not in a group. They're not together. They don't talk into the wind; they only wait on the brake lights that so rarely happen. Still, every new car or bakkie or combi or lorry is a new hope, rising and dying like a beating heart glowing and then spending itself on the pavement, only to live again when the next one comes. Out there in their best clothes, trying to get to the school deep in the veld. At certain moments in the early afternoon the tar road looks like it's burning. A boy kneels and sniffs. There's always one who thinks he can tell how much longer it will be by smelling the road.

"Stupid," another says.

"Not stupid, science. It's about air currents near the pavement's surface. They change when —"

"Ai, go on."

"Where? Go on where?"

They're hungry, but you don't want to pull out food, because no one would want to be caught chewing if the miracle of car does stop. Imagine a comfortable ride in a bucket seat with the radio playing. They keep their bread in their pockets. Boys have it worst. They are chosen last, after old mammies, mothers with babies, old men. Most of the time their only option is a lorry. Lorries don't stop, they only slow down, just long enough for the boys to toss their bundles and leap, before the driver shifts gears and accelerates again. *Klim op!* Then they huddle against each other in the wind and wait for it to be over, as the lorry gains speed and begins to cross bridge after bridge over the dry rivers.

2

POHAMBA

He was a big man and he prayed out loud in a small bed. Through the wall, his face in the mattress, and still we heard him.

> *Out of the deep I call*
> *To Thee, O Lord, to Thee*
> *Before Thy throne of grace I fall.*
> *Be you merciful to me . . . Damn you, to me . . .*

During the day he denounced God as residual colonialist propaganda. "Listen, if He was opium, I'd stuff him in a pipe and smoke Him." Pohamba. Resident Catholic school blasphemer, atheist, revolutionary, provocateur, math teacher. Even he turned to a higher power when the long veld night closed us in. Who else could deliver him from such a place? A farm in the desert? And what kind of god would put a farm in the desert? Pohamba was a man out of options. All traditional and earthly means had failed. He'd sent countless letters to the Ministry of Education begging for a post in a town, any backwater dorp would do. *Dear Comrade, I'll even accept a position south of Windhoek in order to do my share for this budding democracy.*

Every one of them went unanswered. He often conjured those letters, talked about them as if they were castaways washed up on some bureaucrat's desk. And when he got going, a little Zorba in his veins, he'd describe the bureaucrat, Deputy Minister So-and-So. Meneer Deputy Minister Son of Somebody Important in the Movement! Some bastard who spent the war years in Europe while the rest of us sat here *ja baasing* P. W. Botha. He'd give his bureaucrat a smooth, freshly shaved face and a fat-cat corner office in the Sanlam Building. A wristwatch big as a Volkswagen. And a secretary, of course, in a chafing skirt. White. Make her a white secretary. And he'd imagine his letters, his babies, sitting stacked neat, unread, ignored. "Like to burn that office," he'd say. "Watch Meneer Deputy Minister Son of Somebody Important melt. Secretary too. Both of them black as char in the morning."

Nights were different. And some nights it wasn't Jesus he'd beg to but his mother. These were the longest. It wasn't that he kept me up when he talked to his mother. It was that I couldn't hear him. Even with our walls made of envelope, I had to press a coffee cup to the wall to listen. *Mama oh Mama . . .*

She was buried, he once said, behind a garage on a farm north of Otavi.

The hours drag on. Then the inevitable. Through the wall Pohamba moans low. The bedsprings noisy for a while before the death silence of small relief.

But there were, weren't there, also afternoons when you could have almost called him happy? Pohamba on a rock outside our rooms, cooking bloodwurst, thick German plumpers he bought from the butcher Schmidsdorf in Karibib. Pohamba whistling. His tape player spewing that horrid Afrikaner disco folk. Tinny synthesized drumbeats accompanied by sexy panting.

Saturday languoring. Wind, sand, boredom, sweat, visions of sausages. Eating our only glory then. The rest of us loll in the sweaty shade while Pohamba forks bloodwurst. We lick our fingers, slowly. Pohamba moving in time. A big man but graceful. His feet plap the dust. The rocks beneath our heads get hotter. Sleep refuses. Pohamba bobs. He skids. He twirls, juts, swags. He wiggles a booty at us. In the pan, in the holy grease, our beloveds fatten and splurt.

3

THE VOLUNTEER

A brother from the diocese drove me out there from Windhoek. His name was Brother Hermanahildis. He was a silent man with a bald, sunburned head. The single thing he said to me in four hours was "I am not a Boer, I am pure Dutch. I was born in The Hague." He drove like a lunatic. I watched the veld wing by, and the towns that were so far between. Brakwater, Okahandja, Wilhelmstal. Brother Hermanahildis seemed to be suffering from an excruciating toothache. At times he took both hands off the wheel and pulled on his face. I was relieved when we reached Karibib and he turned onto a gravel road heading south. Eventually, he let me off at a wind-battered tin sign — FARM GOAS — and told me to follow the road, that the mission was just beyond the second ridge. When you get there, Brother Hermanahildis said, go and see the Father directly. *Ta-ta*.

With a suitcase in each hand, one backpack on my back, another on my stomach, I followed the road, a rock-strewn double-track across the veld. There were a number of ridges. I looked for one that might be considered a second one. The short rocky hills made it impossible to see what was ahead on the road, although in the distance I could see a cluster of smallish mountains rising. A few crooked, bony trees here and there. Strawlike grass grew like stubble up out of the gravel. Somehow I thought a purer desert might have been more comforting. Where were the perfect rippled dunes? Where was the startling arid beauty? These plants looked like they'd rather be dead. I listened to the crunch of my own feet as I shuffled up and over ridges. There was no second ridge. There would never be a second ridge.

*   *   *

An hour or so later, sweat-soaked, miserable, I stood, weighted and wobbly, and looked down on a place where the land swooped into a kind of valley, a flat stretch of sand and gravel. There was a group of low-slung buildings painted a loud, happy yellow. There was a hill with a tall white cross on top. *Hallelujah!* As best I could I bumbled down the road until I reached a cattle gate made from bedsprings lashed to a post. The gate was latched closed by a complicated twist of wire. As I struggled with the wire, a rotund man in a khaki suit moved slowly but inevitably down the road toward me, as if being towed by his own stomach. When he reached the other side of the gate he stopped. He faced me for a moment before he spoke much louder than he needed to. "Howdy."

"Howdy," I said.

"I see you are having some trouble with our gate."

"A little."

"In fact, you are unable to open it?"

"No, actually I can't."

"Of course not. You're the volunteer?"

"Yes."

"Volunteer of what?"

"Pardon?"

He wore large glasses. Behind them his eyes were tiny, distant, and his head seemed far too small for his body. Behind him, up the road, a group of boys in powder-blue shirts had gathered to watch us. Under a lone and scraggled tree, a bored cow gazed at me in that eerie, death-announcing way cows have of looking right through you.

"And your name might be?"

"Larry Kaplanski."

He pumped my hand from the other side of the cattle gate.

"Pleasure, Mr. Kaplansk. So very good of you —"

"Kaplanski."

His big head winced. He swatted a fly off his ear.

"And your qualifications, Mr. Kaplansk?"

"Qualifications?"

He took off his glasses and examined me. Without them his eyes got even smaller, receded into his head as if an invisible thumb had pushed them in like buttons.

"I see. And what have you brought for us?"

I stared at him. Even with all the shit I'd lugged —

"To be expected!" he boomed. "You came under the presumption that you yourself will be of use to us? Oh, erroneous! Oh, so erroneous!"

"But —"

"Be this as it may, Mr. Kaplansk. Of course it would have been far more advantageous to our development, yes, to our *development,* had you placed cash in an envelope and, well, to be frank, mailed it! Goas, Private Bag 79, Karibib, Namibia, 9000! Alas! You didn't!" He turned and raised a thick, baggy hand and swept it across everything in sight, the blue-shirted boys, the cow, the infinite veld — all of it dry, everything everywhere dry.

"Brother Hermanahildas told me to see the Father."

"Brother who?"

"From The Hague, Brother Hermana —"

"Listen." He grasped the gate with both hands as if he were preparing to vault it. Then he leaned toward me and whispered, "Have you not heard? No man can serve two masters, Mr. Kaplansk." He backed away, appraised me again, gnawing the inside of his cheek. "Do you understand the parameters as they've been succinctly explained this day of our Lord, March the sixth, nineteen hundred and ninety-one?"

I nodded frantically.

"Very well! As long as you're here, you'll teach Standard Six. English and History." He about-faced, whistled once, as if he were followed by a platoon (and it was true, always the principal commanded an invisible army), and marched up the road toward the cluster of school buildings. Some boys came down and helped me with the gate. The cow, without taking its eyes off me, took a long, long piss.

4

—

CLASSROOM

They stand up when I walk into the room. Every morning, first period, they leap out of their chairs. *Goed morro, Teacher.* And every morning, my fraudulence more transparent, I plead, *Sit down. I beg you guys.*

So cold in the shadows and so unbearably hot in the sun, and no in between. I watch the day rise, then blare, then finally leak away through the cracked and broken glass. The boys sit in a swath of dusty light with their foreheads sweating but their feet still cold. The boys who wore their shoes were quietest. The ones who went without, who conserved their shoes for church or soccer, would rub their dry, chapped feet together, and you'd hear it all through class like a chorus of saws.

Rubrecht, Nestor, Jeremiah, Gideon, Sackeus, Albertus, Demus, Mumbwanje, Kalumbo, Magnus, Fanuel (coughing, always coughing, always apologizing for it), Stevo, Nghidipo, Ichobod . . . Later in the term, Fanuel will spend two weeks at the clinic at Usakos. Bloody lung, Sister Ursula will call it. After Usakos, Fanuel will be transferred to Windhoek General Hospital, and from there we will lose track of him.

But right now another boy, one of the smallest Standard Sixes, Magnus Axahoes (his feet don't yet touch the floor), raises his hand and stands and whispers, "May I, the toilet, Teacher?"

"You may."

Magnus walks out of the classroom, then runs across the courtyard, his feet kicking up sand that seems to rise but not fall into the now stark light.

5

THE C-32

I remember the slow roll of a road that seems flat. How it suddenly dips into dry sloots I'd forgotten were there, and that swooning that happens in my stomach. I also think of the old woman who sold rocks at a small wooden table. Who did she sell them to? She sat at a place where the veld seemed to repeat itself, where there was no sense of the land passing, or even of time. Nothing in either direction but fence-line and veld, and then there she is by the side of the road, at the top of a rise. You don't see her until you are upon her. She's there, waiting. Everything about her has shriveled in the sun but her hands. They seem to have grown bigger than her face, and she sits there, lording over the common rocks she calls gems. That's what her sign says: GEMS 4 SALE. She doesn't shout, wave, or cajole. She lets the truth of the sign speak for itself. Those enormous gnarled hands hovering over the table as if she's trying to levitate it. And then she's gone — or we're gone. We never stopped, not one time, all the times we went back and forth along that road. We never even slowed down. Turn your head and she's a shroud of dust.

6
—

WALLS

In the beginning, none of the other teachers would much talk to me. As I had apparently come to Goas on my own volition, I was suspect. Those first weeks I spent a lot of time cowering in my room in the singles quarters, pretending to write tediously detailed lesson plans.

Mine was the room assigned to teachers who came and went. Rooms in the singles quarters were square boxes, each with one window set low in the wall. From bed, I lived eye-level with the veld. My view was of the toilet houses, and beyond them the Erongo Mountains that would always be too far to walk to.

The teacher who'd lived in my room before me had papered the walls with the German beer calendars that came free in the *Windhoek Advertiser*. Everywhere you looked were shirtless blonde buxoms in tight shorts. There was one girl in nothing but a red bandanna and a Stetson staring down from the ceiling above the bed, her breasts like about-to-be-dropped bombs. One day I ripped her down, and was tearing off the others when there came a knock on the wall. Then a voice, my neighbor's, Teacher Pohamba's: "What are you doing, Teacher?"

"I thought I'd clean up a little."

The noise of him lifting himself out of bed. He opened his door and came over to my window and squatted down. Then he stuck his head through the torn screen. Teacher Pohamba yawned at me. It was meant, I think, to be a sympathetic, comradely yawn, but it came out too big, like a kind of maw. "Hand over the tits, Teacher."

I gave him the scraps and he stuffed them in his shirt pocket, but he remained outside my window. Teacher Pohamba pitied me. Me standing there on the cement floor in my Walgreen's shower shoes. "Go to sleep," he said finally. "Don't you know it's siesta?"

When the first study-hour triangle rang, he came to my window again and told me to follow him. Together, we walked across the soccer field to the married teachers' housing, to the circle of plastic chairs in front of Teacher Obadiah's. The old man was holding court. Everybody was still drowsy from sleep and only half listening. Teacher Obadiah wasn't as old as he liked to consider himself, but he was one of those people whose age baffles. He might have been fifty-five; he might have been seventy-five. He reveled in the crevices of his face and his white hair. That day he had a week-old *Namibian* on his knee and was lamenting a story about corruption in the Finance Ministry of the new government. The only thing the white government did fairly, Obadiah said, was teach the black government how to steal.

Pohamba drummed his cheeks awhile and said, "Politicians: black, white, bowlegged — what's the difference? Let's hear the weather."

Obadiah flipped some pages and read. "In the north, hot. On the coast, hot. In the east, very hot. In the central interior —"

"Have mercy!"

Eventually, Obadiah turned my way and tried to bring me into the fold of the conversation. He asked me what I thought of noble Cincinnatus.

"Who?"

"You say you hail from Cincinnati?"

"Yes."

Obadiah made a roof over his eyes with his hand and peered at me. "Well then, of course, I speak of its namesake, the great Roman general Cincinnatus. Surely, you must —"

"Sorry, I —"

"And you have come here to teach our children history?"

"Is he in the Standard Six curriculum?"

"By God, if he isn't he should be! Gentleman farmer, reluctant warrior, honest statesman. When people needed him, he ruled. When the crisis was over, he returned to a quiet life on his farm. Not a farm like this, a proper farm. Had Cincinnatus lived here, he wouldn't have come back. He would have done anything to avoid such a fate — even, I daresay, become a tyrant." Obadiah put his hands on his knees and leaned forward on his plastic chair.

"Why are you here, young Cincinnatus?"

"I have no idea."

"He tore down Nakale's calendars," Pohamba said.

Obadiah stood and began to pace the dust, his hands behind his back. "The beer girls? Interesting. I must admit that on occasion I peeped in there to have a look. I too once had desires. I have since forgotten what they were." He wheeled and faced me. "Why did you do it? Were you intending to moralize?"

"I wanted to be alone," I said.

"Ah!" Obadiah brought his hands together as if to applaud me, but stopped short and whispered, more to himself than to me, "Don't worry. You're alone."

7

MORAL TALE

Morning noise: The murmurs of the boys coming from church, the slap of their bare feet on the concrete porchway, the slow *whish whish* of the lazy classroom sweepers, boys on punishment from the day before.

Every morning meeting, before school, the principal told a moral tale. We'd stand more or less at attention, half listening, gripping our coffee, watching the unburnished gray light leak through the staff room's single window. Not the sun; full sun wouldn't happen for an eternity.

Often the principal's stories came from the Bible. Other times the lessons were taken from the newspaper or from some gossip he picked up at the Hotel Rossman in Karibib. Most of the time — wherever they came from — they were somehow related to the principal's guilt over one of his own vices. That morning he must have been suffering pangs over his embezzlement from the school till.

He wore a different tie for each day of the week. It's how we knew what day it was. As he spoke, his Adam's apple thrashed beneath his yellow Wednesday tie, as if, as Obadiah once said, his poor conscience was trying to escape his lying throat.

"Listen, colleagues," he commanded. "Seriously and piously. This happened near Angra Pequena a hundred years ago, but indeed, it could have happened yesterday." He paused and swallowed, allowed this thundering fact to settle upon us. "Let us say it did happen yesterday. Yes, yesterday. Three skeletons were found in the unforgiving sands of the Namib. God didn't create our desert. Hark!

14

The Namib was born of God's forgetting. He'd always meant to come back and put something here, but alas, he didn't. So it goes with this country. Let us return to today's tale: Two of the skeletons were found together, the third on a dune about a kilometer away. All three were partially covered by sand and of similar age and weathering."

He paused and eyed us all, one by one. He lingered at Pohamba, who was teetering, fighting hard to keep his eyes open and his knees from buckling.

"Erastus?" the principal said.

Pohamba had a new girl in Karibib. He hadn't landed on his own bed in two days. He still had on his white ducks and silky disco shirt #7. The principal was the only one at Goas who called him Erastus.

"Erastus, will you summarize?"

Pohamba licked his chapped lips. "Three skeletons," he said. "Two found together. The other not far away. It is curious. In fact, I would even say it smells."

The principal resumed, not satisfied, but not willing to derail the tale at this point for the sake of telling Pohamba what he thought of him. "Indeed. The first two skeletons were found with their heads staved in. The head of the third was uncrushed. And in the thin whitened bones that once enjoyed the skin of a fist, the third held" — he pointed a vicious finger at Pohamba — "what?"

"His member," Pohamba said.

Even the principal laughed, his cheeks filling up and exhaling like bellows. The problem was, we laughed longer, and whenever that happened, he changed sides. He ducked under the table and returned with his shoe and proceeded to pound, Khrushchev-like, for order.

"No, Erastus, he didn't need that anymore. And mark me: *Yours too will wither.* No, I speak of something far more lasting. In the hand of the third skeleton . . . diamonds! After he murdered his two friends, he was going to leave the desert a king. In the wind and sand, he gripped those immaculate stones. Imagine how tight and with what hope he must have clutched them in the long Namib night!"

Now the principal guffawed, happy to pawn his shame off on

someone else. "Oh, you smelled something, Erastus." He brought his fingers to his nose and gave them a smell. "Oh yes. And I do also. Satan lurks this morning. I smell corruption. I smell evil. Is not lust merely another form of avarice? God forgot the Namib, but he remembered to punish the third man, and He, in All His Glory, won't forget grown teachers who chase young strumpets and neglect their duties to learners either. When are you going to be too old, Erastus? For the love of God, woe unto you, woe!"

The principal took a breath, crossed himself.

"And yet, I do forgive you, Erastus, I forgive you your filth, your rot, your disease."

That afternoon, we climbed up the hill and sat beneath the cross. I watched the Erongos retreat beyond the blurry sheen of afternoon heat. The sky was like watered-down milk. The goats wandered languidly along the paths in the veld. And we talked and we talked. Pohamba said he had a brother Josiah who worked for CDM in the south and got caught stealing diamonds he'd shoved up his ass. Obadiah said, You've got more brothers than the principal has sins to atone.

"Truth," Pohamba said. "They caught him on X-ray. He's still in prison at Oranjemund. That was four and half years ago."

"How'd they get them out of there?" I asked.

"Laxatives."

This all got Obadiah started in on the diamond fields and how Adolph Lüderitz bought a tenth of the world's wealth for three hundred breechloaders and a wagonload of cheese. And of course Vilho — who everybody said still had faith in God (that's how people described him, *Vilho who still has faith in God*) — couldn't help himself from adding that Lüderitz drowned in the Orange River after his boat tipped over. "He never got rich," Vilho said. "The man didn't live to sell a single stone."

"And his descendants?" Obadiah shouted. "And his descendants' descendants' descendants?"

But Pohamba didn't want to talk about history or the wicked getting their just deserts or God's sense of justice. He wanted to talk about his brother Josiah, who was still in prison at Oranjemund for shoving diamonds up his ass. "One carat," he said, and turned around, bent over, and talked to us, his big melon head between his thighs. "Or two?"

Vilho rubbed his hands together. He wanted to pray for the deliverance of Pohamba's soul, but wouldn't dare do it in front of him.

8

A SPOT NORTHWEST
OF OTJIMBINGWE

*You claim that you are sorry that I do not accept German
protection. You seem to think that I am guilty even of this . . .
This is my answer: I have never in my life seen the German
emperor and am sure he has never seen me.*

HENDRIK WITBOOI, 1885

*In the event you should intend to fight me further, I have to ask
your Highness to provide me with two more boxes of Henri
Martini cartridges so that I can respond to your attack. So far we
have not really fought each other . . . A great and honest and
civilized nation such as yours should not stop ammunition for its
enemy. In the event that I should have enough ammunition, you
are welcome to conquer me.*

HENDRIK WITBOOI, 1893

The story goes that it was the most savage raid on colonial
forces in the whole bloody history of German South-West
Africa. Hendrik Witbooi and his men — answering a call from
God — made a surprise attack on the German base at Otjimbingwe. Five thousand imperial troops led by Herman Goering,
hapless father of the more successful future reich marshal, were stationed in the barracks, fast asleep on a sweltering summer evening.
The raid was so successful that Goering himself was forced to flee
and, in what must have been a particular humiliation, reduced to
begging the protection of the British garrison at Walfish Bay. Not

surprisingly, the Germans did not allow the attack to go unanswered and stormed back three months later, following the arrival of fresh recruits from the Fatherland. Witbooi retreated to the uninhabitable sand wastes and clay buttes northwest of Otjimbingwe.

One Monday morning Obadiah, carrying a long stick, marched his class, thirty-eight Standard Threes in those powder-blue button-downs, holding hands, two by two, away from school, up the dry riverbed. After trudging through the sand for what felt to the boys like twelve days, Obadiah abruptly stopped. He jammed his stick into the sand.

"Cherubim! Who can tell me what makes this place significant?"

None of the boys said a word. They tried not to even breathe. At that time of day, late morning in March, everything looked bleached. The sand, trees, bushes, even the cows, were all the color of plaster. Above, the sky allowed for no variation in the glare. All around the boys was semidesert sameness, and they were hungry, so so hungry. Teacher had made them skip morning break for this expedition. Pocked across the dry riverbed were hoof- and footprints accumulated since the last time it rained. Plus all the goat shit in neat little piles, like tiny pyramids. What here could be worth all that walking?

"Fortitude," Obadiah said. "An important word, leprechauns. It means having the courage to fight when your body says, *Asseblief makker*. No more, I beseech You. Hendrik Witbooi had it. Write it in your notebooks when you return to class. Use it in a sentence. For instance, 'Witbooi had fortitude, indeed.' Look at this staff, my children, alone, here in the sand, silent as a pillar. Even fortitude needs to rest sometimes. The great Hendrik Witbooi, after fleeing the garrison at Otjimbingwe, rode northwest toward Goas — yes, even Goas has a place in history — and he stopped at this precise spot."

The boys looked languidly at the stick leaning crookedly out of the sand.

"This spot! Even fortitude must stop and take a breath of pure desert air, this air of freedom. Listen, boys. You hear them? The *Schutztruppe* in menacing pursuit. Think on it, little men of Goas. Of being chased, of riding for your lives. But think also of all those killed in their beds. Yes, criminals, colonizers, but also men with beating hearts. Death to them, absolutely. But with their heads on their pillows? Was it not something Witbooi might have learned from the Germans themselves? Take a pause. A great man rested here. Was it a victory?"

Obadiah seized the stick, hoisted it to his shoulder, and scanned the line of boys.

"Hendrik Witbooi was the greatest shot with a gun since Jonker Afrikaner's father." Obadiah lowered his rifle. "He was also a Christian down to his eighty-year-old feet. I repeat, think on it. A heroic act of independence? Certainly. But the beginning of a time of slaughter as well. I bring you here to Witbooi's place of rest to remember the price of one man's greatness."

With this, Obadiah thrust the stick back into the sand and began to walk slowly away, back toward the school. Over his shoulder he called, "I provide no answers."

They stood and watched him. They'd heard about this from the boys in the grades above, about drunk Master Obadiah's stick in the veld, but now that they were out there alone, they did what other boys before them had also done. They stared at it. Now more awake, they stared at that stick. All thirty-eight boys, silently, still gripping hands. One boy considered knocking it down. Another thought of taking it and using it to smack Reginald Eiseb, his enemy. Another, of riding on it, as he'd seen a white witch do in a picture book. But one boy, Jacobus Tivute, listened for the pant of a hunted man and actually started to hear it. The noise was coming from the boy whose hand he held, an asthmatic, but it didn't matter. Jacobus was hearing that awful gasping. The Germans will hunt Witbooi to the end of the earth. Then they'll shoot him seventeen times at Vaalgras. He'd heard that story from his father. Looking around at the cragged trees, the tangled patches of sharp bushes, the wide, waterless river snaking away ahead, Jacobus thought, Bravery is more hell than cowardice. He hoped to grow taller and never have either, and he swore to himself he'd remember this. Then Jacobus said a short prayer asking God, politely, to have mercy and let him leave this desert place one day so he could go live in a town. After that he turned from the stick and, with his wheezing partner in tow, followed his teacher.

9

ANTOINETTE

Sometimes, as now, on the edge of morning, she hears the stifled cries of the Hebrew women giving birth in secret. Pharaoh's men are tossing boys into the Nile. Antoinette wakes and stands in the dark and prays for them, and for her own lost, her first, a daughter, taken away before she had a name. Aren't daughters supposed to be allowed to live?

She bows her head to pray, but she will never kneel. Not in church, not anywhere. Since she was a child, she's known this. To ask something of God is not a humble act. It's a demand. Why try to disguise it by doing it on your knees?

Eyes closed, she listens for the birth cries of all the lost children. With her rheumatic fingers, she makes her hands into a basket; but she will never kneel. She waits for the noise of the cries to fade, the voice of her own blood and the blood of so many others.

They never named her. You don't name a child until you hear it scream, and this one was born silent. The death certificate, the only relic holy enough to store in her Bible, is written in highfalutin Afrikaans. *Herewith on said day the following unnamed personage . . .* They paid ten rands for it. Ten rands for a fact anybody could tell just by listening to her not scream. Still, there are days when she takes it out and rereads. The paper is worn away from rubbing. At the folds are dirty creases; the certificate is breaking apart. She thinks how it must have lasted longer than her daughter's bones.

Born in peace, weren't you?

*   *   *

She leaves her house and her sleeping husband (asleep again in his chair) and heads across the sand to the boys' hostel. It will be another half hour before the light spills over the mountains and floods the veld.

10

A DROWNED BOY

Among the farm's ghosts was the soul of a Standard Five. One morning, nineteen years earlier, the boy had drowned while swimming in the far dam, up near the ruined, roofless buildings of what was still called Old Goas, where the original farm had been. In theory, we lived at New Goas, but nobody called it that. Back then, the far dam had been used for the cows' midday drinking. This was when Goas had more cows. There had once been a fence around it so the farmhands could check for missing cows after they were corraled. Now the fence was gone, as gone as the water, although you could see the remnants of it flattened into the dust by years of hooves.

He wasn't a very demanding ghost. Some mornings he'd come and stand by our coffee fire. In the lingering dark, we'd huddle, jostling each other with our empty cups, waiting for the coffee to percolate. You knew he was there, because the smoke started wafting in the wrong direction, into the wind. Obadiah said the boy was using whatever breath he had left to push the smoke out of his eyes. The dead can't use their hands, Obadiah said. He also said the boy was a Twsana, the only Twsana at Goas at the time he drowned, and that he visited us for some warmth and to be remembered a little. A boy who died so far from his people. There's nothing criminal about needing to be spoken of once in a while. But it happened so long ago, no one remembered anything else about him other than that he died and that he was a Tswana. So whenever anybody claimed the smoke wasn't behaving according to certain meteorological laws, we made things up. It didn't matter who said what on those mornings. We were too cold to care, and people murmured into their coats. We all claimed the mantle of being as lonely as that boy must have been the moment he went under.

"Born in Gobabis, son of a rich chief," said one voice.

"True," said another. "His father — before the drought of seventy-nine made him a poor man — owned four hundred head of cattle."

A third voice, or maybe it was the first. "But at Goas, the boy roamed in bloody feet."

"Why bleeding feet?"

"Someone stole his shoes."

"Ah yes, and rich men's sons are tender-footed."

"That's true."

"Tender-footed, but he knew how to swim."

"True. He had lessons at the swimming pool for whites in Windhoek."

"So what happened? If he knew how to swim, why'd he drown?"

"Sadness."

"I see, yes."

"And then he sank."

"There was enough water to drown?"

"A rare year."

"And they didn't find him until the cows began acting strange."

"They wouldn't drink any of that water."

"Then they trampled the fence."

"Yes, and then a shepherd — not Theofilus, this was even before Theofilus — pulled himself up and looked over the edge."

"That boy's head was floating like a cabbage."

Our feet were cold, our hands; we crowded to the fire and hunched toward it with our empty coffee cups. We watched each other's breath more than we listened to any words. Those mornings, it was less that the sun would rise than that the darkness would simply pale. And it always, always came back to his loneliness, how he was the single Tswana on a farm of Hereros, Damaras, Namas, Coloureds, Ovambos. There were even two Bushmen at Goas then, two Bushmen who could at least talk to each other. We forgot about the stampeding cows, something nobody ever believed anyway. Cows at Goas never did anything that dramatic.

Our voices in the changing light:

"Forsook, the boy was."

"Aren't we all?"

"Our Lord, the same."

"And he didn't call for help. He knew nobody would come. The one certain thing about calling for help."

"And the cows?"

It was a rare woman's voice that answered, a voice we didn't recognize.

"The cows watched."

Nobody said anything after that. There was the slow rise of the smoke. Then it wandered away, toward the boulders beyond the toilet houses.

11

GOAS

Seasons at Goas, as much as you can call cold, hot, and more hot seasons, catapult into each other. Days too. Winter mornings bleed to summer afternoons. And memory is as much a heap of disorder as it is a liar.

The spiraled ash of a spent mosquito coil. A book with a broken spine lying facedown. A row of tiny socks drying on the edge of a bucket.

12

STORY OF A TEACHER'S WIFE

Tuesday and the beautiful and sleek and unsmiling and too good for us Mavala Shikongo is gone. The only single woman teacher to bless an all-boys boarding school so far in the veld even the baboons feel sorry for us. They come and shit by our doors. Yes, Mavala Shikongo has escaped Goas after a scant three weeks. Three weeks; the universe had only just begun to be merciful. The word is, she's found a better posting at a junior primary in Grootfontien. But twenty-one days was enough for us all, single or divorced, or wanting to be divorced, decrepit or spry, morally repugnant or generally decent — every last one of us — to fall, to stagger, to cave into love with Mavala Shikongo.

She had arrived not long after I had. No longer was I the new teacher. Anyway, my novelty was short-lived. I wore pants. The brief moment she graced the farm, Mavala Shikongo lived a quarter mile up the road, cloistered, in a room that had once been the principal's attached garage. She was Miss Tuyeni's, the principal's wife's, sister.

She ignored us. Three weeks we were invisible. Long school-day afternoons she never once stopped by Auntie Wilhelmina's fence to monger the latest lies, only went back to her room at the back of the principal's house, to her books. Festus reported, having spied the mail, that she was studying for a university course in England by correspondence. She's not satisfied, it was said. She doesn't even want to be a teacher, it was said. She wants to be an accountant. This was swooned over. She's going somewhere in this world, Mavala Shikongo is. She's not going to lie down with the cows at Goas. Women rise higher now. The war did it. Because — not only skirts, not only textbooks — Mavala Shikongo's a genuine hero of the struggle herself. An ex-PLAN fighter. Not even twenty-five and this girl's shot her share of Boers. Those blinkless eyes, it isn't hard to imagine them staring down a barrel. How many times those days did we moon by her classroom windows? On our way to the toilets, just to catch a glimpse. Three weeks we circled, coward vultures from a distance. And now look: Mavala Shikongo's battered mustard suitcase is riding away in the back of the priest's bakkie. How are we going to get up in the morning without the sight of her charging across the sand in her saucy black heels, those inspiring city shoes? Only Mavala Shikongo could lure us away from our dirty dreams on the coldest mornings. Days when our fingers cracked like the branches in the coffee fire and our scrotums didn't loosen until after third period break. How to warm a desert winter now?

We're all deep in mourning in the singles quarters and nobody feels like walking out to the road to wait for a hike into Karibib. Obadiah wanders over to my room and offers me a freshly peeled carrot. He invites me for an afternoon drink in his Datsun. I follow him out to the car. Obadiah's Datsun is mired in the sand behind his house, near Antoinette's chicken coops and laundry lines. An old Windhoek taxi, it will never, come the Second Coming or even the Third, drive anywhere again. Still, Obadiah has prophecies. Prophecies of the engine one day combusting, the carburetor carborating, the upholstery growing fur again. In the meantime, we talk in it. I take a nip of Zorba and say, Farewell, Mavala, if only we could have opened that mustard suitcase, taken one final whiff of you.

Obadiah adjusts the rearview. He's wearing his TransNamib hat, the hat his cousin Elias gave him when he retired from the railroad. Its peak grazes the top of the crumbling roof of the car, which, every time he moves his head, snows chunks of old yellow foam.

With his left hand at the top of the steering wheel, he gets right into it. It's another story, he says. A good many years ago, he says, another new teacher arrived at Goas. He hadn't been here long. Three weeks, perhaps. But three weeks is always enough for a man to fall in love with another man's wife. The Roman Empire? It took Nero one drunken night and a box of matches to burn the place down. The Hundred Years' War? An exaggeration. Advertising for Joan of Arc. God's Flood? You think he needed forty days and forty nights to drown every man and beast and creeping thing? He — how do you put it? — overdid it. He was irritated. Wouldn't you be? Five chapters in and already you've got to start again.

Obadiah moves the steering wheel only slightly, as if we're moseying along a mostly straight road. Outside, around the car, the scrabbling chickens peck the dust.

So, Obadiah says, three weeks and the new teacher is insanely, lunatically, in love with another teacher's wife. The teacher with the wife taught Standard Four math and the new teacher taught Standard Five Afrikaans. One day the husband noticed that the new teacher's class was cacophonous, more cacophonous than usual. He went and stuck his head in the window of his new colleague's classroom. *Where's Teacher?* he asked. Thirty, forty voices answered, *We know not, Teacher.* But the teacher with the wife could see something in the eyes of those boys. They were mocking him. This happened in the seventies. Boys were less innocent then. The war made them more worldly. These boys didn't want to study fractions, they wanted to kill whites. They used to climb up the hill by the cross and shout: *Boers back to Kakamas!* And what is it about war and lust? So yes, they mocked that teacher. Although their lips were tight, he could see the laughter in their eyes. *While the cat's away, the mice will play!* The teacher then walked slowly toward the singles quarters. He didn't knock on the new teacher's door. It happened, by the way, in Kapapu's old room, the room next to yours. A few minutes later, his wife followed him home across the sand, naked and guilty as Eve, clutching her clothes to her chest. We all watched — I am shamed to confess it — from our classroom windows. Neither the teacher nor his wife nor the new teacher left their room for the rest of the day. That night the teacher with the wife returned to the new teacher's room and killed him with a bicycle spoke. But here is the strange part. His wife accompanied him. In the morning we found them together, leaning against each other outside the new teacher's door, sleeping. Odd thing that, except for the blood on their clothes, they could have been angels. Lovers entwined. Romantic. The magistrate at Usakos sentenced them both. Eventually the husband was released — his offense being merely a crime of passion — but the wife remained in prison, she being guilty, under the laws of the time, of not one but two heinous crimes.

Obadiah reaches across me and pulls a rusty nail clipper out of the glove compartment and begins to trim his cuticles. Now that he's stopped driving, the coming of the winter night, the flat dim bluelessness we wear along with our double sweaters and bed socks, gives me a weird sense that we've really gone somewhere. I watch the shadows Obadiah's billowing shirts make as they swing on the line in the wind. Near the ashes of the fire pit are the remains of a laceless tennis shoe and the torn cellophane of an empty potato-crisp bag pecked clean by the roaming chickens.

The room next to mine?

Obadiah nods. To kill a man with a bicycle spoke is an ugly thing, he says, as he sweeps the nail slices off his shirt into his hand and tosses them out of what used to be a window. The new teacher's stomach was so ripped apart, Obadiah says, the constables had to collect his insides up in a bucket. To many people the question was: Did she take part, or did she only watch? Yet I was never interested in this question. To myself the murder itself has never meant very much. It was the vigil by the door. Over the years what has remained is the way we found them slumped in the morning. Vengeance, true, but something else perhaps, something more difficult to define. I ask this: However it came about, there must have been satisfaction in such exhaustion, no? A sense of things being finished at last? Might it be that those two spent their best hours out there waiting for the light?

He stoops and begins to work on his toes.

Antoinette comes from around the front of the house and, without hesitation, chooses a bird from the coop, twirls it by the neck. It's a circling. You flap your useless wings, you splay your crooked feet. Maybe Mavala Shikongo will hate Grootfontien, I say. Maybe she'll come back.

Obadiah is too polite to laugh at anybody. Nor does he point out every time you're a goon. He says nothing. In the waning, in the doomed light, I watch Antoinette raise a rusty cleaver on dinner.

13

UP ON THE HILL BY THE CROSS

The school hunkers in the center of the farm, near the intersection of three dry rivers. It was thought that this would ensure enough groundwater to support the teachers and the learners, even during the driest years.

The view from the top of the hill extends all the way from the mission — the school buildings, the church, the hostel — to the base of the Erongo Mountains. And you can see all three rivers, channels of grassless sand, meeting for a stretch near Goas and then parting for good. The Gamikaub heads straight north across the veld, ridged as a tar road, while the Kuiseb meanders west, where it snakes a narrow gorge into the Erongos, the beginning of its long desert haul to the Atlantic. The Toanib River, the Goas favorite, has no sense where it's going. It winds beneath Krieger's gleaming razor-wire fence, but then wanders back onto Goas, twisting south, where it seems to die out in the scrub.

Every evening the five of us — Pohamba, Obadiah, Festus, Vilho, and I — we'd stretch out on cushions stolen from the staff-room chairs and pass around a two-week-old *Windhoek Advertiser*. You didn't read the *Advertiser* for news. You read *The Namibian* for news. But who wanted news? After a week in the classroom, we wanted the real dirt, the smut and the glory. A fifty-thousand-rand sweepstakes on page 3 and multiple sets of naked breasts (in rainbow colors, spirit of the new nation) on the foldout. It was a good newspaper. Pohamba had it first and read out loud a sampling of that day's headlines:

IDI AMIN HAS ADVANCED SYPHILIS
NAMIBIAN WHITES PLAN MASS EXODUS TO PARAGUAY
US VP QUAYLE TO VISIT WINDHOEK
DOG POISONER ACTIVE IN TSUMEB
TWISTED AND HORNY, WIFE TAKES GRANDPA LOVER
MISS NAMIBIA PAGEANT BATHING SUIT MISHAP. PHOTOS,
    PAGE 5

"Hey, let's see those last two," Festus said.

And when we were through with the paper, I'd either sleep or watch the veld. Pohamba liked to say the only absolute of Goas is this: The same veld that wishes you good night will kick you in the head in the morning.

But Obadiah would say, That's blindness. "Empty? The veld? You must be looking into your own heart, Teacher Pohamba." Obadiah would say the veld changes so much, it's hard to keep track. One day you'll be out walking beyond the Voortrekker graves, and there, in a place where there had been nothing the day before but nameless scrub, will be a rare clump of stinkbush. Another day, in that same spot, poison mustard berries, or the more deadly euphorbia. It's not that nothing grows on Goas, it's only that it's nothing we can eat. And the grass? The Boers call it upslang because it shoots up overnight. After rain, it's green for a day. The next day it's dry as straw. Watch the dry grass alone, he would say. How some hours it leans with the wind, other hours fights against it. And more than movement — consider the light. In late morning, the Erongos to the west look like mounds of peppered cheese. And think of the mirages that pool at the base of those mountains. You walk and you walk and that water stretches away, but also, at every step, gets bigger. A pond becomes a lake, becomes an ocean. It's merely a collision of heated and unheated air causing an optical refraction. But what, I ask, do climatological proofs matter to a thirsty man?

14

CLASSROOM

Let the truth out: Kaplansk has no grammar. I am an American from the 1970s. In Miss Eckersley's English class, we sewed puppets while Miss Eckersley played guitar and sang.

Again, today, I drone onward, reading to my learners out of the book. English Lesson 12: The Simple Future. I drone as if droning itself is to have faith in something . . .

"To express a promise, willingness, as well as futurity, we use I (we) will and not I (we) shall. Remember, for the interrogative we use Shall I? in all cases, not Will I? Now, Shall I or Shall we? often has the meaning Do you want me to . . . ? or Would you like me to . . . ? E.g., Shall I open the window? Shall I get you a cup of tea? Shall we go to the theater tonight? Will, on the other hand, is another can of worms entirely. Will expresses not a question but rather a determination. For instance, I will study my grammar during study hour. I will not beat children who are smaller than I. This sort of thing. Any questions? Confusions? Bafflements? Things of this nature?"

"The simple future as opposed to what?" Rubrecht Kanhala, class genius and sweat-inducing burden on the teacher, asks.

"Excellent question, Rubrecht. As opposed to, well, the complicated future, which we don't have to worry about right now."

Resume drone.

The other boys' heads remain steady; for a while the droop is only in their eyes. Then slowly, one after another, their heads begin to drop, and I watch them catch their heads without their hands, raise them again, and try so hard to listen.

"All right, then. Does anybody remember what an interrogative is?"

Silence, tomb-like. Even Rubrecht is tired of this. None of the boys wear watches and there's no clock on the wall, but Jeremiah Puleni, famous for knowing the time in his bones, has begun to rub his feet on the sandy floor. Half an hour left now and everybody knows I'll talk it to the grave. Jeremiah, barefoot farm kid so much taller than the other boys, older too. He started school years late because he was needed on the farm. His brother was up north in the fighting. He's never caught up. He just sits in class after class and smiles. Jeremiah Puleni smiles across years. Not a word of English, he speaks only Damara and Afrikaans. When I look at him, he's always staring, silent, concentrating. I wonder, Concentrating on what, Jeremiah? A big oaf of a kid, always looking for a reason to laugh. We know he's doomed, and for this we all love him more. Goas is a haven for some. No one wants to think about what will happen to Jeremiah Puleni when he finally finishes Standard Seven and there's no primary school left for him.

"Good. Now copy this chart."

I watch the sun streak through the tall windows. Dusty yellow bars reach across the room, crashing into the heads of the taller boys. Jeremiah's face awash in light, and still he narrows his eyes at the rules on the board, copied by Teacher but not understood by Teacher. To this day, not understood by Teacher. And Jeremiah Puleni? Him staring politely, his lips quivering, as if it all makes perfect sense, is perfectly reasonable.

15

GOAS MORNING

Not yet morning and Obadiah sits in the paling darkness in his blue chair and caresses his new Grundig radio. The batteries are spent and the generator's been off for hours, but still he imagines what it might tell him or what song it might play. So much going on — even now, even all the way out here — in this silent little box. A cacophony of unheard voices, and here he sits in a robe and slippers listening to possibility. Astonishing, isn't it, that there is ever silence in a world so vast and full of voices? Today in class he will yank out all the great maps from the locked cabinet and tack them up all over the walls, show the children the North Pole, Siberia, Alaska, the Philippines, Addis Ababa, Cairo, Montevideo. He will thrill the children with the possibilities of maps. The world sits flat and conquerable. All pilgrimages possible! Maps — his heart soars — is there anything so glorious as a map? Even for a man who rarely ventures farther than the Pick 'n Pay in Karibib?

Antoinette sleeps. In the darkness he sees her without needing to look toward the half-open bedroom door. She sleeps with her feet sticking out from under the blankets like two paddles she'd smack him with. Her mouth gripped tight. She sleeps with her teeth clenched, in case she should die. Her soul might escape, she says. She breathes, noisy, out her nose. When they were younger, he used to kiss her as she slept. He'd pry her mouth open with his tongue. Was that myself? I'd like to do it now. Why can't I? He lets go of the radio, but remains where he is, looking at nothing and everything. The newspaper photographs thumbtacked to the wall behind his head. Nkrumah, Bobby Kennedy, Miriam Makeba, a handcuffed Zephania Kameeta. They all stare at him, waiting for him to do something. Do what?

What would you gallants have me do? He'd like a nip. A half-pint's in his closet, waiting for him in a worn-out loafer, its copper top peeping out like a baby's head. In the hostel, the boys are sleeping. In Windhoek, his sons, Thomas and Matti (both employed), are sleeping. In Tehran, two lovers, Tehranians, sleep. In Moscow, old cosmonauts gracefully sleep. In Peru, Morocco, Flanders. Why? Why can't I?

The windmill behind the mission garage begins to move, one hesitant creech, then another and another until it reaches full squeal. He sees it looming above the mission garage in the dark. *Aermotor Chicago*. On the other blue chair is Antoinette's unfinished needlework. He wants to touch it. Touch whatever it is she's making now, to twist his fingers in that scrumble of yarn, but he doesn't move, doesn't reach for it. Only thinks about what it would feel like if he did. Which is different, isn't it? He listens to her gusty breathing in the bedroom as the light turns from fog to yellow. Antoinette's cocks crow all night. They never sleep either. To them it's always dawn. Even so, he thinks, isn't there always a darkening before morning? Why not touch? Why not go to her now? Why are there times — he's thought this before — we'd rather want than grasp?

16

DIKELEDI

With Mavala Shikongo gone, our lusts still maintained a constant: Dikeledi. Pohamba once worked up the equation: $p = \Box d = 2 \Box r = Dikeledi$. Impossible that she was Festus's wife, and yet she wore it proudly. She dominated Festus in ways we didn't even try to fantasize about. It was rumored that when she wanted him — as in when she wanted him wanted him — she rang a little bell, a little tinkle tinkle only he could hear. These were the sorts of disgusting particulars we had to endure. Festus and Dikeledi were the farm's abhorrent newlyweds. It was said she washed her teeth in fresh goat's milk every morning. We all wished she'd sleepwalk over to the singles quarters, because that was the only way she'd come near us. She must have cleaned their little purple house all day. Somehow she successfully banished every grain of sand, every crunchable beetle underfoot. I used to watch her looking out the window. She didn't seem to have any interest in watching our soccer field antics up close, but she always watched from the window. And so we made a point of putting on shows out there for her. That time Pohamba challenged every boy in Standard Five to wrestle him all at once. My job was to make certain no older boys snuck into the match, so I'd lined them up and crosschecked them against the Standard Five register. I set them up in three clusters, ripping off a dumb line from my junior high gym teacher: *All right, halfwits, listen up. I want half of youse over here, half of youse over here — and half of youse over here.* Pohamba with all those boys hanging from his neck, and the rest of us jeering him to scrum the Standard Sixes too. I look toward Festus's purple house and there's Dikeledi in the window.

Her head was shaped like an egg we all wanted to cradle. Sometimes she'd send a boy with marinated chicken and rice and syrupy peach halves to the singles quarters. Other times, potatoes and creamed corn from a can. But this was only charity. Her love for Festus unnerved us. Her face hid nothing. It was there in those teeth, in her nose, in the delicate porches of her ears. She looked at him a hundred different ways, but the one I remember most was curiosity, as if one of the reasons she loved him was that she was unsure of what he'd do next. No one at Goas was more predictable than Festus. He was the farm's most unsecret agent. He was so reliably duplicitous, he circled back around to trustworthy. Festus was a man who cahootsed with both sides of the Goas power balance. When the principal wanted something, Festus hopped to it, believing one day he'd become assistant principal, should the principal ever deign to appoint one. Same went for the priest, though the reward might have been more intangible. (Then again, maybe not. It was said that the Father was a hoarder of both money and frozen steaks.) Above all, what Festus cherished were his hushed conferences in either the rectory or the principal's office, his proximity to power.

But the question was: Why couldn't he just be content to make love to Dikeledi? What makes an already rich man need more? Everybody was waiting for her to get pregnant, as this would, we thought, take the sting out of her being so close and yet always behind that window. Obadiah wrote it in a poem. *May we rejoice in the sadness / of your milkplump breasts.*

17

TYPING

It was rumored Pohamba had a wife, an actual wife, and that she lived in Otavi, and that some nights he would lock himself in his classroom and bang out letters to her on the school's ancient Olivetti.

Festus and I would knock on the classroom door. We'd call out to him that we were going hunting, one of Pohamba's favorite leisures. We hunted for the spoor of the elusive dwarfed hedgehog (*Potamochoerus porcus*) of the central Namib escarpment. Hunting entailed borrowing a couple of Auntie Wilhelmina's whelps and marching around the veld with umbrellas. Pohamba said this is how real men hunted. So when he was holed up in there, we'd slip him notes under the door with bloody drawings of bludgeoned hedgehogs.

But when he was typing he never answered the door. We'd stand outside and listen to the rattle of the typewriter. Festus said that the wife had run away with a Boer. When the Boer tired of her she went back to Pohamba, but he wouldn't take her, and neither would any of her people, so she had to go live in a cave up in the mountains of Damaraland. Festus said Pohamba sometimes took pity on her and every once in a while sent her a letter, which was delivered to her by a man on a donkey.

Obadiah said nonsense. He said Pohamba was just in love and that he wasn't writing to his wife but to a floozy in Windhoek. He said the girl's father was a SWAPO bigwig in the Justice Ministry and had forbidden her to marry a failed math teacher with a big strutting stride. That Pohamba had once tried to meet Bigwig at his office in the capital, but Bigwig's secretary said he had to make an appointment two months in advance. After that Pohamba smashed his fist on the glass reception table and started shouting that this was his independence too, and that if he wanted to see a government employee in his own country — the one he fought for, the one the blood of his comrades gave birth to — then he wasn't waiting two minutes, forget two months. So they threw him out, and almost arrested him, Obadiah said.

All I really know — and this is only conjecture, because Pohamba never said one way or the other — is that the typing, whomever he was typing to, was one of the few things he refused to make a farce out of. I think he was writing to someone, but that someone was either dead or so far gone from him it amounted to the same thing.

When Pohamba wasn't around, we used to hunt his stuff for the pages, but we never found anything. He might have burned them. Or maybe he saved on paper by not using any, banging away at a dead ribbon.

One night I outlasted Festus and read as I listened to him type. I sat against Pohamba's classroom door. In the early evenings, boys would climb the hill and do pull-ups on the cross. Every night, there were these silhouettes rising and falling in the half-light. Rubrecht Kanhala was up there then. I knew it was him because he was the best. His long body flinging itself up and over the horizontal bar of the cross. Rubrecht did what looked like fifty or so pull-ups, and the boys were chanting his name, begging for more. I gave up reading when there was no light left, but Pohamba plowed on, without a candle, the typewriter ringing as he reached the end of line after line.

18

RAIN

Rain, those few times it came without thunder. You could feel something bloated about the air when you breathed, and you knew. You also knew it would disappear as quickly as it arrived, that by tomorrow the dark stain in the sand would be as gone as the silence of the rain itself. I'd learned at least this, that the rain carried its own engulfing silence, and that it, too, would leave us. As if none of it ever happened. Then the Erongos would emerge from the clouds and loom again, and the relentless sun would pierce our thin walls, and we would curse the rain for bothering us in the first place.

It had been a glorious downpour, but it had gone on for nearly three hours. It was no longer a miracle, and however fleeting and teasing, it always started as a miracle. Now it was just rain again. We were waiting for after rain, when the sun would rise, battered, like a wet loaf. When Antoinette's chickens would shake out their dirty feathers and saunter again. When the younger boys would start whittling sticks to spear the fantasy fish the older boys lied to them about: *Don't you know? They swim down from Ovamboland when the heavy rains come.* Those boys — lying on their stomachs, watching the amazing river of actual water, looking for barbel or pink-bellied scroot. But the only thing the momentarily flowing Kuiseb carried along was a few drowned mice.

The earth slogged. The water curdled in our footprints in the sand. All was mud now. We'd all retreated to our rooms when Pohamba knocked on the wall. "Mother Goas has birthed another lunatic!" Then he came to my door and ordered: "Come and see." Wet feet, towels over our heads, we went out to the edge of the soccer field. And there was Dikeledi at mid-field, whirling. The rain was still falling in gray veils. Festus was out there too, on his back, playing his fatty chest like bongos. She was wearing his stupid straw hat and laughing, her arms stretched out, her wet breasts swinging as if they were trying to reach out to her hands. Rain-worn, we craved her more. Pohamba kicked his door shut and yowled about his fucking toe. I rammed my door also. For once our envy of Festus spoke with one voice. It was too much. We shut up our windows and listened to the silence of our rooms, of our beds, as the dread rain pounded, pounded our corrugated roofs.

19

OBADIAH

My love's been out rescuing the laundry from the rain. Sad that we must save our clothes from what's so welcome. She flings a heap on the kitchen table and begins draping our sheets, our pillowcases. Over the table, over the stove, the counters, chairs. From the light fixtures, from the doors. She hangs an undershirt off the back of my own head. Our life as shrouds. When she's done, she crosses the worn linoleum in her wet feet, slapping prints with detached toes. Where'd your toes go, my Toinette? She fills the kettle with a bit of water to rinse it, not too much, dumps it in the basin, fills it again. The drum of the water draining into the kettle joins the rain. How easy, how simple it is to merely fall. As if it never forgot. As if it always fell like this. She rips a match. The suck of the gas of the Primus. The flames reaching out from under the kettle like desperate blue tongues. Soon the kettle will scream as if it's screaming only for her. Then her pruned hands will hold a mug. My wife or my mother? Am I remembering this or seeing it? What house of my life doesn't have wires for laundry behind it? What kitchen of my life doesn't house a woman making tea? Your drenched body, its outlines. If I could pull you close. Three hours of hard rain at Goas? Did gorging ever make a man starve slower?

20

SECOND COMING

My sweaty hand is writing sentences on the board for copy-ing. Days of woozy heat have followed what is now known as the "Deluge of Dikeledi." It was three days ago and already we're lying about it. It rained for twelve hours. No, twenty-six. Theofilus had to go around and rescue the goats with a canoe.

1. The atom bomb is a frightful thing.
2. My father is an Elk.
3. Will you please iron my shirt after you finish the dishes?
4. My sister has a Mexican jumping bean.

Pohamba's shadow looms across the threshold of my classroom.
"May I have a word, Teacher Kaplansk?"
"Certainly, Teacher Pohamba."
I go out to the porchway. "What is it? I've got another fifty min-utes to murder."
Pohamba cups his hand to my ear, murmurs, "She's back."
"Who?"
"Che Guevara."
"What?"
"In a skirt."
And then she's there in his eyeballs, strutting across his undrunk morning pupils.
"Mavala Shikongo?"
"In the exposed flesh."
"Wow."
"There's more."

"What?"

"She's with a child."

"She's pregnant?"

"Not with. With *a*. Note the article, English teacher. He's about a year old, maybe a year and six months."

"Wait. She didn't look pregnant."

"Kaplansk! Think. She's been gone less than a month. It was born already, see? She went somewhere and picked it up."

I take a step back. "Oh. Hey, how much cologne have you got on? I'm getting dizzy."

"Not cologne. Eau de toilette. Stag. I'll get you a bottle."

"How'd she get here? I didn't hear any car."

"Walked."

"With a baby she walked?"

"All she needs now is a basket on her head. A modern girl, our soldier."

"Where's she now?"

"With the Commandant."

I look down the porchway, toward the principal's office. The mustard suitcase is in the courtyard, standing on the well-watered grass where we took our school pictures. On promotion day, the principal would stand on that green patch and hand out pens. He called it Ireland.

By this time, all my learners have their heads out the windows. Pohamba glares them back to their chairs. Then he whistles to one of them, the boy closest to the door, Magnus Axahoes. The boy comes out and stands before us. He's nervous. He comes up to just about Pohamba's thigh.

"Go to the principal and get the toilet key," Pohamba says.

"Yes, Teacher."

"And come back and tell us what you see in the office."

"Yes, Teacher."

But Magnus doesn't move. He stands there looking up at Pohamba.

"Go."

Magnus bites his lip. Then, after a moment, he flips around and sprints down the porchway.

"Who's he?"

"Magnus. Never says a word. Mostly he looks at his feet. He writes well, though. He wrote a composition about a baboon who becomes a police officer."

"They're already baboons."

"This one drove a flying donkey cart and rescued dogs."

"Rescued from what?"

"I don't know. Just rescued."

"Make him talk. You should hit him."

"No, quiet's better. I might start hitting them for asking questions."

Across the courtyard, from Obadiah's classroom, the boys are reciting geography. "Labrador, Lagos, Lancashire. Now you try. *Labrador, Lagos, Lancashire.*"

Usually when the principal speaks in his office we can hear him across the farm, but today we hear only Obadiah and his boys. That mustard suitcase stands like a sentry. Magnus comes back, holding the key, which is attached to a wire, which is coiled around a brick. He stands there, but he doesn't say anything.

"Well," Pohamba says.

"Excuse? Teacher?"

"Tell us what you saw in the office."

"Mistress Shikongo is there, Teacher. With Master Sir."

"And what are they doing?"

"Excuse?"

Pohamba nearly shouts: "What are they talking about, you little fool?"

"Not talking."

"Not talking?"

"Yes, Teacher."

"So what are they doing? Sitting and looking at each other?"

"No, Teacher. Master Sir is looking at Mistress Shikongo. Mistress Shikongo is looking nowhere."

"What do you mean nowhere?"

"Not here."

"What?" Pohamba raises his hand. The boy flinches, but his eyes remain steady — as if he's trying to show us what not here looks like. He cradles the brick to his chest. We wait, listen for a moment, as if we can hear all this looking and not looking. From Obadiah's class: "Now again, angels, try it again. Lausanne."

"Looo Zaaaaan!"

"Brilliant! Just as the Swiss —"

"And the child?" I say. "What's the child doing?"

"The small boy is beating his mother, Teacher."

And then, from down the porchway, the principal doesn't laugh at her, he erupts. The noise of him swooping, coughing, happily retching —

"Take back the key," Pohamba says.

That night we staked ourselves out on the blue chairs in Antoinette and Obadiah's living room and waited. The shelves of musty books made everything smell like old cheese. It was a crowded little room. The floor was scattered with open books, facedown, and various unmatched slippers. One naked bulb hung over our heads, muted by a scarf fashioned into a shade. In the corner was Antoinette's dressmaker's dummy. We pretended to listen to the radio while we waited for Obadiah to proclaim whatever there was to proclaim.

The chimes of Big Ben ring out. What's some clock in London to Mavala Shikongo? The news we wanted wasn't on the BBC. Our oracle stood on a piece of carpet sample and curled his toes. He turned up the radio so he could talk more freely. Antoinette was in the kitchen, plonking silverware, one crash after another. Whatever it took to call us lazy. "She went to see my fedder," Obadiah said quietly, under the noise of the radio.

"Your what?"

"My distaff."

"Huh?"

"This long disease called wife."

"Will you simply tell us," Pohamba moaned, as he reached out to fondle the breasts of the dummy. "One time, simply talk straight."

The cricket news: *Pakistan eight wickets over Malaysia in a test match* . . .

Obadiah sighed. "This modern age. You want it all right off. Nobody has time for a preface anymore. There was a time when the beauty of a story was in the meander. Take your hand off Magdalena. All right. Your pretty soldier asked my wife to watch the boy while she teaches. She said the boy might be a bit difficult to handle. She even offered to pay —"

"And so?"

"You don't know my wife? 'Pay me to care for a child!' Even before the girl came to her, she had dragged up an ancient universe from under the house. A crib, a high chair, a stuffed giraffe, a bassinet — You see, this is how women join clubs. It's true that men often join secret societies, but the societies of women are so secret even they don't precisely know —"

"Where'd she get it?" I said.

"The bassinet? From beneath the house. Didn't I —"

"The kid. Where'd she get the —"

And so we began to wonder. Us in the blue chairs, Obadiah on the carpet sample, wondering, which led to conjuring, which led to certain lovely visions of coitus. Latin, Obadiah informed, from the past participle *coire.*

"Virgin birth," Pohamba said. "Who could get their sausage anywhere near her but Him?"

"Wait, what's a past participle?"

Antoinette appeared. Cotton balls in her ears to keep out the noise of us, but even so, she heard every word anybody ever said. Your own thoughts unsafe — she channeled them through her cotton balls. She didn't say anything, only raised a fork, tiny, but in the light of that single bulb, in that cave-like room, it loomed. She'd skewer us gossips up like shish kebab.

And maybe she was more imposing now than she was in the old days, the days Obadiah often waxed over. *Had she been Turkish,* he'd say, *my wife would have been a pasha*. Her standing there in her brutally ironed gray dress, holding that fork. Why waste words when you can lash with your eyes? Cowards. Leave that girl's life alone. Enough for her already without you sloths mongering. Father? What father? Who cares about a father? Any.

21

BROTHERS

Late. Pohamba pounds the wall. "My dreams are too loud," he says. "Aren't yours?"

"No."

"It's her. She's walking on my head with those heels."

"Go to sleep."

"She's put me, you know, in a manly state."

"I don't want to hear about it."

"And you're not hungry?"

We had chunk meat for dinner, which I now can't remember eating. "What have you got?"

"Canned snoek."

"Use the Primus?"

"No. Outside."

In front of our rooms he builds a small fire by the garbage pit. I hold my flashlight while he pours oil into one of Antoinette's big black pots. He slaps the fish out of the tin. "One-sixty k from the ocean," he says. "You wouldn't know it from the fish we eat."

I listen to the crackle of the oil. Above, a crowded bowl of stars and a dented orange moon so low in the sky, it looks like it's squatting in the veld.

"Another thing."

"What?"

"Lowest population density of any country in the world, and I live in a two-and-a-half-by-four-meter room. Explain the incongruity."

"I can't."

"Have I told you about my brother Moola, the scientific social-ist?" he asks.

"Is he the one who lost his hand at the canning factory?"

The wind is so dead at this hour, I can hear him swallow. He doesn't laugh. "That was Simeon."

"Oh."

"My father's sister's child. To myself, this is a brother. I called him Moola. His mother called him Bonifacius. We went to junior primary together at Otavi. Then to Dobra for high school. The boy liked to dance, I tell you. Run also. Up in the mountains above school. Had he lived he would have become as fast as Frankie Fredricks. Running in the Olympics. Money, cars, women. He also read more than any of us. Fuck this school, he said. He said the rest of us — no matter how poor our fathers — were peons of the whites. Sellouts. He said he was willing to die so we could rule our-selves and work together, because, he said, you, my friends are the *proletariat* . . . It was going to be beautiful. We were going to build community halls, post offices. He always talked like that, us holding hands and building post offices together."

The oil in the pot splutters and Pohamba pokes at the fire with the edge of his boot.

"We formed an underground organization — Moola called it the League of the Just. We would meet in the veld, and Moola would teach us, lecture us. So when the time came, I left school and fol-lowed Moola north and joined the struggle. Understand, we hardly had boots. They had planes and tanks. But wasn't our cause righ-teous, eh? "

He pauses, cracks his knuckles, all of them.

"Myself and Brother Moola. We were part of a platoon that worked reconnaissance. In country. We'd spend our days sleeping in the bush. Nights, we'd sabotage. We were saboteurs. Ha! Our job was to create fear. Not to win, only to keep the whites afraid. We'd get them while they slept. We'd steal their women, their children. We were spooky terrorists. We were the gorilla in guerrilla, get it?

Oh, were we good! And Moola was our fearless leader. Then — it happens. We're all sleeping in the bush, middle of the day, up near their air base at Ruacana, and — suddenly — a helicopter lands on us like a weaver coming home to roost. Two Boers hanging off that metal bird with howitzers. Out of seven comrades, four dead, rest of us wounded. Myself in the left leg."

He swallows loud, and rolls up his left pants leg.

It's small for shrapnel, it seems to me. Still, I gasp. *Holy shit.*

He's quiet for a while, satisfied. Lets the thud-like truth of the wound settle.

"Only one of us, you see, wasn't there. One of us, you see, had, *fortuitously,* crept away before the ambush. Have a good sleep, my comrades. Oh, he used to cheer the good fight with his right hand raised! Mandela! Nujoma! Toivo ja Toivo! We tracked him the next day." Pohamba burps, looks at me over the pot. "Watch the ones who talk too much."

"Why'd he do it?"

Now he laughs, waves his spoon around. "Why does anybody do anything? Money or women. In this case it was money." He sings, *"Money makes the world go round the world go round the world . . .* We found five hundred rand in his boots. A few thousand more in his underwear. My dear brother sold us. He was trying to get out. Maybe he wanted to preach the revolution in Paris or somewhere. Fuck some French girls for Trotsky. I don't blame him. Do you think I blame him?"

He reaches into the pot and feels the fish with his fingers.

"The fish is done."

"What did you do to him?"

"Oh, the natural thing." Pohamba takes his spoon and glops some fish on my plate.

"What's that?"

"Eat your fish. Don't you want some chutney?"

I point the light in his face.

"What's the natural thing?"

He yawns. "We tied him to the back of a lorry and drove. Drove till the veld shaved the skin off his body. You could hear him moaning on the Champs-Elysées. Then we cut him loose and let the birds eat out his eyes."

Pohamba takes the pot off the fire and sets it on a rock. I hand him back my plate. I want to believe him. I want to believe him in the way you want to believe the one story people tell (he told so many, but he really told only one) to be the truth. He's stacking himself up against the soldier.

"She's not that hot," I say.

"No, only that arse."

He hands me back my plate heaped with blackened snoek. I shove the fish in my mouth with my hands. When I'm through with my second plate, I watch him eat. Pohamba's a dainty eater. He changes the subject, tells me how he'd like to open a shop at Goas and sell cooldrink and candy to the boys. Easy money, he says. A monopoly. Some cooldrink, some chocolate. Simba raisins and peanuts. "Wouldn't you like to open a shop?" he says.

22

TO RETURN

We pretended not to notice. Bastard children were normal for country people, farm people. Or men. (Pohamba claimed legions.) Not for a woman teacher. Not for a woman teacher at a Catholic school. And certainly not for a woman teacher at a Catholic school where her brother-in-law is principal. To parade around as if it was nothing (as Miss Tuyeni put it to Antoinette, overheard by Obadiah, who reported to us) was more than an embarrassment; it was a disgrace. The girl goes off to fight a war and now look at her, toting a child without a husband. Which is what men want. Any man. To plant seeds without staying around to water the garden. The price respectable women charge is marriage. There is no other fee.

But not only Miss Tuyeni clucked. It was all of us. Nobody greeted Mavala Shikongo when she returned. And everyone, myself included, wore an air of Nope, we're not surprised. We expect nothing less than humiliation here.

In morning meeting, the principal acted as if she'd never left. Vilho had been covering her classroom, running back and forth across the courtyard. All day, every day, for nearly a month, he had done his best to control two rooms of squalling boys, his own Standard Fours and her sub b's. Supposedly, the principal had put a call into the ministry for a replacement teacher, but no one had turned up, and now no one needed to.

And so the prodigal daughter went back to her class, as if she'd always been a fallen woman and not the up-and-comer in a new nation. Even true heroes became no one at Goas. That's what you get for walking around wearing your head so high. Now we don't consider ourselves so far beneath you. A similar thing happened with Pohamba. Once, he made good on his daily threat to leave and was gone five days. His previous record was three and a half. When he slouched back up the road in the same disco shirt he'd left wearing, no one reminded him of his vow that he'd come back to this farm only as a corpse, and even then his ghost would flee.

Now we don't have to be so discreet when we again pilgrim by her classroom on our way to and from the toilet houses. Ignominy has given us license to spy more openly. She's taller than she was when she was a myth, and not every move she makes is so utterly graceful. She stomps around her class with a book open in her hand. Her short-short hair and her eyes that gaze restlessly up at the ceiling in the middle of a sentence. She does not baby her sub b's as Vilho did. She reads fast and doesn't pause to explain what the words mean. And when she teaches the alphabet, we note with interest that she does not sing it. But the small boys seem to love her more for not talking down to them, for treating them like her little soldiers of the dangling feet.

23

STUDY HOUR

Another of the principal's tortures, a bit of daily imprisonment in the name of holy education. *If they refuse book learning, then we must foist it upon their shoulders so that they may carry it like honorable oxen.*

And it's an hour and a half, not an hour.

Pohamba and I are on duty. We sit bunkered down in the staff room while mayhem reigns in the unsupervised classrooms. From the Standard Fives, the sound of broken glass. In the courtyard, a couple of Standard Sevens are fencing with our teacher brooms. We hear nothing, see nothing. We're eating yesterday's cold fish and chips and playing War. Fast rounds, plapping down the cards as quick as we can. It's the Cincinnati Kid versus the Man. Three out of five for who gets to leave early. In between chips, Pohamba chews on a chicory root, which is supposed to improve his virility. It isn't making him very good at War.

"That was my take," I say.

"I had a jacko," Pohamba says.

"Three's wild."

"Seven."

"It was seven last time."

"Where's the vinegar? How can the Man eat fish and chips without vinegar? It was seven."

"Three."

"Take it. It's your conscience."

Next round he loses again. I get up to leave.

"Wait," he says. "Did she speak to you?"

"No."

"Look at you?"

"No."

"Play for Thursday."

"Your credit's no good."

He snaps off a little chicory. "What if I give you some of this here root, Kid?" Whence from beneath the outside ledge of the staff-room window, a TransNamib hat rises. And a godhead thunders:

Hear this, idle suitors! While you sit there playing games! Know this: During the great Herero rebellion, during a break in that slaughter, two German officers once played cards — cards! — on the naked buttocks of a captured Herero princess. Imagine it. Think of a card slapping on flesh and its reverberations. Titillated? Go ahead, be titillated!

Forgive us. We got titillated. Because he invited us, cajoled us, and the hour and a half wasn't getting any shorter. And so — mid-War, the cards in our sweaty hands — we indulged. We thought of her young body arching off a table, and cards —

Then the hat in the window rumbled again.

Thrilled? All right, then. You had it your way. Now see it another. Think of how still that girl must have held. How long the game lasted. What the smoke was like in the tent. Was ash flicked on skin? Was it better than what else she knew could happen? Or did that happen too? Of course it did. Her relatives who live among us are all the evidence we need. Yes, it certainly got worse some nights. And you may in the filth of your imaginations take it that far. But I ask that you consider only the rudimentary evil of the game itself. Now add a voice — Gruss Gott! — And laughter and the reek of the cigars . . .

There were afternoons when any sort of idle entertainment spurred his umbrage. Such diversions, Obadiah said, contributed to the disintegration of civilization. Thus, he ambushed us with history, rose up from the window, and bombasted.

"Revolted?" he said.

We nodded.

"It won't do. Revulsion only makes a man turn away. I demand you look at her again, see her again —"

"Demand?" Pohamba said. "We're only trying to get through the day here."

Obadiah raised the brim of his hat and peered at Pohamba. Of all things, this he understood, but when he was sober, he pretended he didn't. Drunk, he carried his own aches. Sober, he lugged the burdens of the world. Today on his back were the miseries of a long-dead Herero princess. He left us, slowly, hunched over. I slid the fish and chips to Pohamba; he slid them back to me. A six of diamonds and a body seized beyond fear into stillness. Fingers clenching the edge of the table.

24

AUTIE

I f you bothered to wash up at Goas, acceptance, or at the very
least toleration, was pretty much guaranteed. Auntie Wilhelmina
was an exception, as ignored as she was ubiquitous. She was the
minor character who always insisted she star.

A Wednesday? A Saturday midnight? Auntie was all day all days.
The most prominent thing of many prominent things was the noise
of her. Her fat twangling, her fulumping down the ridge toward
the singles quarters. The jangle of her hundreds of stolen bronze
bracelets. The barking of her retinue of sycophantic dogs. The
heaving of her breasts. She was a big heaver of her breasts; Auntie
heaved at the slightest provocation. Her turtled skin. Parts of it were
long past withered; other parts were new, infantile, as if she had the
power of selective regeneration. You see, once you start to describe
her, there is no end of her. A wildebeestian woman, the only answer
is to look away, but it's impossible. Her eyes — no, stay clear of her
eyes. Her cheeks sag off her face like grocery bags overstuffed with
fruit. Her teeth, cruel, sharp, heinously white — on the days she
wore them in. Without them, her mouth looked full of bloody
thumbs. There was a fresh wart on her chin, not like a dead thing,
but a happy thing, very much alive. She groomed her beard a lot like
Obadiah's, a bit pointy off the chin. Beyond ugly, Auntie Wilhelmina, beyond ghastly, and this was the fundamental problem.
The woman was a fascination. The boys said that if you stared at
Auntie Wilhelmina long enough from a certain angle, you'd never
stop wanting her. Ever.

She lived at Old Goas, in a ruined pondookie up and over the
ridge, only half of which was roofed. Vilho, who was here that far

back as a learner, remembered that one day she materialized. That one day Auntie Wilhelmina was simply in the veld, rooted, like something that had always been right where it was. You just hadn't seen her. Like a hill beyond another hill. Or as if, Vilho put it, Goas had come to her, not the opposite. Obadiah refused to indulge in anything so metaphysical about Auntie. He only said: That old bitch talks too much.

Auntie Monologued

She had an extremely hoarse voice, like an old dog's after it's spent the day barking and can hardly do it anymore — but bark onward it must. In that terrible voice, she would go on about her royal lineage and her family's personal relationship to Jesus. She said she could trace her family back to Kambonde on her father's side and Impinge on her mother's. She said her paternal grandmother's eldest brother was Mpingana, who was assassinated by Nehale. And she said Mpingana's son, Kwedhi, her great-uncle, was the one who, after banishment, started to associate with the Germans. She said the Germans might have had their faults, but we must always bless them for bringing the word of God to this heathen place. Eventually Kwedhi was baptized and declared himself king — hence, as she, Auntie, was the great man's niece, everyone owed her fealty for freeing them from the bondage of paganism. In Auntie's universe, four hundred years of colonialism and apartheid never happened. And she carried her namesake, the last Kaiser — Wilhelm II! — proudly.

"Murdering fop of a Kaiser," Obadiah said. "And there is nothing, zero, in the historical or anthropological record to support a lick of her stories. That obese woman bastardizes history! Christianization was a gradual process. It occurred over decades, centuries. No one man determined anything. Her Kwedhi was no Constantine, and for that matter, neither was Constantine. Faith is not something commanded by a despot. The woman's a fake and a liar."

"A fake what?"

Obadiah didn't answer. He was going to condemn her for making up stories? For exploitation of history to suit her own ends? For lying for the sake of the good of the story? This sin?

Auntie Filched

Initially the priest had hired Auntie Wilhelmina as an undercook in the hostel kitchen. Then one day she walked off with two forty-kilo bags of carrots. Dragged them behind her in broad daylight, her philosophy being that stealing in public is no sin. *Robbing His children under His watchful eye is no transgression.* If it was, she said, wouldn't there be thunder and lightning? How do you argue with this? The priest fired her, but he didn't have either the heart or the stomach to banish her off the farm for good. So he let her live up there in her half-roofless house with the dogs she stole as whelps from farmers up and down the C-32. A good, quasi-socialist thing about Auntie Wilhelmina was that she stole only expensive things from the government (rands from the tuition scholarship fund) and the Church (a year's supply of communion wafers and a golden chalice). From us, she took double-A batteries, lightbulbs, mosquito coils, your last nub of toothpaste. Her dogs were especially fond of gnawing rolls of toilet paper. She'd knock on your door and there she'd be, every glorious boozy inch of her. "I bestow my blessment upon this dwelling." And you'd be faced with a choice that wasn't really a choice. Let her in and let her take whatever the hell she wanted. Or listen to her.

"Come on in, Auntie. I was actually just on my way to choir practice. Make yourself at home."

"Sing well, White Child, raise high your voice."

Auntie Promised She'd Die

Like all descendants of Kavango royalty, Auntie said, she could not allow herself to die a natural death. As with Jesus, as with the lineage of Kwedhi. When her time came, she said, the oldest male was supposed to strangle her to death. She often hinted that such time was nigh, but Obadiah, overanxious, would ask, "Is it not yet time to perish, O Queenly Queen of Queenishness?"

And she'd say, "Patience, little brother, patience. Soon, soon, the royal murder."

And Obadiah would stroke his old callused hands as if to sharpen them.

25

UP ON THE HILL BY THE CROSS

Mavala Shikongo walking along the road to the principal's house. Us watching from the top of the hill, the gust in our faces. Obadiah says, There are sixteen kinds of wind, but only one that lifts a skirt like that.

He stands and whaps the cross with his hat.

26

GOAS LOVE

And still the bedraggled pigeons fuck. Everywhere they do it.
No place is sacred, or depending on how you looked at it, all
places sacred. Every mapone, every acacia. Toilet pit, dam, trough.
They fuck on the road to Krieger's farm. We blame it on the late
freak rain, the theory being that somehow it had lodged into their
chickpea brains that the world was all greenfull and pleasure from
now on. Couldn't they see the land was already parched again?
Obadiah caught nine of them orgying in the backseat of his Datsun
and attacked them with a broom, which seemed only to increase the
rapture all around. The noise of their foul love deafening but inde-
scribable, and yet I hear them still in my sleep. That gurgly, broody,
out-of-breath whorling. Ecstatic death throes that went on death-
lessly across dusk, night, dawn, coffee — feather-flapping fuckery. They
do not do normal pigeon activities. They do not roost. They do not
sun themselves. They do not harass your feet while you are eating an
egg sandwich. They fuck. After that they fuck. Pigeon-mating season was supposed to last two weeks in the drier season — dry, drier,
drought — and so was considered by the regional government to be
only a minor plague on the list. As it has now gone on a month, we
would welcome any other wrath, because those birds are such an
affront to the general celibacy of Goas. Toads, serpents, locusts,
boils, blains — at least they wouldn't mock us. Leprosy? Give us the
spots. Of course, Vilho counsels love, his finger holding his place in
Matthew 13:37. He calls them doves, not pigeons. "He that soweth
the good seed," he says. "What would Jesus say?"

Pohamba blows him a kiss. "Jesus would stomp these flying rats
with a fat hairy sandaled foot."

*   *   *

A moment of reprieve. Mercy of a soft thud. One drops dead in the soccer field right in the middle of it. Just rolls off and that's it, motionless feathers. We go out there and hold an impromptu funeral. We ring around him, we figure it's a him. "Same thing happened to Nelson Rockefeller," I say. "Died on top of his secretary." People ignore this, like a lot of things I tend to say.

Beerless, we raise plastic cups of lukewarm water and toast this pigeon's flight to hell. Sheeny blue-green body, deviled orange eyes. All around, his countryman haven't noticed, haven't flagged. A fundamental truth we didn't want to be reminded of: You die, everybody else goes on fucking. That's when Vilho, smelling our vulnerability, flaps back to the Old Testament, starts in about the murder of the Kenite, Sisera, by Jael, the wife of Heber. How Jael, clever wench, lured the sex-starved Sisera into her tent with the promise of her favors, her charms. How she gave Sisera butter. Then, as soon as Sisera got comfortable, she smote him on the head with a nail. "*At her feet, he bowed, he fell, he lay down.* A Kenite," Vilho says. "God reviled him, but still his death is grace. Who among us will not die on a bed of sin?"

We look at Vilho. We look at the deceased. As if one or the other could provide an answer, but to what? Even Pohamba is silent. Butter — absolutely — but to be smote on the head? Theofilus brings back a shovel from the mission garage, and we, bereft, bury our old tormenter amid the racket of the continuing deliciousness of his fellow foul fowls.

27

MID-MORNING BREAK

She never laughed. Even during break, when Obadiah would retell that morning's moral tale, doing his best imitation of the principal's self-flagellation (which was, by his kind of osmosis, our flagellation):

Oh, savage gluttony! Ye who fare sumptuously while others go without. Do ye not ache for your lack of guilt? Consider for once the Ethiopians, the Irish, the Chinese. Have you no pity? No, it is only, More meat, more crackers, more cheese. Ye who would not offer a finger dipped in water to a thirsty —

Mavala sitting in the sand, leaning against a barrel, unpeeling a hard-boiled egg. Not hearing a thing. Us all trying not to watch her bite the top off that egg. Obadiah said it was the struggle. All those years of believing the end of the war would usher in Paradise. He said Mavala Shikongo was even more beautiful for believing in all that. Now she carries an attendance register and wipes snot from under sub b noses? She's old, Obadiah said. No matter what her legs look like. It's all that believing. A woman with a Kalashnikov isn't anything new. My Lord, think of the Amazons of Dahomey. But believing — it's like seeing a bronze-winged courser this far west of Gobabis.

28

SIESTA

We must raise the political and social
status of teachers. They should command
the respect not only of their students, but
also of the whole community.

DENG XIAOPING

After classes, after lunch. A consecrated time of languishment. A flopped, dead-eyed hour. Our beds damp oases, narrow paradises of our own orificial excretions. And here we wallow in moist, sweat-clammy bliss, until the study-hour triangle rings us back to bondage.

One siesta — hark — treason! A boy (ruffian! villain! bandit!) whistles — loudly — as he wanders by Obadiah's open bedroom window. The insomniac inside just so happens to be asleep this day. (Taped to Obadiah's screen, facing out for the world to be inspired by, is a photo of Mandela after his release: that peppered hair, that raised fist, that loving-even-my-jailers smile.) But Obadiah, now that he is awake, is no gentle spirit of the nation today. He's belligerent. Nonetheless, to temper his fury, he uses the language of diplomacy. Hence, the following resolution is translated from the French:

Be it known that Head Teacher Obadiah Horaseb of the Goas Primary School RC *calls upon* all boys of Goas to heed the following . . . That Head Teacher *recognizes* the need for spontaneous joy in young plebeians who do not yet comprehend that life on earth amounts to nothing but sorrow, regret, failure, and, ultimately, humiliation.

Furthermore, that Head Teacher *reaffirms* such young plebeians' inherent, nay, inalienable right to express such bonhomie in certain proscribed instances, such as the Lord granting me a decent night sleep. However, be it known that Head Teacher henceforth *forbids* the expression of any such jollity — particularly by way of infernal whistling — at any time during siesta, which, be it also known, is the only remaining solace for those who do understand that life on earth amounts to nothing but sorrow, regret, failure, etc., etc. The Head Teacher *decrees* that punishment for whistling — which may, in the instant case, be defined, to wit, as: to emit or utter from the mouth or beak a shrill sound or series of sounds — shall be the SEVERANCE of said offender's lips from said offender's mouth, through the deployment of Theofilus's unsharpened sickle.

Mindful of this day of non-repose,
Head Teacher Horaseb
Adieu.

29

SHOE WAR

Miss Tuyeni had much of her sister's beauty, but wore it all wrong. She had the same long legs, the same jutting chin and huge blinkless eyes. But Tuyeni scowled constantly, so, unlike her sister's, there was no mystery on her face. The world never ceased to find ways to disappoint Miss Tuyeni. We noticed her much more after Mavala came back. Before that, she had seemed to be merely a better-looking appendage of the principal. She was childless. As far as anybody knew, she'd never been pregnant. This led to all kinds of talk, most involving the besmirchment of the principal's manhood. But it wasn't true that she was a complete nonentity. She wielded a quiet sort of power in her own right, and you could sometimes feel it during staff meetings. When she didn't like something he'd said, she had a way of letting him know. All of sudden he would veer away from a topic, and we knew it had something to do with her. But we never cracked their intimate marital code. Mostly she kept to herself. She never was treated quite like a traitor. After all, she had to live with him, and people couldn't help but feel a little sorry for her for that. The only person she ever talked to was Antoinette, as if Miss Tuyeni, for her part, acknowledged the one true authority on the farm.

Still, as I say, the fact of Mavala made Miss Tuyeni more present, because how could we not compare them? And maybe she realized this and tried to compensate. Even though Mavala had dishonored her family in the eyes of the Lord, Miss Tuyeni started wearing high heels to school. She had no mastery of this delicate art. The truth: We all took sadistic joy in watching Miss Tuyeni totter across the sand toward morning meeting. The treacherous crossing, books in arm, one unnimble step after another. Sometimes she would tip over and the principal would send a boy to help her up.

Then Mavala would come charging down the road, always on the edge of being late. We speculated that the reason Mavala was so good in heels, her gravity-defying sense of balance, had something to do with — combat. Everything that was wonderful about Mavala Shikongo had to do with combat. You see how she twisted us?

30

MOSES

The boy who the priest caught jerking off to the statue of the Virgin in the church grotto. The boy who burned down the science class. The boy who tried to poison the farm's water supply with diesel. The boy who stole Festus's classroom door. The boy who . . . The boy who . . . None was mightier than Moses, the Standard Seven who slaughtered a neighboring farmer's cow with a pocketknife and lived off it in the veld for two weeks. Moses out there alone, a small cooking fire, only the eyes of the dead cow for company. But he's eating meat; Lord, is he eating meat. A boy who got tired of mealies every day. He was a poor boy, an orphan. Yet a child born of this earth is entitled to some meat now and then. Is he not?

"In those days the boys ate meat only on holidays," Antoinette says. "Now we try to give it to them twice a week, if we have enough paraffin for the refrigerator."

Antoinette speaks of Moses in the way a lonely mother might go on about the antics of the favored bad child. If anything remotely like this happened on her watch now, she'd thrash him. Uncountable lashes for a boy so bold. But Moses — she'd pull him to her bosom. Have some tea with four sugars, my wayward boy.

We are in the kitchen of the hostel dining hall, a wide, cavernous, many-windowed building beyond the soccer field. It reminds me of an air hangar or a floor of an abandoned factory. The windows are fogged from the steam rising from a vat of burbling pap. The boys are lined up outside the door, banging one another on the head with impatient spoons.

She lays out clean bowls on the tables as she talks. Antoinette tells

73

stories only during the heat of work. A Moses without a basket. A Moses without a people to lead. Only his own poor hunger. After the constables finally found him, they beat him until they got bored. What could they take from him other than his blood? Then they brought him to the farmer, who beat Moses until he too got bored with it, and that was the end of it. God only knows where the boy is today.

Outside, the boys begin to clamor louder. Antoinette walks the tables slowly, ladling thick pap into bowl after bowl. Today is krummelpap with a side of toast with jam.

"But forget the end," Antoinette says. "Go back to the beginning, think of murdering a cow with a pocketknife. Cows don't fight back, but this doesn't mean they die easy. They stand and bleed. It took hours. It took the boy all night. It wasn't rage. It was work."

She points to the door. I open it. Then she steps past me and stands before the motley line of boys and raises her oven-mitted hands for silence. The boys file in, trying to be slow, trying not to dash, the big ones yanking the little ones back, toward their waiting, steaming bowls.

31

BY THE PISS TREE

Obadiah and I doing our part, watering the desert.

"Teacher Kaplansk?"

"Yes?"

"I should like to know your candid opinion of Woodrow Wilson. It's my contention that despite his having a horse-like face, he had a certain fastidious decorum. And I do not doubt his sincerity. And yet, I must tell you straight out, and you must pardon any offense: Your man Woodrow was a cabbage. Not only was he ultimately responsible for fascism, he also left us, our dear insignificant country, in the lurch for seventy years. And South-West Africa shall be a sacred trust of civilization. Sacred trust of *whom*?"

"He wore a top hat," I said.

"I wonder why. To make himself taller? Napoleon did that."

"I think he was tall to begin with."

"Hmm. Interesting. A tall man in a tall hat. May I ask you another question? Apropos perhaps of nothing?"

"Sure."

"Your quite un-Wilsonian surname. What sort of name is Kaplansk? It seems highly original."

"It was Jewish Polish until the principal lopped off an —"

"Polish! I should have known! How many names under the sun rhyme with Gdansk? Ah, and a Semite? But your hair —"

"What?"

"It's orange."

"Yes."

He leaned toward me and examined my face. I breathed in his

sweet, malty breath. "Hmm. Yes, well, *Hosanna!* My first Jew! I've waited a long time."

"You're my first Damara."

"Half. My father. My mother came from Angola."

"First half-Angolan also."

"My father's dead. Yours?"

"No."

"Jewish as well?"

"Yes."

"A rebbe?"

"No."

"A scholar?"

"Not really."

"A dealer in ancient manuscripts and maps? A cabbalist? A loan officer? Pardon any offense."

"He's a dentist."

Obadiah thought a moment, a bit dejected, but after he zipped up, he brightened. "Ah yes, a most basic and elemental human need fulfilled, no doubt honorably, by your Hebrew father."

"He left my mother. Ran off to Memphis with a hygienist named Brenda."

"I see, nonetheless, teeth . . ."

32

OBADIAH (3 A.M.)

Every moment is a death. We may go back and haunt them, but we may never possess them again. Who designed such a cruel mechanism as memory? Imagine yourself on a train. You see a boy walking the veld. He begins to raise his arm, his mouth widens. He's about to shout to you — and then nothing. The boy's gone before you even started to see him. I was on a train only once, the most dawdling train anybody ever bothered to build — the Windhoek-Swakop line. Pushing a team of wheelbarrows across the Namib would be faster. But even the slowest train in creation is still a train. Even a wooden seat in a third-class carriage rocks you like a mother. See him out there beside the tracks? Trousers too short for him, shirtless, carrying a staff tied off with a red kerchief? And still I can't hold him, his rising arm, his almost shout. I float by. Something he needed to tell me? Something I needed to know? So I died then. That was twenty-five years ago, the occasion of my exile. Are that boy's words still on the wind? A warning? At the temple courts, Jesus wrote with his finger, in the dust. What words? Nobody knows. Do you see what I'm trying to say?

33

IN THE NORTH

I'm not talking about some fucking Gandhi refusing to step on ants," Pohamba says.

He tells this often. It happened up north in the bush near Oshikuku, he says. An SADF tank is roaming the veld looking for terrorists, when suddenly — Pohamba loves the word "suddenly" — an old man with leaves on his head jumps out from beyond a clump of bush and begins to beat the tank with a stick. The two troopies inside watch him for a while through the heavy windows. It's a pretty good show after two months of wet Ovambo heat. They listen to the crazy smacking, which reverberates, so that for every hit they hear it twice. *Someone's knocking on the door,* one troopie sings. *Someone's ringing the bell.* He points to the other troopie, who opens the hatch and shoots the man with leaves on his head once in the arm, but this doesn't stop him. He keeps at it. Whack whack. The troopie shoots him again. Single pistol shots sound almost funny in a bush war like this, Pohamba says. Normally you hear only the bursts of automatics. But the second shot doesn't slow him down either. The man with leaves on his head is dancing now. Dancing around the tank, bleeding and hitting. Now the tank is polka-dot red. It takes two helmeted troopies ten shots, Pohamba says, and even then he never lets go of the stick.

"And do you know what?"

We know. It's me and Vilho and him, and we're lounging on the mealie sacks outside the hostel kitchen, waiting for Dikeledi to hang her laundry. Holy laundry, blessed laundry. Pohamba slides his mirrored sunglasses down his nose and peers at us, repeats, "And do you know what?"

I stifle a yawn. "I can't imagine."

He leans back against the mealie sacks, sighs. Then he drags it out, slowly, dramatically: "He   wasn't   a   he."

"Tut," Vilho says, without looking up from his book. "Tut, tut, tut."

Pohamba sucks his teeth and starts again. "Once upon a time in the north . . . You see, the north isn't like here. Things *happen* in the north. Things *have happened* in the north. This is not a place to live. Cows eat sand for breakfast. In the north, the baobab trees grow so big they use one as a post office."

"A baobab isn't a tree," Vilho says. "It's a succulent."

"Once upon a time in the sacred north," I say. "An SADF tank is roaming the veld when *suddenly* a man with leaves on his head . . ."

". . . begins beating the tank with a stick," Pohamba says. "And beating and beating and beating and beating . . ."

". . . until one of the troopies inside gets tired of it, so he shoots the man . . ."

". . . who isn't really a man," Vilho says.

"Yes," Pohamba shouts. "The end!"

We sit there. It's still too early for Dikeledi's laundry.

Vilho looks up from his book. "But why would she want to die like that?" he says. "Why would anyone choose such a graceless death?"

"Graceless?" Pohamba says. Then he stands up and does Christ. This is a new wrinkle in the story. He droops his head, reaches his arms out wide, contorts his face into his idea of rapturous agony. Crucifixion atop the mealie sacks. "You prefer this?"

"Our Lord didn't have a choice," Vilho says, looking up at him. "He didn't want to die for us, he wanted to live. That's the whole message."

And Jesus did nudge Vilho with his toe. His arms still stretched out, his head lolling, Pohamba says, "You see, they've killed everyone in my village. All the terrorist old women and all the terrorist babies and all the terrorist chickens. Only I was left alive. So what must I do? I gather leaves. I find a good stick. Now do you understand?"

"Even their abominations do not justify."

Pohamba twitches and takes a sniff of an armpit. "Whew, brother, too long on the cross!"

"Let her live," Vilho says, squeezing his eyes shut. "Next time you tell it, let her —"

"What?" Pohamba plops down heavily on the mealie sacks. "You want her to wait around for it like a goat?"

34

DROUGHT STORIES

Drought stories were told the same way war stories were — they filled in the gaps of the longest days — except they were more true and left less room for dramatic acts of bravery. You don't fight the Almighty. You don't sneak up behind lack of rain. You don't sabotage clouds. You die. At least back in the old days. Now drought means you breathe up dust and the food prices are higher at the Pick 'n Pay and salaries remain the same and the government has to import mealies from Zimbabwe. And cattle suffer.

But in '79 the drought in the Koakveld (this happened to other people — to be a victim of drought meant you were a farm person, and no one at Goas was a farm person, Goas being a temporary stop, no matter how many years of your life you spent there) was accompanied by an epidemic of rats. Rats who became just as hungry as the people. What happened was, a rat ate a baby. This happened to a family no one knew personally. Antoinette told it while she was hosing down her tiny garden with water pirated from the science lab. She grew wild onions and radishes and small tomatoes. She was wearing her green Sunday dress. It was Sunday, after church. During the drought of '79, in the Koakveld, up in Africa, she said, not here, it didn't happen down here, a starving rat ate a starving baby.

35

MAVALA

I watch her shadow as she stalks across the courtyard, her heels stabbing the sand. She avoids the patch of the principal's Ireland and steps up into the open door of his office. He's either on the phone or about to be, his big hand reaching for it. Who he talked to we never knew, although he always seemed to be ordering supplies and books we never saw.

I'm doing a reading-comprehension drill. I have just read them a story about a mischievous boy named Tom and his wily teacher, Sir Joseph Blinks. *Now the question is: Why does Sir Blinks mistrust Tom?*

I stand near my open classroom door. I hear her ask for construction paper. I look back at my class. Most have their heads down and are doing their best to write something, except for Rubrecht Kanhala, who knows I'm only trying to run out the clock before third-period break. He's thumping the end of his nose with a pencil. Sir Blinks doesn't know shit.

I step out and wander halfway up the porchway and listen.

"You need to fill out a requisition form."

"Give me a form, then."

"The forms are finished."

A long silence. Outside Pohamba's class a boy whacks two erasers together and gags on the chalky smoke.

The principal is sitting. Mavala is standing. His finger is poised in mid-dial of the rotary. She watches his face. If only she'd slacken a little, this young sister of his wife, and behave more like a woman is supposed to. He could make things easier for her. She need not acknowledge his authority — of course she needn't go that far —

82

but for God's sake, won't she look at his existence as flesh, as a man with hands and blood and cock and need and eyes?

I don't have to see any of this — it's all there in the silence. Power is easily spent — you can always get more later — but as far as she's concerned, he can keep it and play with it. He sees this, and it only makes him sweat watching her. Her: Go ahead. Cower beneath me with your principal stomach, your principal key chain, your principal phone in your hand. She doesn't leave, only stands there, in her sleeveless blouse, with her bare shoulders. Stands there like a taunt. A few minutes more she's in that office. Maybe she's going too far — stepping on him too much, too easily, too early. She hasn't been back a month. There's no more talk of construction paper or forms.

She leaves empty-handed and heads back across the courtyard — this time she tromps straight across Ireland — toward her class, which is waiting silently (itself a miracle at Goas). She'll ask Obadiah for some construction paper. No, a better idea. She'll take her boys to the veld and let them draw on the rocks like Bushmen. A few minutes later, I watch them file out, her ducklings, two by two.

36

COFFEE FIRE

W hat does she want, then?"
   "Not to be a teacher, obviously."
"Who wants to be a teacher?"

"Not me."

"You degrade the profession. Shame —"

"Well, she was probably expecting more. Look at Libertine Amathila. Now she's Minister of Health. Didn't they name a boulevard after her in Otjiwarongo?"

"But Libertine Amathila's a doctor. SWAPO sent her abroad to study. Easy to come back to the country a hero when you're a doctor."

"And now she's got her own avenue!"

"Boulevard!"

"Yes, even better!"

"Miss Tuyeni says one day she just left and crossed the border. They didn't hear from her for two years. They thought she was dead."

"How old?"

"Seventeen or so. The mother nearly died of grief over it."

"How did she come to teaching if she hates it so much?"

"She taught school up in the camp."

"Teacher and a soldier?"

"Yes."

"Not the only one."

"Who else?"

"I'd rather not boast."

"Well, it's understandable."

"What is?"

"To want more after something like that. After committing so much to the cause, wouldn't you expect —"

"What? More than Goas? Everybody deserves —"

"Always more. Why can't anyone ever —"

"And the kid?"

"Ah, yes — the child."

"That child's demonic."

"Shush — that's a beautiful lamb."

37

ANTOINETTE

Just past noon and the boy is, at last, sleeping beneath the kitchen table. *Difficult,* the girl said, as if the child was a problem to solve. Now she understands. There's some rage within him — his little fists are constant. Unless, like now, he's sleeping, his anger gone. As if sleep possesses us, infuses us with a goodness that isn't really us. She peeks at the boy, at his tiny unclenched hands, at his dirty elbows, at his stomach rising and falling. Or what if it is us? What if asleep is the only time we are true? If so, who are we when we're awake?

She takes Obadiah's glasses out of her apron. Often he declares them lost and she finds them at various places around the farm. She begins to read.

Most days she lets the wind decide the page. Other, rarer times, like now, she goes back to the beginning.

The beginning? Does one remember being born? I was always at Goas. Even before I was at Goas, I was at Goas. Before the dry land was the water and the firmament. Out this window, I see the dry land. At night, I see the firmament. Where's the water?

They say there was an ocean here once. It must have dried up.

And the boy, scrambling out from under the table, makes for the door.

38

OBADIAH (SHAVING)

Two souls abide, alas, within my breast,
And each one seeks riddance from the other.
The one clings with a dogged love and lust
With clutching parts unto this present world.
The other surges fiercely from the dust
Unto sublime ancestral fields.

GOETHE, *FAUST*

I stand before this mirror an orphan. Of my own body I would say I have decidedly mixed feelings. It is tall. It carries my head. It seems my left leg is longer than my right, but this has never been proven. There are days when I see my feet as if from a great distance. When I was young, in my vanity, I favored turtleneck sweaters to accentuate what I considered to be my Corinthian neck. That I am now ugly is of no concern. My mottled, sagging skin. My berried nose. That my face fails to present my beauty and originality is not a failure of my maker. Rather, it is a testament to the unsung nature of my uniqueness. That the philistines cannot recognize my soaringness only makes it truer. More than truth. Is there a higher highest? A truthlier truth? My head carries my thoughts and my legs carry my body. And yet touch — physical — I long for it again. *Don't you remember?* When you used to do do do Meneer Oblongsky? Remember? Your thimbled fingers? When I was poor but also beautiful? Now I'm poor and ugly? Meneer Oblongsky hangs limp like a wrung chicken's neck, and still I'm sick with desire?

Lame men make lusty husbands? Would it were so, Poet. Now I ride the donkey by memory. And yet it isn't merely youth I lust for, but last week. Give me back last week. My Antoinette in her chair rubbing her feet with camphor.

39

ANTOINETTE

and shall cleave unto his wife: and they shall be one flesh.

Love? You want to know where love went?
   Easy. Same place as all the water. Now enough. I have stomachs to satisfy.

40

GOAS

The first recorded attempt to escape Goas occurred in 1930, when a Boer farmer named S. J. Dupreez tried to trade the farm for a lusher parcel upcountry.

OFFICE OF THE MAGISTRATE
KARIBIB
12 JULY 1930

My dear Sir,

As you no doubt know I have been a heavy loser of stock, having lost all owing to the latest drought. It was my intention to quit the country altogether but owing to the pleas of my motherless and unmarried daughter Grieta I have decided to try again but in another district. With this end in view I paid a visit to the north and was very much taken with the east side of Outjo District, particularly the vacant farm Weiseenfels. What I propose to do is effect an exchange of my farm Goas with that of Farm Weiseenfels, the hectarage being roughly the same. Goas as you know is occasionally well watered, and will no doubt make a most valuable addition to the Otjimbingwe Native Reserve, an opportunity for an enterprising kaffir. In penning you these lines I do so in the hope that you will kindly forward same with your recommendation to the proper quarters.

Your Obedient Servant,
S. J. Dupreez

SECRETARY FOR SOUTHWEST AFRICA
F. P. COURTNEY CLARK
WINDHOEK
8 DECEMBER 1930
RE: FARM GOAS

SIR, I beg to forward herewith for your consideration a letter received from Mr. S. J. Dupreez, owner of the farm Goas in this district. There has been no rain on the farm since early last year, and Mr. Dupreez has lost all his cattle throught [sic] drought. I have informed Mr. Dupreez that the Administrator does not contemplate purchasing any of the farms adjoining the Otjimbingwe Native Reserve owing to the depletion of stock therein, and there is little likelihood of his proposal being accepted.

Acting Magistrate
T. Miller

OFFICE OF THE MAGISTRATE
KARIBIB
12 DECEMBER 1930
RE: FARM GOAS

With reference to your minute No. 2/4/2/4 of the 8th instant, I shall be glad if you will kindly inform Mr. Dupreez that it is regretted that the administration is not at this time prepared to entertain his generous offer.

SECRETARY FOR SOUTHWEST AFRICA
F. P. COURTNEY CLARK
WINDHOEK

Thus, Dupreez's proposal (i.e., this farm is so useless you may as well give it back to the natives) failed. He did, however, establish a precedent of unrequitement that would reign at Goas for the next sixty years: a great urge to leave, matched only by total practical impossibility. Eleven more years Dupreez hung on in the wind and sand. In March of 1941, he died of gout. His bloated corpse was buried between his long dead wife and his (still unmarried) daughter, Grieta, who had died of consumption the year before. Moss doesn't grow on graves in the desert. At Goas they are known as the Voortrekker graves, in honor of the great trek the Boers took to reach this paradise of their dreams. In his will, S.J. bequeathed the farm to the only one who couldn't refuse it, God, through his fiduciary on earth, the Roman Catholic Archdiocese of Windhoek. There are two ways of seeing this at Goas. One is that he may have thought he'd get a place in heaven for this bestowal. In which case, the line went, he burns in hell for trying to stiff the Almighty. The other: He knew exactly what he was doing. As a Dutch Calvinist, he wanted to stick it to the Catholics.

The diocese didn't know what to do with Goas. There was an idea of turning it into a leper colony, but apparently they couldn't find enough Catholic lepers. Finally, the bishop sent two German monks, Brother Sebastian and Brother Gerhard, out there to raise karakul sheep. Even at that time those two monks were well into their last years. But the diocese needed cash, and karakul was where the money was. Either way you looked at it, a win-win proposition. If the brothers made good and raised capital, praise be. If they dropped dead out there, God's will. The plan failed on both counts. The sheep died and Brother Sebastian and Brother Gerhard didn't.

In '42, their inaugural year, drought wiped out half the herd. In '43, the rains came, but so did blue tongue. In '45, more drought. In '46, they held on. In '48, they had too much rain. The Swakop River swelled and another third of the sheep drowned. And yet the two monks lived on — and on — thereby establishing another tenet of Goas: Its misery is hearty. The lashing wind and the frigid mornings and the eyeball-melting afternoons eventually become what your life was always supposed to amount to. Two monks, exiled in the wind. Raising karakul even under the best of conditions — they are a finicky, wimpy breed — was an enterprise born of love and despair. Year follows year and Brother Sebastian and Brother Gerhard don't die. Their nights are long. The bleat of the parched lambs keeps them awake. They aren't exactly missionaries. There are no native heathens here to preach to. The monks carry God's Word to a veld that never even sends back an echo. Weren't there days when they wondered whether they were still alive, when it occurred to them that they might no longer be living, breathing men, holding sheep shears and praying?

The fifties were as hot and desiccated as the forties. And yet because of a year like '53, they endured. In '53 there was enough rain. The sheep got fat. The shearing went on into the night for weeks. The sort of year that makes all the suffering worth it, until the next drought comes and all that's left is to tell stories of '53.

You recall '53, Brother Sebastian?

Oh, happy times, Brother Gerhard. Happy times.

Then one afternoon Brother Gerhard didn't come home from a walk in the veld, and Brother Sebastian went out and searched for him. He's still searching. Of all the ghosts at Goas, and as Obadiah says, for a small place, our ghosts are legion, none is more bewildered than Brother Sebastian. Awkward, naked, and cold — and dead himself now too — and still Brother Sebastian keeps searching for Brother Gerhard's body. He senses him in one place, then another. People hold out hope that Brother Sebastian will one day stop looking and be at peace. In the meantime, it is Brother Sebastian who digs those strange, unidentifiable holes we sometimes find by our doors in the morning, too big for a rabbit and too small for a hedgehog. Each one like a tiny, empty grave.

In 1967, with the Group Areas Act forcing black schoolchildren out of the towns, the Church found another use for Goas. A school! Why hadn't anybody thought of that before?

* * *

It would be difficult to find a place more unlovingly built. Two parallel rows of classrooms, concrete blocks, repainted yellow each year by Theofilus. The boys' hostel the same — narrow, barracks-like. A church that could double as a storage area. Small houses for the married teachers. A bachelors' quarters for the single males. In spite of the new paint, the place is already in a state of minor crumble. We live amid newish-looking ruins. And yet after a while you start to see that maybe there's a logic to the place, that the buildings of Goas are only as temporary as the people who pass through them.

Hereby established a Native School (Inboorlingskool) situated south of Karibib and maintained by the Archdiocese of Windhoek resident at 2013 Peter Mueller Strasse, Windhoek, was duly registered under Sub-section (1)(a) of Section one hundred and five Education Ordinance, 1962 (27 of 1962) made under the ordinance.

DIRECTOR OF NATIVE EDUCATION
WINDHOEK
27 JULY 1967

And when the wall of night fell on the first boys in the hostel, boys who had come here from all parts of the country, where did they think they were?

41

THEOFILUS

He was easy to forget, though he was always among us. At least when he wasn't in the veld mending a fence or milking the cows or shooting a kudu for meat for the boys or disinfecting the toilets or regreasing the generator or smoking bats out of the hostel — or any other of the thousand things he did every day that made us feel our laziness so acutely it was like a wound — Theofilus was among us. Maybe not even listening, but near. His hands momentarily still. The farm would have collapsed without him within a week, and yet we so often forgot him. In hindsight, this seems surprising, because, to be honest, he was so shocking-looking. Theofilus was albino, but this was never mentioned out loud. Not white exactly, his skin was more like faded red leather. And nobody made any of the usual cuts about black albinos either. Nobody said his eyelids got seared off when God kissed him out of heaven. Nobody said he was a photographic negative with legs, or a milk kaffir, or that he was the ghost who nibbled children's feet at night. People talked only about his graceful, motor oil–stained hands and how there was nothing he couldn't fix except Japanese cars, which was all right, since Jesus himself couldn't have healed Obadiah's Datsun.

He slept on a cot in the mission garage. His bed was always neatly made with a single blanket. I never saw a pillow on it. He kept his second pair of boots under the bed, along with a cardboard box where he stored the clothes he wasn't wearing. There was also, sometimes, a shadow made by his bed that stretched across the oily pavement of the garage, depending on the time of day and the angle of the sun coming in through the cracked windows.

Every third Saturday of the month, Theofilus would leave the farm and its cattle and goats in the charge of two Standard Sevens and take a donkey cart to visit his wife. She was attached to a farm near Wilhelmstal, halfway to Okahandja. It was said she couldn't move out to Goas and live with Theofilus because keeping a wife didn't come with his job. Once a month, he ironed his suit and white shirt on an old unused door held up by two upturned paint cans. Once a month, his tattered blue jumper swung in the wind on the line behind the garage, waiting for him to put it on again Monday morning.

The boys were having a soccer tournament that Saturday, so we were out there on the sidelines, sitting on desks we'd dragged from our classrooms, watching and betting on teams. Bufula Bufula were 2 to 1 over Pepsi All-African Stars, 8 to 1 over Omaruru Toyota. (Pohamba's odds.)

Theofilus on his donkey cart in a pressed black suit and shined shoes. He was all hitched up, the cart standing near the far goal, in front of the mission garage. The unfair thing was, he had always been kind to them, never beat them at all, much less very hard, and he never picked on the lazier of the two, a nameless grizzle-haired black and brown who often let his friend, a gray shaggy named Oom Zak, carry most of the weight. He fed those two donkeys more carrots than they could eat. It was as though they'd talked it over and decided that day to go on strike, Theofilus and his mercy be damned. We could see, from our seats on the other side of the field, that he at first considered it an aberration. He beat them a few times, gently. Still, they wouldn't budge. He beat them harder. Nothing. We watched him look curiously at the stick, as if it were the problem. Then Theofilus raised the stick over his head and calmly began to flog them.

He kept at it.

Finally, even the boys noticed and stopped the game to watch Theofilus crack those donkeys so hard and for so long that we could see the blood of the lazy nameless one flicking off the stick. The whole time he stared straight ahead, like none of this was happening, as if the whole farm weren't watching. A man on his way to see his wife but not going anywhere. His long legs at perfect right angles, so that they looked, from where we all were sitting, like a solid table. We all watched — the teachers and the boys. Him pretending it wasn't happening, even as the blood began to splatter his clean suit, and still those two stood motionless, as if today they were no longer farm donkeys but dignified statues of their supposed cousins, horses.

Theofilus straddled up there in his best now-ruined clothes. There was something almost obscene about how we couldn't take our eyes off it. It was Mavala Shikongo who finally said something. She was sitting with that baby, Tomo, clawing around, biting her ankles. She'd begun to join us. Tomo had come first. He couldn't be contained in that little room that used to be the principal's garage. And Mavala had followed. What else was there to do at Goas, ultimately, but join us?

She gets him a day a month?

I didn't hear it when she said it. Do you know what I mean? At first, you don't hear something, and then you play it back in your head and you hear it perfectly?

She didn't say anything else. Still, she shamed us. We hadn't thought of his wife. Maybe we figured we didn't need to. We'd seen so many like her, old mammies walking along the goat paths that ran beside the tar roads, scarves wrapped tight around their heads. Why be more specific?

Theofilus didn't break the bastard stick across his knees. He set it down on the floor of the cart like it was made of glass. He looked exhausted, as if he really had gone to her and come back. His pale, sun-ravaged face. He got off the cart and unbuckled the harnesses the same gentle way he always did. Then he walked to the mission garage and hoisted the door and went inside. The boy who had been closest to the cart, the keeper, Skinny Hilunda, walked up and gave the donkeys a few punches in their flanks. They didn't notice. Later, both of them wandered away to the veld, because they felt like wandering away to the veld. Theofilus didn't work that day. He didn't come out of the garage. And we sat by the soccer field and thought of her watching the road he wouldn't come home on, wondering if somehow after all these years she had got the wrong Saturday. Are you next week, Theo? Always she hears him before she sees him. The axles beneath the cart shriek, and if there's no wind, she can practically hear him from as far as Vogelslang — then him coming into view over a rise in the highway.

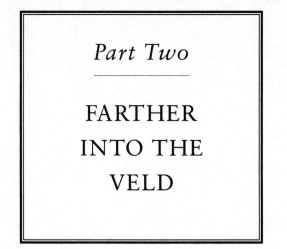

Part Two

FARTHER INTO THE VELD

God preserve me from love.
— Bessie Head

42

NIGHT

Summer or whatever you called that even hotter time before summer even started when your skin wasn't used to the night heat yet and the mosquitoes began their bloodlusty moaning. How their noise changed as the night went deeper. At the beginning of the night they were feverish because of the unbearably beautiful proximity of your flesh, and yet the netting and the coils worked for the most part and the lust changed to frustration and you'd listen to their hunger for you rise and dissipate, rise and dissipate, until you sank into a sort of stupor that didn't feel like sleeping, though you woke up in the morning and realized you had slept, that it hadn't all been a waiting. And in the morning, the hopeful ones, the hangers-on, were so drowsy from unrequited aching outside the net they were simple to kill, so on hot mornings you'd hear, from every room in the singles quarters, the sound of joyous acrobatic whacking, easy rolled-newspaper slaughter, even from Vilho's, all that love-thy-neighbor talk and he was as much mass murderer as we were, and then we'd show off the carnage on our walls, give each other mini-tours of death, Got this fucker with my pinkie, all the flat black asterisks, and the lucky ones also, the ones sated with our blood, them massacred now too, us thinking we've reaped our revenge, always forgetting that tonight our victories will mean nothing, that they'll all be reborn, reincarnated fifty, a hundred, a thousand times, and that killing them will always be the same as not killing them.

43

POHAMBA

Spacious days yawned on. We put off everything we had to do, because there would always be time for it later. This afternoon was tomorrow. Night was Madagascar. We'd stand before our classes and say words, slowly, languidly, words. It was as if we were talking under water. These were days Pohamba couldn't contain himself. He was sweating for it, working long hours of love, going to Karibib every chance he got (hitching rides, taking Festus's bike), and straggling back to Goas at sunrise and not changing his clothes for school, just appearing in the staff room for morning meeting with enormous ovals of sweat staining his silken armpits. Even the principal respected Pohamba's work ethic and didn't ride the Good Book too hard on him.

He'd often run out of money. Only Vilho would still give him any. That saint would look at him with his sad, empathetic eyes and stick the rands in Pohamba's pocket like a bouquet. And still Pohamba would feel the need to explain it: "Can't be a sugar daddy without any sugar, hey?"

Those days were hardest on his Standard Sevens. The more fatigued he was, the more he expected of them, up there in front of his class roaring: "Differentiate the following: Y equals 1 plus X divided by the square root of 1 minus X to the second power."

"But, Teacher —"

A bleary, too-caffeinated man pacing the rows with a ruler in one hand and his big deadly wooden protractor in the other. "Do you want to end up at Goas like me? Don't you boys see I only want the best for you? No fingers. Calculate!"

44

TOMO

What kind of person hates a baby? That's no baby. He only looks like a baby. Mavala called him her monstrous, her squirmy, her rodentia, her bedlam. He had squat little legs like a miniature Greco-Roman wrestler. We called him Little Festus. He was not yet two but was seen by reliable witnesses lifting a wheelbarrow over his head. He loved a toilet house, especially when you were in it. (As good a time as any to mention that the only toilet house that locked from the inside was the principal's private one. It would have been considered tantamount to a coup d'état if anyone else shat in it.) Tomo's ferrety, chicken-greasy fingers in your pockets. He ate everything. He noticed everything, understood everything. I remember his eyes staring at me through the slats of a chair, just his eyes, holding me, knowing me, hating me back. We were jealous of him. Of what his eyes had the privilege of seeing in person. An outside shower, the spigot in the back of the principal's house. Tomo sits in the muddied sand while she . . . she . . . she . . .

I'd try to hold him tender — my false hands — and his body would seize. And that thing. All babies do this, but Tomo did it with particular vengeance. That thing they do. You'd be playing with him, or think you were playing with him, having a good time making gurgling noises and chasing him around, and then he'd fall over and he'd raise his head and think about it a moment, make the calculation. Decide whether it was in his best interest to cry bloody murder. In my case he always wailed like the tornado drill at Wainscott Elementary on North Clifton in Cincinnati. The way he could turn it on, turn it off. Blast. Modulate. Blast.

Upside-down in his car seat, his feet where his head should be (one bootie on, the other long gone), that big head dangling down. How those eyes never seemed to bother with seeing anything superfluous. Like your lying-ass smile. He sneered right through you. He couldn't talk yet, and maybe this was the true source of his power. Words would only get in the way of his seeing the essentials. Who would hate a baby?

We said Mavala Shikongo never laughed. It wasn't true. It was that only he could make her do it. I mean laugh. Laugh like a banshee, as if she had the whooping cough, uncontrollable seal barks you could hear all the way from the principal's house. Small, easy things like brushing his hair with a toothbrush, like stuffing a little mashed potato up his nose, would get her going with her croaking.

45

LATE DUSK

Goats skitter in from the veld through the late dusk, the blue light like falling smoke. Pohamba's asleep, his early evening nap. I take a tub of Rama out of the food cupboard and scoop the margarine out and toss it onto the garbage pile beyond our fire pit. One of Antoinette's roosters, the one with the spiky tuft of green hair, immediately converges, stunned — never has such a mother lode of butter been delivered with such nonchalance. I leave him to his wonder. I walk up the road toward the principal's house. She's sitting on a bench outside her door, stirring pap over an open fire. Tomo sits up from rolling in the dirt at her feet and glowers at me. I hold up my empty tub.

"Anybody home? We're out of margarine in the quarters, wondering if —"

Mavala jabs her thumb toward the window. Beyond the curtain I can see the fuzz of the television. The principal can't get any reception from Windhoek, but he and Miss Tuyeni like to sit there and pretend they're watching the shows they read about in the paper.

"My sister and her husband are being entertained," Mavala says. "Would you like to sit and wait, Teacher?"

Her feet are bare. It's either bare feet or heels. Immense attention is paid to Mavala's footwear in the quarters.

"I asked if you'd like to sit, Teacher."

"Sure." I sit down next to her on the bench. She leans over the pot and stirs some more, then sets the spoon on the bench between us. She crosses her legs one way, then the other. Then leaves them uncrossed.

"You know, I wouldn't be so fat if I was home working in the mealie fields. In the north, you strap a baby on your back and go to work in the fields."

We'd been noticing this, that she'd sometimes say things that made you think she'd been having a conversation with herself and your presence was only incidental.

"Who said you're fat?"

"I heard English whites don't like fat women. The Boers like them fat."

"I'm not English."

"I'm bored," she says. "Aren't you bored?"

I watch her scratch her left ankle with her right toes. I stoop and pick up Tomo. I want, for a moment, to be closer to her feet. I start to bounce Tomo on my knees, but he goes for my eyes and I drop him. He snatches up my margarine tub and tosses it in the fire. She doesn't seem to notice any of this. She looks at me, her eyes too big. Pohamba said no woman should open her eyes that wide, that a woman who advertised like that was either lying or crazy. I stare back at her with what I'm thinking looks like sensuous, but also intellectual, meaning.

She looks back at the pot.

"Why don't you cook inside in the kitchen?"

"It seems my sister thinks my morals contaminate the food."

"She said that?"

"She said I'm a slut."

"Sluts don't use kitchens?"

"Apparently not."

I lean toward her sideways, with my eye on the small scoop in her neck, thinking this is the right angle for something, but she's already off the bench, moving fast into the darkened veld, up and down a small koppie and out of sight.

She shouts to me, "Feed him for me, will you, please? Wait for it to cool."

I spoon the pap into his bowl and set it on the bench. I watch the steam rise for a while. Then I call the monster and the monster comes. He plumps himself down against my leg and waits for his bowl.

Down the road, Antoinette hollers wash. "You boys, I want you washed, scrubbed, and pious. Ten minutes!" And the boys shout it back in all their languages. A babel of voices hollering wash.

In the house, there's the subtle flick of the constantly changing white light. Miss Tuyeni laughs at something she thinks she sees. I watch Tomo eat.

46

WALLS

A boy in the hostel has night terrors. We are all accustomed to it now. We wait for him. It's as if he does our screaming for us. He's screaming right now.

Pohamba bangs the wall. "Can't sleep?"

"No."

"Which boy do you think it is?"

"I don't know."

"What's he afraid of?"

"Look, let's try and —"

"Mobutu can't sleep either."

"What?"

"Mobutu Sese Seko and his leopardskin hat. What keeps him awake? What's he fear?"

"It's two in the morning."

"He fears Patrice Lumumba. Want one? A bedtime story?"

"Leave me alone."

"Come now. We've nowhere to go but sleep. Answer. Why does Mobutu fear Patrice Lumumba?"

"I have no clue."

"Good. You shouldn't. Because Lumumba's gone. They chopped him up in pieces and threw him in a barrel of acid."

"So he's dead. Let Mobutu and me go back to sleep."

"Is the mind always logical? Mobutu lies in his big golden bed and he can't sleep for fear. So he calls in his security chief and says, 'Security Chief, I want you to do something for me. Go kill Patrice Lumumba.' 'But, master,' the security chief says, 'The postal worker's been dead for years.' 'You think I don't know that? The people — don't you understand? — the people still love him.' So the security chief calls his men and tells them what to do. They're confused also, but the security chief shouts at them, 'Do I pay you clods to ask questions?' His men shrug. It's not hard. They go out and murder a guy. The security chief brings the body to Mobutu. 'Here's Lumumba, master.' 'Good,' Mobutu says. 'Now go and do it again.'"

Pohamba blows his nose, honks. "So every night, in Kinshasa, they murder Patrice Lumumba. Well, it's Africa, no?"

"Good night," I say.

"You think *this* isn't Africa?"

"What?"

"You're not afraid?"

"No."

"I am."

"Why?"

"I'm afraid I'm Lumumba."

"Nobody wants to kill you. Sleep."

Vilho taps the opposite wall lightly, whispers, but these walls make no difference. "Patrice Lumumba was a martyr," Vilho says.

Pohamba clears his throat like a drumroll. "And how do you know I'm not a martyr?"

Vilho ponders this. We can hear him. He sighs when he ponders. Vilho wears a nightshirt to bed. We can see him tucked in there snug, in sheets so clean they squeak. We find sleep listening to him ponder. The three of us breathe in the dark behind our walls.

47

VILHO

Vilho who is always cold. Unlike the rest of us, whom the sun warms too quickly after the cold mornings, he remains bundled, wool-hatted, scarfed. He accepts chill as his fate. He never complains. We complain. We complain about the heat. We complain about the cold. We complain that Vilho never complains. He's the confusing sort of lonely person who does not seek to be unlonely. And beyond this, the most alarming fact of all: It's not the terrible coincidence that Vilho was a learner at Goas and is now marooned here again as a teacher. It's that it's not a coincidence. Upon graduating near the top of his class at Dobra, Vilho requested a posting at Goas. *"Requested!"* Obadiah cried, incredulous. "It means our poor Puck outcasted himself!"

If you didn't know he was a teacher, you'd mistake him for a learner. His face is so smooth, hairless, supple. He seems, also, not to salivate over women. Not Mavala. Not even Dikeledi. Pohamba says it's impossible. An African man? Vilho? A moffie? But Obadiah says, if it's true, we'd certainly be more cosmopolitan, a bit of Cape Town in the scrubveld. Even so, with all Vilho might hide, he's the only one at Goas who seems unburdened — and so, naturally, we foist our various aches on him. Antoinette knits him scarf after scarf to keep him warm.

48

THE SEVASTOPOL WALTZ

I must say I'm pleased we're all in the road," Obadiah said. "Does anyone have a theory as to why?" No one had a theory. No one intended to have a theory. Still, he waited. Morning break and the heat's already risen and we're under the single tree closest to school, which happened to be in the road.

"We're not learners," Pohamba said. "Aren't we the teachers?"

"Wrong!" Obadiah shouted. "I'm tickled, good people of Goas, because the place for stories is in the road. You don't tell stories inside a house. This was my father's rule. When he wanted to tell a story, he herded us outside. My two brothers and four sisters, the whole family, except for my mother, who used to say my father made dead dogs look unlazy. She'd come out, however, but she never stepped into the road. Now understand, we lived on a dusty street full of rocks and garbage and sleeping tsoties with hats pulled over their eyes, and my father would tell stories of gone days in the Old Windhoek Location, before they came with the bulldozers and moved everybody to Katatura. My father spoke of the Old Location as if it were God's humble paradise. Then he'd look around at our road, at all the houses — not houses, he never called our houses houses; they were pilchard cans pushed together with our tribe and number on the door — and he'd say, 'I'm an old man, and they expect me to fight. With what? These shaky hands?' My father was a proud man, a cultured man, a Pan-Africanist, a Garveyite. He didn't condemn men for picking up arms, he begged mercy on the devils who forced them to do so. He'd quote Senghor: *Lord, forgive those who made guerrillas/of the Askias, who turn my princes/into sergeants.* It was only that he was convinced there was a better way.

111

He believed in education as a way to revolution. Books, he'd say, are the great topplers. Tromp the Boers with *Tristram Shandy*! The poor man. For my mother, it was one settler, one bullet. My father shamed her. She'd only laugh nastily at his memories, which she said weren't even memories at all — but colonialist propaganda.

"And once, out in the road, my father told us about the dance hall that used to be in the Old Location. 'So big that dance hall, it felt like being in a small country.' From the other side of the fence, my mother said, 'Dance hall? You want to thank them for a dance hall in 1942? Other husbands go to jail.' Then she spat."

Obadiah paused a moment to think of his mother. Mavala closed her book, but held her finger in the place where she'd stopped reading. She gazed up at the sky. The sun was faint, like a useless bulb in a day-lit room. Pohamba was marking quizzes. Festus was asleep with his head on his knee.

"No, she wasn't a lady, my mother," Obadiah said. "And she would have gone and beat the Boers herself if she didn't have to prepare mealie pap for six of us. My father feared her, but in public he pretended he didn't, so he hushed her, told her, 'Go home, woman. Go make your man some Ovaltine.' She didn't move. Neighbors had gathered around. Any activity in the road was better than nothing, and if it wasn't a riot, at least they could watch my parents battle. 'Size of Lesotho, that dance hall,' my father said. 'And in that great hall they held competitions, fierce dance competitions, and during one such event my wife and I — that belligerent woman standing right there — placed first in the Sevastopol Waltz.'"

Obadiah leaped up and stood before us. "Like myself, my father was a skinny man. His clothes never fit properly. When he waltzed in the road with my second sister, his shirt flapped in the air so that he resembled a bedraggled bird with shoes." Obadiah held his arms out and gripped a woman only he saw, his body erect, one hand cupping an elbow, the other flat on an invisible back. "Ready position!" he called. "And a one and a one, and a two and a two. Swing forward, swing back —"

Whatever he was doing didn't look like a waltz. It didn't look like much of a dance at all, really. He was still a little drunk from the Zorba he'd had in his morning coffee, and he was flailing — a slow flail in loose loafers. He was a little drunk and loving his father and his father's story, and we weren't listening, because it was too hot and we had to haul ourselves up and teach in less than five minutes and we were just trying to get a little rest by the only shade tree.

He was still circling, alone, when Mavala dropped her book in the dust and stood up and joined hands with him. After a bit, he said, "You can't dance. How can a woman with so much natural finesse —"

"And you're an old souse," Mavala said.

"Try," Obadiah said. "Try and dance."

And they did try, the two of them, in the road, in the sand. Mavala pulled off her heels. Even without them she was as tall as he was. Still, they were an awkward pair. When he went forward, she went forward, and their heads knocked together. Finally, he dropped his hands and peered at her curiously, as if he were trying to read something in bad light. "There's something else," he said. Up the road, the boys were coming back from the dining hall, gripping half-eaten carrots.

"What?" Mavala said.

Obadiah moved toward her, and reached out to her without touching; his hands only hovered over her shoulders. "My father never drank a drop. But — and I have never in my life forgotten this cruelty — that day as my father waxed triumphant in the road about the Sevastopol Waltz, my mother said, softly, because she knew she need not shout it, 'Better a man drink.'"

Obadiah stood in the road and looked at his feet. Mavala raised her hand and swatted, almost gently, the beak of his TransNamib hat.

The triangle rang, and we stood up and brushed off our pants and gathered our stray pens. There was a knob on Festus's forehead from his knee. As we started back to our classrooms, Obadiah called out, "May I add an addendum?"

Nobody turned around.

"My mother had, it's true, exquisitely long legs. Are there not days when a son may imagine how they might have looked?"

49

HYGIENE PATROL

One woman delouser. Pest Control Queen. Antoinette stalking the rows of beds in the boys' hostel. The only instruments necessary are her hands, long-fingered, clawlike pinchers. No meek shampoos. She needs to feel the crush of death in the skin. One by one she tweaks the lice and squeezes. Hygiene as spectacle and Antoinette the unhooded executioner. Boys at attention! Your bodies are living, breathing, sweating violations! Their bunks are so close together she has to walk sideways. Boys, boys, boys. So many heads to inquisition. Boys, year after year, boys. Scalps! Underarms! Pubic nesting grounds! Lift your arms, Matundu. Pants down, Shepa. Your head, Titus, bow it! And then one day a boy simply says, No. My head is my head. Unhooded halts. Examines recalcitrant. Eyes his eyes, her pupils colossal. Antoinette is less alarmed than fascinated. Being stood up to is always something she's wondered about. A tyrant without opposition gets very bored. Napoleon was said to have dreamed sweetly of defeat. And didn't Stalin await the poison, half loving the notion of martyrdom? Antoinette halts, looks the boy up and down. He's sitting on his bunk. His feet don't reach the floor. She doesn't know him. He's not a thief, a vandal, or an arsonist. The good ones blur together. Why is it we remember only the hoodlums? His defiance isn't even very spirited, and yet it's unequivocal. His little legs in shorts. The dirty bottoms of his little feet. His clean powder-blue shirt. (Clearly he follows some regulations.) His slightly ovaled head and bags beneath his eyes. Does this boy ever sleep? He stares: Do what you want to me, old bitch, but my head is my head.

"Surname?"

"Axahoes, Mistress."

"Common name?"

"Magnus."

"Standard what?"

"Six, Mistress."

"So small a Standard Six?"

He doesn't answer this, looks at his feet as if they explain so small a Standard Six.

"From which place?"

"Andawib West."

"Farm?"

"Of Meneer Pieterson. Kalkveld district."

"Parents?"

"Father."

"Mother?"

He sits silent. One leg twitches.

"Stand up."

He gets up off the bed. The other boys stand mute, but their eyes are swarming.

"Bow your head."

"No, Mistress."

"Why not? You suspect vermin? An infestation? You're afraid?"

His eyes want nothing, not even for this to end. Such a rare thing. You can't drain the want out of your eyes no matter how hard you try. Even the dead want everything back, which is why the undertaker either closes their eyes or blocks them with a penny. But this boy. Not even sorrow, as if he knows that above all sorrow is only pride. Train your eye to watch a single mosquito. You can never concentrate enough. Since she was a child, she's tried to follow the course of just one. It's impossible. You can only hope to get lucky when it flings back into your vision. But this boy's eyes, because they see nothing else, could probably do it. She thinks: Your mother, child. The world is full of dead mothers, to the hilt with dead mothers. Jesus in his meekness, and you claim the right to be haughty? Your affliction's greater? Still, she pities him, she loves him. This is not a standoff. This is a breath before a rout. She raises her hand and breaks him on the hostel floor like a donkey.

50

NOTES ON A MOSTLY ABSENT PRIEST

Storyless lump. To Goas his sole importance was that he had transport. A car, two bakkies, a lorry, a tractor. Our Father of Goas captained a fleet. It was like being on a desert island with half a dozen rescue boats. Except there was a catch. Only Theofilus was permitted to drive any of them, and he could use them solely for official church business, which did not include the business of teachers.

For a mostly doughy man, the Father had very square shoulders. In his robes he looked like a box dressed in a tablecloth. No one knew him well enough to hate him. He'd been at Goas only a few years. He spoke in an oddly high-pitched voice, and, it was said, there was something in it that harked backward. Whether fair or unfair, people sometimes said it was because Father was "coloured," and so a half-step closer to being white under the old — just recently old — laws. Myself he ignored. He once asked me what my faith was, and when I told him, he said, "So Windhoek sent us a pagan?" Then he shrilled something that might have been a laugh and marched off.

He kept a German shepherd in a pen — sequestered from Auntie Wilhelmina's whelps. He loved the dog and would feed it fresh kudu bones. One day this pampered dog escaped and stepped on a puff adder in the veld. It dragged itself back home and stood howling in front of the rectory for its master. We all stood around and watched its neck balloon. Then the dog begin to convulse and choke. Eventually, Father came out and brained it with a hammer.

The priest had two rules, as opposed to the principal's countless ones. No drinking and no fornicating among unmarrieds. The first one wasn't enforced (the priest was known to indulge in vermouth). The second didn't need to be.

Why the principal, by far the loudest Catholic on the farm, and Father despised each other was a mystery. It probably had something to do with the nationalization of schools, which happened after independence. This made for a sense of confusion as to who truly ruled Goas. The principal ran the school, but the school was on Church property. The teachers of Goas saw it this way: The principal owns our asses; the priest, whatever's left of our souls.

There was a strange story about the two of them. An inexplicable story, with no beginning and no end and no point whatsoever.

One morning the priest found the principal asleep on the rectory roof.

What was he doing up there? Spying?

Nobody knows.

Why'd he fall asleep? Was he drunk?

Wouldn't you get drunk if you had to spend the night on a roof?

Yes. *What was he doing on the roof in the first place?*

I said, Nobody knows . . .

51

ENGLISH NIGHT

Even more than her lipstick and her baby-blue eye shadow and her skimpy skirts, it was Mavala's enthusiastic organ playing that drove the priest out of his gullet. Wednesday night was officially English night in church. Any ordinary Sunday or daily morning Mass — if he happened to be at Goas, often he wasn't, the Erongo region being short on priests — the Father spoke a kind of apocalyptic-sounding Afrikaans. *Nothing but hell awaits you boys who flout your immorality under God's all-seeing eyes* . . . Wednesday nights, though, he left off the pulpit fist-banging. It was said that he resented the edict handed down by the bishop in Windhoek, out of deference to the new constitution, that English be spoken in church at least once a week. It seemed that Father wanted to show everyone that Afrikaans was still the language of a thunderous God. So, on English night, he tweeted his homily. And the boys took his cue. They knew it was safe to fall asleep in church on Wednesday. The older boys brought pillows and sprawled out on the back benches. In the front pews the sub b's fell asleep, collapsed onto one another's shoulders, their little heads lolling, their tiny kneecaps digging into the wooden slats as they endured painful but merciful sleep.

After dozing through the service, the boys perked up when Mavala played. She said that in spite of everything she was still Catholic. Whether they wanted her or not. The organ didn't work very well. The pedals often stuck, and the notes reverberated even longer than they were supposed to, creating a sort of bleeding music that layered on itself, as if every note she played were happening at the same time. By the end of a hymn there was always total cacophony. It never mattered. And the boys irritated the Father further by singing in English. *O food of exiles lowly, O bread of angels holy* . . . Their voices carried across the farm — out to Theofilus in the veld; up to the top of the hill by the cross, where Pohamba sat alone, boycotting church.

As a supposed living embodiment of the virtues of speaking English, I made a point of going to church on English night. I sat with Vilho in the back pew and tried not to think of her legs pumping, her feet pumping. Mavala closed her eyes when she played, her head tilted slightly toward her right shoulder.

One Wednesday, I waited for her after it was over and everyone but Vilho had filed out. He often remained. He once told me there was something unusually calm about a just-emptied church. Together, Mavala and I walked up the road toward the principal's house.

"The wind's up," I said.

(*The wind's up. The wind's down.* Sometimes we thought it, said it, just to have something to think, to say.)

"Yes," she said.

"It was down before."

"Right," she said. "It was down before, wasn't it?"

We passed two boys, Obadiah's Standard Threes, Siggy and Petrus, who were sitting at the remains of the stolen picnic table, practicing introducing themselves in Obadiah's King's English; which king was never clear.

"I should be honored, kind sir, if you would favor me with your name."

"I was christened Siegfried, but please, I insist, call me Siggy. Dare I inquire of yours, friend of my youth?"

"Ah, kindred spirit! I'm known as Petrus."

They smoked pencils like pipes. They tipped imaginary hats. From their faces they both seemed to be in great pain. English was often associated with constipation.

The two of us went on up the road. "Like a zoo, this place," she said.

"They love it when you play."

"Oh, that."

"You inspire them."

Mavala popped her forehead with her palm. "You know what? I forgot the kid."

We headed down the road again, walked across the soccer field to Antoinette and Obadiah's. Antoinette was standing at her guard post, her open kitchen window. Tomo was doing a headstand on the steps.

"And how was my angel?" Mavala said.

"He abused my chickens. He fouled my radishes." She shoved down the window. Antoinette's smiles were vague and fleet. Her face was blurred in the gloom behind the glass.

Mavala scooped up Tomo and kissed him all over. "How could I forget this boy? A boy such as this boy?"

We started back up the road a second time. She put Tomo down and he refused to walk, so she yanked him through the sand and he plowed along like an evil little water skier. Then she dropped him, and he scuttled after us.

"What were you saying?"

"That your playing —"

"Oh yes. That I inspire. On English night I do inspire!" She paused and looked at me. "Don't I?"

At the missing picnic table, Siegfried and Petrus were still at it.

"And may I inquire from where your people hail?"

"I was born and bred in Swakopmund, my friend."

"Oh, the sea. Its extravagances."

Mavala squeezed my elbow. "What do you call that?"

"At least he's teaching them some English. Better than I can do."

"What about teaching them to know who they are? Is that who they are? This place is a hole and he's president. God bless poor Antoinette."

"I'm running for vice president of the hole," I said.

"Happy for you. When are the elections?"

"So why do you play in church? If this place is so doomed. Why give the boys a false sense?"

She didn't answer. We reached the principal's house. It was dark. He and Miss Tuyeni had gone to Karibib. Mavala let go of Tomo's hand and he tore off toward their room. He couldn't reach the knob, so he stepped back and began ramming the door with his head.

The wind was up. The air had sand in it now and it began to peck our faces. Mavala looked down at the ground as if she'd dropped something. She had a slight widow's peak I hadn't noticed.

"Why do you play?"

"Stop thinking about me."

"I asked —"

"I'm finished with that."

"With what?"

"Being thought of."

She left me and went and stomped toward the kid.

52

HUNS AND KHAKIS

Our guru was musing about the difference between certain colonial powers. I don't remember where we were. We may have been at the urinals in the rank men's room behind the Mobil station in Karibib, or at the Dolphin in the location, or at our table at the Public Bar, or in a lorry heading back to Goas, a week's worth of groceries between our knees, sweating, passing around a warm Fanta, so thick it was more like molasses — but it was Fanta and we had it, so we drank it. We might have been out beyond the dry Kuiseb River, where Goas ended and the real desert began, hunting the spoor of that elusive dwarfed hedgehog of the central Namib escarpment. We may have been anywhere where Obadiah felt the need to hold forth, to educate us, to alleviate the burden of our fathomless ignorances.

"Now, the Germans at least were honest. They said they were going to steal our land and they stole our land. They said they were going to kill us, and by God, they killed us. Now, the British were less — how shall we put it? — forthright. They said our land was ours and they stole it. They said they were humanitarians and they bombed the Namas. That was in 1922. A year later, they cut off King Mandume's head and made a parade of it. So who's the devil's favorite? The Germans go before God with reeking, unwashed hands and say, See, Father, see what I have done. Now judge me. The British? Those khakis knock on heaven's door and offer plum pudding."

Obadiah paused and straightened the collar of his frayed tweed coat. Wherever we may have been, I can say with certainty he was wearing his piebald-colored tweed coat. He wore it summer or winter, teaching or not, shirt underneath or not. (When he was shirt-less, small tufts of white hair spaghettied out between his lapels.)

"Indeed, we've had ample opportunity to observe these two giants of the enlightenment. As an aside, I might say that the Boers never had to shoulder the burden of being enlightened . . . But the Germans and the British! Consider the idiot carnage of what they call the Great War. It even reached us out here at the far-flung edge. Shakespeare versus Goethe in a battle for thorn scrub. One British general wrote to the King, 'Your Majesty, this land isn't fit for baboons or Bushmen.' Now, one may well ask, Then why send men all the way down here to die?"

"Good question," Pohamba said. "Why in hell —"

"Never ask it. The lives of soldiers, even white ones, have never been worth more than baboons or Bushmen."

"So fuck them both," Pohamba said.

"Must you vulgarize?"

And I seem to remember Obadiah squinting at Pohamba then. So maybe we were outside in the glare. Let's say we were — us tromp-ing across the veld toward the Erongos.

"Fuck the Swedes," Pohamba said.

"What'd the Swedes do to you?" I asked.

Pohamba shrugged. "Fuck Hawaiians."

"Fuck Bulgarians," I said.

"God Save the King," Pohamba said.

Obadiah ignored us and held forth to the afternoon. "The British vanquished the Germans at Korub Aub. In the histories, *their histo-ries,* they call it a white man's war fought in heathen Africa. As if we weren't even here at the time. The simple truth is this: They wouldn't have won without us. The British promised us land — our own — if we helped them."

He kicked off one of his sandals and dug a craggy toenail into the dry earth. It was a long time before he spoke again. Afternoon fell. The mountains ahead of us blued. A cloud, miserably pallid and empty, lazed slowly by. We'd failed at hunting again.

"When it was over," Obadiah said softly, "there was a great deal of euphoria. A delegation of native soldiers went to military head-quarters to present a petition to the British on behalf of the people. It expressed gratitude to the King and reminded him of the promise of unconditional return of ancestral lands. The soldiers waited two hours before a sergeant in leather hip boots appeared."

Obadiah paused again, gulped some wind. Slowly, he cleaned the dust off his teeth with his tongue. We did the same.

"The sergeant didn't read it. Instead, he flung that petition across the room. The men watched it float slowly to the floor. Then the sergeant barked: 'Your hats! All subjects must remove any and all bonnets in the presence of an officer of His Britannic Majesty George V!' Then some galoots came and tossed that delegation out the door."

That was it. Enough alleviation of ignorance for a hot and useless day. We followed Obadiah along a goat path, into darkness the color of a new bruise.

53

KARIBIB

A forgettable sun-worn place with too-wide streets (an old German mining town, the boom never quite happened), midway between Windhoek and Swakopmund on the coast. A popular petrol and toilet stop. There's a tiny (still) white dorp and a location across the rail tracks, north of town, where most people (still) live. There's a hotel, a grocery, a few shops, and some scattered bottle stores, around which revolve much of the life of the town. So unimportant a place, Pohamba said, that during the struggle SWAPO didn't even try to blow up the post office.

Still, since we were always trying to get there, we had to pretend Karibib was somewhere. It was our Mecca, our Bangkok. Sometimes we'd go to Ackerman's, the furniture store in the dorp, and spend the afternoon loitering on the comfortable couches on the showroom floor. Pohamba knew the salesman, a former learner named Wilbard Lilonga. The manager lived in Swakop and came in only on Saturdays. Wilbard would let us laze around. We'd read magazines or just sleep on the deep plush. Love songs gentle on the Muzak. Velour, camel, horsehair, Fontainebleau. Our feet on what Wilbard had once told us were called occasional tables. For what occasions? Ackerman's had those plastic tints on the windows so the world outside was dyed blue. We'd loiter and watch the blue people walk down the blue street.

Pohamba leans back, his feet on the table, his head resting on the top of the ridge of his loveseat. He looks up at the ceiling.

"Wilbard!"

Wilbard doesn't answer. He's in the back smoking, ashing his cigarette on the carpet.

"Who buys all these couches?"

Wilbard still doesn't answer.

"Wilbard? Wilbard!" Pohamba thunders. "Wake up, you lazy shitter! I want to know, who can pay four hundred rand for a place to sit?"

54

BUTCHER SCHMIDSDORF

The choice is clear-cut: either the West
predominates in South-West Africa, or there
will be a triumph of naked barbarism over
Western civilization . . . The hour is late
and the danger is great.

ANTHONY HARRIGAN,
RED STAR OVER AFRICA

This happens. Two whites alone together as we're alone together in this tiny butchery next to the Mobil station in
Karibib, and it's back to the war, back to the glories of counter-
insurgency. "Think about it." The butcher Schmidsdorf, one bug eye
a widening orb, the other squinting, whispers, *"The South Africans*
would not use their navy because of the Soviet threat."

"I'd like a kilo and half of pork loin," I say. "And some lard."

He takes the pork loin out of the case with one hand and carries
it to the slicer. Pork loin's on special. There's a sign in the window.
He glances toward the door and says, "You must understand. It
wasn't a war. It was a police action. We were fighting Sam Nujoma,
not Brezhnev."

The butcher Schmidsdorf is a very thin, mostly insane man with a
flat nose and up-turned nostrils that face you like two black holes,
abysses, hairy pistol barrels. He hates Commies, Jews, and kaffirs.
A good butcher, Antoinette says. He even makes some cuts like a
great butcher, though as a general rule, butchers shouldn't be so
bony. Engelbert Schmidsdorf, famous for his bloodwurst, boer-

wurst, leberwurst, fleishwurst, weisswurst, zungenwurst, and occasional schinkenwurst, as well as for his chronic wifelessness and the fact that he was one of the few German Southwesters who fought side by side with their ex-enemies, the South Africans (i.e, the British and the Boers), against the only true enemies, Commies, Jews, and kaffir terrorists . . .

"You know what?" I say. "Maybe make it two kilos."

He peeps over the counter at me. "I was stationed at Ruacana. Greenest place in this dry hole of country. And there were terrorists on every side — black shadows."

He rubs his nose upward with the palm of his hand, and those nostrils have me in their sights again.

"Did you ever see a black with a shadow? Out there at that school? We lived in a guest house, soldiers, and we had maids, black ones in white shoes. In the mornings we went out and got killed, but didn't we sleep well at night?" He pauses, looks down at the loin on the slicer. "Since then, I am dead."

This happens also. The butcher says he's dead. He fondles the pork loin on the slicer. People say it's the bug eye that does the talking, and that it's the other eye, the one that squints, that's the lonely one, the one that never wants you to leave him. Antoinette says the man is so lonely he forgets to eat. All the meat under the sun and the butcher starves. There are days, Antoinette says, she'd like to drag him out to Goas and make him listen to the boys sing in church.

"How fatty your loin?" he says.

I wiggle my hand. "So-so fatty."

He holds a slice up for my approval.

"Little more."

He finishes the slicing and wraps up the package, holds it out to me with a bloody paw, just out of my reach. He sneezes, a small, forlorn sneeze. He wipes his nose with some bloody paper.

"How much lard?"

"Five K bucket."

"No fleishwurst? It is very fresh."

"Maybe next week."

*   *   *

Outside, I wait for Pohamba. He's next door in the China Shop buying a pair of snakeskin shoes. You could find anything in the China Shop, including Chinese people. Across the road, in front of the takeaway, I watch two drunks hold each other tenderly, like two drunks.

55

SISTER ZOË

O n the wind of talk, word carried — from Usakos to Omaruru to Karibib, and then even out to Goas — that's no real nun. It had, people said, something to do with her mouth, or more specifically, the way she bit her lip with one jagged, vampirish incisor. People said this wasn't the way you walked around penitent. Not a bride of Christ, this one. Her catechism is nothing but lies. It was about desire, how it eats away at you when it's stifled, and just because you hide in the sisterhood doesn't mean you don't sweat the sheets. Sister Zoë, her serious, tired face, her generous hands. She was from the south, a Nama from Keetmanshoop. She ran from her mother. She ran from Keetmanshoop. Anybody would run from Keetmanshoop, where the sun does nothing all day but lash your neck and look for plants to kill. At least up here we've got three scrawny trees a kilometer.

Now they say she's back down south for good.

Sister Zoë worked at the clinic at Usakos, and she used to come every first and third Saturday with Sister Ursula and Sister Mary, out to the farm for sick call. The boys would line up in front of the hostel dining hall and go in one by one to be examined. There wasn't a boy at Goas who wasn't deathly ill those particular first and third Saturdays. If only to get touched by Zoë's hands and sent away, condemned healthy. Sister Ursula was German, gaunt and old, with cracked hands. She's been a nurse so long among blacks, people said, the woman thinks she's a doctor. Sister Ursula would usually stand off to one side and wait, haughty, for hard cases. She carried antibiotics in a padlocked handbag. Sister Mary was the one the boys went to when they were actually sick, so sick that even the touch of Zoë meant nothing. Sister Mary was a large, shaky-breasted woman with a pocked face. She was from Malemba up on the Caprivi, a place, she'd said, that was so thick in the bush that once you left, you could never find home again. She laughed at the boys who were sick, called them God's paupers. Come, little pauper, come; we shall take your temperature and then see what we find in Sister Ursula's magic handbag. Sister Mary always gave out free Q-tips and plastic rosaries in multiple colors. But mostly those Saturdays were about Zoë and her hands on your body. Pohamba would stand and supervise the mob, and every once in a while walk to the front and push his way inside the dining hall and announce to Sister Zoë that he had cancer.

"Cancer all over. Heal the sick, Sister."

And Sister Zoë would gaze at him from under the habit that people said was fake, a prop, and say in her soft, beautiful English, "Teacher, I counsel repose." Because her hands were only for the boys. And Pohamba, who when he really loved was a total coward, would go back to policing the line. Later, he'd go on about how all he wanted was to lift her habit, not take it off, only lift it.

We'd see them come up and over the ridge, moving steadily toward the cattle gate. Their walk, how one never got in front of the other. Their white gym shoes. Their habits lifting vertical in the wind like the scarves of old-time pilots. And the boys would catch a glimpse of the top of their heads and begin shouting, "Swestas!" They always parked on the road, because once Sister Ursula got the van stuck in the last dry riverbed and vowed she'd never go through that hell again. Also, didn't it look better for the Lord's healers to come on foot?

One day only two appeared over the rise.

The story that got back to us was that she'd gone to administer shots in the location and was raped by a bostoto. Sister Ursula sent her back to Keetmanshoop. The boys — for months and, who knows, maybe years — thought only of her hands, how they barely touched you when they touched you, sending you away. Move on, healthy boy, move on.

56

THEOFILUS

Nothing is beautiful here except the beginning and the end of the day — which is never the beginning or end of his work — so beauty happens in the middle of unfinished jobs. There are dusks when night is less about light than the mountains. When the ridges of the Erongos seem to huddle and move forward, as if they — not the sky — will bury us.

Day work means the veld. Night work means the generator. It runs from around seven-thirty to eleven. Since it is constantly breaking down, Theofilus acts in the capacity of a nurse. He sits beside the generator in the generator shack, listening to the motor, waiting for some wrong sound in all that jangle. Those hours we have electricity, he sits there until eleven. When the lights suddenly pop off early, we know his fingers are working in the dark.

When he does finally go to his bed in the mission garage, he lies there and sips warm beer, if he has any, and falls asleep with his eyes open. His blue jumper hangs on a nail by the door.

57

ZAMBEZI NIGHTS

Night swelt. The only wind is my own breathing. It's after eleven and I'm marking compositions by candlelight. I've invented a candleholder. I propped a candle in a boot and tightened the laces. Boot light. The papers all begin with the line: Out in the veld I saw . . . *Out in the veld I saw a kudu. Out in the veld I saw a broken tree. Out in the veld I saw too many dead people. Out in the veld I saw no money.*

There's a long scratch at my screen. I leap and knock over my chair.

"Who's out there?"

"Did I scare Teacher?"

I carry my boot to the door. Her face is always different in person than when I think about it. Her face looms so large in my mind that when I see her I'm surprised how small it is. Only her eyes are huge tonight, like bobbing olives in the light of the candle. Tomo is slung on her back, his head lolling over her shoulder. At her feet is her mustard suitcase. She's got on long pants, a rare thing.

"Scared me? You?"

"I saw you jump."

"Normally my guests knock."

"Ask me what I'm doing."

"Not that I have any guests."

She sits down on the suitcase.

"What are you doing?"

"Leaving."

"Again?"

"For the moment, however, I'm moving over here."

"Here?"

"Next door."

"Next door? To Kapapu's old room?"

"Yes."

"You don't want to do that."

"Why?"

"A teacher got stabbed in there. With a bike spoke. You never heard the story? A new teacher comes and falls in love with the wife of another teacher and —"

Mavala snorts. "The stories of this place." She stands up and seizes the handle of the case. "You aren't very hospitable. Don't you want to invite me in?"

I give way and Mavala's in my squalor. My first official guest after Pohamba and Auntie. Goas is a life lived outside rooms. If our rooms aren't sanctuaries, at least they are places to hunker in private. Mavala sets Tomo down in my laundry basket. He takes right away to my reeking socks. Then she pushes away my books and papers and clothes and takes a seat on my bed. I go back to my desk. Moths batter against the torn screen and for a while we listen to the soft thumping. Mavala begins to knead the mosquito netting and I remember it's something my mother used to do when she came home from work exhausted, sit on her bed and knead the blanket.

I point to the candle on the desk. "What do you think of my boot?"

"Why don't you stick it in a bottle?"

"No. See the boot is the whole point."

"The whole point of what?"

"I don't know."

"There's probably a regulation against it."

"I'm sure. And isn't there a regulation against single women living in the quarters? Didn't the principal do a tale on it?"

"Ask me if I'm going back there."

"Something about temptation and how to keep it at bay. That the sobering influence of married people acts to tamp down —"

"Go ahead. Ask me."

"Are you —"

"Die first."

"I see."

"I loathe this place."

"So why'd you come back?"

She doesn't answer, still that kneading. A moth careens into the flame. It tries to fly with a wing on fire before that's the end of it. A sound like a wrinkle and smoke.

"Festus said you had a good posting in Grootfontein."

She sighs, bounces a finger against her lower lip. "There was no Grootfontein." She looks at Tomo, who is now on his stomach in the basket, his arms spread out like a tired swimmer, a pair of my underwear on his head. "Tomo was Grootfontein. He was waiting, at a friend's. I never thought I'd come back. Then I thought with him so young, it might be easier here for a while. At least there's a job, and I thought my sister —"

There's a slowness in the shadow her elbow makes as she rubs the back of her head. The shadow creeps and retreats in the spastic flame. We watch each other. A mosquito weens in my ear, now soft, now blaring.

"Your sister?"

"Yes. I thought —" She leans back on my bed. "I don't know what I thought." Neither of us says anything else for a long time. Mavala stares at the ceiling.

A pound on the wall wrecks it, the silence of the night and of Mavala in my room, on my bed. Then more pounds. Three longs followed by two shorts followed by two more shorts and another long. "Has anyone been alone on this farm?" Mavala says. "For five minutes? Alone?"

"Not that's been documented."

"What's he doing?"

"It's Morse code. You were in a war."

"We used satellite phones."

I put my head to the wall and take in the pounds. Now it sounds like he's using his feet.

"What's he saying?"

"He says there's a sale at the Pep Boys in Usakos. Thirty-five percent off on all beachwear and towels."

She looks down at the bed. Her fingers are still crushing the netting. "Beachwear?"

A moment later, Pohamba's colossal head rises from below the window. He puckers the screen like a fish. I run to lock the door, but I'm too late and he explodes into the room in nothing but flip-flops and briefs, leaps up on my bed. "Deliverance!" he shouts. "Mercy, mercy me! Comrade Shikongo joins the bachelors!"

"Shhhhhh, the kid," she says. "You'll wake the kid." And Mavala wraps her arms around Pohamba's bare legs and I watch the two of them leaping and laughing in the now frantic light. I remember this, how I sat there at my desk and watched them.

"Teacher!" Pohamba yells. "Boot's on fire!"

We mobilize our nightclub, which Pohamba calls Zambezi Nights, after his favorite bottle store in Otavi. I pound the other wall and wake up Vilho, who begs to be allowed to sleep, but later materializes with a half bottle of Fanta. Pohamba goes to fetch Obadiah and Festus. Festus bolts right over. It will take Obadiah a little longer because, as everybody knows, Antoinette sleeps with one Cyclopean eye open. Later, he toddles over with a fresh pint of Cardinal Richelieu. "Brandy in the age-old French tradition," he says. "For the European in all of us." Pohamba fixes the tape player with a pen, and we, again, listen to Whitney Houston — before the tape player breaks (again). Pohamba rolls the last of his dagga. I boil spaghetti. Festus and Vilho dance to the memory of "I Wanna Dance with Somebody (who loves me)." Mavala and I sit a little out of the circle, away from the fire, beneath the acacia. She takes a slug of the Richelieu and passes it on. Pohamba says Vilho dances like a Boer having a shit. "Move those hips, dear brother!"

"Oh, I gotta feel some heat with somebody," Festus sings. "Yeah I really gotta . . ."

"It's wanna," Pohamba says. "Wanna feel the heat."

Speaking of heat, we've none left. I'm still amazed by how it disappears in the night, even in summer, torn out of the sand by the dark.

"Is this the piss tree?" Mavala says.

"No, the piss tree's behind Antoinette's."

She sniffs. "Are you certain?"

Mavala droops against me, then wakes, rights herself. Festus and Vilho collapse in a heap. Tomorrow morning looms. Festus gets up and dusts himself off, joins his plump hands in prayer. "Well, I'm off to bed, brothers and sisters. There's Mass in the morning."

"The priest is here?" Pohamba says.

"Back this afternoon from Swakop."

"Bugger the pontiff," Pohamba says.

"Please," Obadiah says.

"I'm not Catholic," Pohamba says. "I'm a Marxist revolutionary, and during the war I —"

"Taught fractions," Festus says.

Pohamba stands. Sometimes when he's drunk, he looks for reasons to pummel Festus. And Festus stands there blinking, waiting, trying to decide if he should run. Instead, Pohamba begins to sway — not to our dear Whitney, to something else. He dances by himself for a while, then slowly turns and looks at Mavala and begins to ramble, not angry, quiet, under his breath. "My mother was Catholic, bless her soul. But my own father fought barefoot at Omgulumbashe, and during the struggle I too —"

"I believe you," Mavala says. "I believe you."

Obadiah was holding up the bottle, toasting the ungreen earth and all of us impoverished beneath its moon, when the principal stalked into our circle from behind the toilet houses. Even then he wore a tie, yellow and blue stripes for Thursday, rammed up tight under his chin. He stood by what was left of the fire and looked us over. His glasses caught the last spark of flame in the coals. Obadiah crawled over to him on his knees and offered him the final swig of the Richelieu. Then he passed out at his feet. The principal seized the bottle by the neck and tipped it back. Then he nudged Obadiah with the toe of his shoe. "This is the Head Teacher with whom I am to build a new nation out of the ashes of war? Ha! Even Goas will fall into the sea."

Without moving his head in her direction, he said, "A word, privately, Miss Shikongo?"

This was followed by a brief and strangely quiet exchange between the two of them in Kapapu's old room. Pohamba held an enamel mug to the door but couldn't catch a thing. That door, behind which so much else had happened. Then the principal charged out and headed straight across the soccer field toward his office without a word. We watched him unlock it and go inside. He sat there in the dark.

Mavala refused our help, either with her suitcase or the kid, who was in full fury at being woken up and taken from my sweat-reeking clothes. We watched her pull the case through the sand, up the road to the principal's house, as Tomo flailed at her back.

58

VILHO

Vilho shivering ecstatically in the cold church before the light. His knees on the concrete.

I only want to be alone, and still there's desire? I don't want Your blood, only Your touch. Sleep is only a brief reprieve. You watch. I wake slow. I come here and I bring You my tiredness, my empty hands, my inabilities, my bitterness, my unsatisfaction, my disgust, my cold knees. The fierceness of silence in the cold. The way each movement echoes here. You above on the wall. Plaster, broken-off leg. But it's You, isn't it?

59

GOAS

An abandoned swing set. A single seat dangling from the cross-bar. It was behind the hostel, where the reek of raw sewage made it a no-man's-land. The smallest and poorest boys would go back there to shit. They couldn't afford the toll the older boys made them pay to use the toilets. Some boy must have braved the stench to float for a while. You'd hear it. The screech was loud, and you could tell how fast he was flinging himself by the intervals when the swing reached as high as it could and the screws and the rust of the chain contracted. We'd hear it during class and wonder which truant was back there. And we could, if we bothered to, remember what it was like, that jolt, that drop.

60

MORE GOAS LOVE

Festus points to one of Auntie Wilhelmina's whelps that's trying to mount another of Auntie's whelps and says, "That dog's penis is too big." Festus says things like this, things you might think but never say. Mid-morning break and us watching it. The dogs in the puddle beneath the standpipe, failing at it. The one dog, the mangle-eyed one, trying, trying again. His terrible red penis. It wasn't that she was averse.

The dog, front paws paddling the air again, hind legs surging forward, a feeble dance. He's on again. Whoops. No go.

Why remember this? Why relate it? Things that are not worth telling force themselves out in the open anyway. Like that sad dog's unrequited erection. Animals fail to fuck and we get a half hour's free entertainment. Antoinette damns us all to yet another level of hell. We liked to think Festus wasn't as complicated as we were. He had too great a love of obvious observation. Things you were looking right at. But he was right, wasn't he? That dog's penis was too big.

"I didn't think it was possible," Mavala says.

"Oh, it's possible," Pohamba says. "Either that or her Switzerland's too small."

The triangle jangled and we all went back to class, left those dogs to themselves. Except Festus, who stayed to watch.

Later, after school, he told us that she finally gave up on him and bit Mr. Big Cock in the neck. And that's when I tried, Vilho-like, to yank a moral out of it. I said, There's something sad about those two unashamed dogs. The public nature of such doomed love. Their complete lack of grace. Those dogs are us, our own pathetic natures, our own fundamental inability to connect . . .

Festus taught science. He said it wasn't sad.

"What, then?"

"A matter of proportionality. It will never fit. I waited. I watched."

"And if they love? Isn't it sad that —"

Festus stared at me for a moment. "It doesn't fit," he said. "That's all." Then he scratched his belly and walked off toward his house, toward Dikeledi, and we watched him, squat and round, walking away. Festus was said to be trying to emulate the principal's stomach. In this he was succeeding. And we thought of how unfair it all was, of a house free of sadness, of a floor free of sand, of soft underwear (Antoinette, who did our laundry, was morally opposed to fabric softener), of those waiting Dikeledian arms . . .

I turned slowly to Pohamba. This our revenge? That Festus and Dikeledi can't consummate? That no sexual congress convened in the purple house we're all so jealous of?

Even we don't wish this on Festus. We tried to think only happy thoughts. Nothing too big, nothing too small. Finally, Pohamba couldn't help himself.

"Oh, that poor poor poor girl."

"Don't you go save her."

"Do you think I am that low?"

"Yes."

He shook his head. "Never to friends." He brightened. "Wait — Festus isn't a friend."

"Close."

"Close isn't a friend, friend." And he bopped off toward the quarters and his waiting bed.

61

SIESTA

I always said, Sure, it's hot here, but you don't get the humidity like we do back home in O-hi-o. You see, back home in Hamilton County, we get what we call a wet heat, and no matter how bad it gets around here, there's no humidity, and so it's really not so . . . I stop saying all that.

Bloat of eyeballs. I have returned to a liquid state. I am a broiled pig melted down to sap. No cold water anywhere on the farm. We'd sent a boy around to beg for some, but neither the priest nor the principal would answer their doors. Water from the tap was at least eighty degrees. We had no choice but to remain in the sweaty, greasy shade of our rooms until the principal headed for Karibib and one of us could hitch a ride and bring back some Fanta. I lie on my bed and pant. I try to read Turgenev. *Until his dying day, Chertopkhanov remained convinced that the blame for Masha's treachery lay with a certain neighbor, a retired captain of Lancers by the name of Yaff, who, in Pantelei's words, got his way just by perpetually twisting his whiskers, thickly oiling his hair and sniffing significantly . . .* I toss Yaff on the floor and lust the walls, try to put together the pieces from the remains of my German calendar girls. Mother of God, to have them back intact. Unhelpful body parts bob across my salt fat eyes: How do you letch an elbow? I can't sleep, won't sleep, will never sleep. Too hot even for self-delight, the only exercise any of us ever got during siesta. And then in the swamp of this lost time, a faraway click. A sound like a door opening. I try to sit up and I think I see a blurry vision of Mavala moving toward my bed. She stands and looks down at me. Her eyes are still, but her lips are moving without words. Through the sog, I think I hear her breathing, but it too sounds as if it's so far away. She kneels and rests her head on my stomach, where it rises and falls with my panting. That's all. She says nothing.

At three-thirty, I woke up alone to Pohamba gargling.

62

OBADIAH

We of course don't have anything approximating your autumn here, but I have often imagined it. Beautiful, but also violent, no? Those leaves, not yet deadened, ripped off the only mother they've ever known, their hold on a branch. Here the sun beats and beats, and the plants, perhaps, come to expect it. Every day the homicidal sun. Your autumn, I've read about it, seems much like a sudden, wrenching death. Or do I misunderstand it from the leaf's point of view?

63

MORNING MEETING

Murmur not among yourselves.
JOHN 6:43

This morning the principal is lustful by way of Isaiah. Thus: so are we. Yea, we are greedy dogs who can never have enough. Thou shalt not. Thou shalt not what? Thou shalt not everything, because, yes, sinners, it's everywhere. Lust grows out from under the rock like wattle bush. Lust needs no water for a thousand days.

And Mavala, next to Vilho, who's next to me, reaches her foot over and nips the back of my shin with the tip of her heel. Then she says something into her coffee that I can't make out. This is how we sometimes communicated, all of us, during the moral tale — through our slurps. And the principal is so loud we can sometimes talk under him. I drink and keep my nose deep in there, lean closer to Vilho, who pretends not to notice. I point my cup her way.

"What?"

"Bored."

And myself, still early-early-morning dopish, gurgle back: "What?"

"*Bored. I'm very bored.*"

"Hast thou enough meatflesh, you insatiable whoremongers?" the principal booms.

And the fog begins to lift, and in a greedy yes covetous yes carnal whisper I nearly shriek into my coffee: *Okay, so . . .*

She waits a moment. The principal is working himself up into a hyperventilating frenzy, dramatically flipping pages. "Siesta," she breathes.

"He goeth after her straightaway as an ox goeth to the slaugh —"

"Where?"

Mavala aims the bottom of her cup at me, her eyes giant over the rim, steady, blinkless. "The graves," she says. "The Voortrekkers."

"Or as a fool to the correction of the stocks!"

64

ANTOINETTE

She keeps them in an empty tin next to the Rooibos tea in the kitchen sideboard. Her vice. Her weakness. Her raisins. What is it about them that makes her crave their shriveled little bodies with such abandon? What makes her lust so overpowering there are times when she slinks into her own house in the smack middle of a working day to stuff a pluck of them in her mouth? Ugly emaciated things, like the shriveled tops of fingers left too long in the wash water. She hardly chews one before it's gone and all she's left with is an insatiable need for another. Savage gluttony. The original fruit comes wrapped in a package from the Pick 'n Pay. The devil is crafty. There is a psychologist in the office block next to the Mobil station, and there was even a time when she almost knocked on the door. I have only a small question, Doctor, concerning a small fruit. Otherwise I am healthy in the head. All I want is to control the passion. To bring it to heel. To leave a boiling cauldron of mealies, my post, my responsibility, to feed my face? Like an old hoer stealing across the sand to a tin in the sideboard. Hand pushing the door. The glant of sun on the sideboard. Fingers seize the tin. Leave your nose among them. How at first they don't smell and then they do. A snort of sugared earth up the nostrils. Oh, filth. Ravish them. A vision of herself scurrying across the sand, the midday sun. Soon the boys will be lining up at the dining-hall door for lunch, spoons in hands. Temptation, fulfillment, emptiness. How can it be that the only cure for sin is more sin?

65

GRAVES

Instead of walking up the road by the principal's, I took the long way around, out past the cattle gate, and doubled back behind Dikeledi and Festus's. The Boers were buried near the banks of the dry Toanib River, where it looped out toward Krieger's farm. It was a kind of ghost river. Not only was it dry like the other rivers, but there were days it was gone, when you couldn't distinguish it from the rest of the veld.

She was already out there, sitting on one of the black granite graves. The graves were three narrow slabs, with a tall headstone at the front of each. The only shiny things at Goas; I wondered how they could still look like this after so many years. Mavala was sitting on Grieta Dupreez, the unmarried daughter. Around Grieta was a moat of white gravel. Below her name: *Rus in Vrede*. Rest in peace. Beyond the graves, in a small rutlike gully, a place where Theofilus sometimes burned garbage; the ground was strewn with ash.

She was making piles out of the gravel, making piles and then slashing them. She didn't look up at me. "I thought you weren't coming."

"I had to make Pohamba a sandwich."

She made a roof with her hand and squinted, looked me over. "Are you the houseboy now?"

"We switch off."

"What kind of sandwich?"

"Turkey with chutney."

"Chutney?"

"What's wrong with chutney?"

She drank from a water bottle she'd been holding between her knees. The water spilled out from the edges of her mouth and ran down her neck, soaking her shirt.

"Is it all right?" she said.

"Is what all right?"

"To come here."

"Yes."

"You don't want to sleep?"

"No."

"You look tired."

"I guess I've gotten used to siesta."

"So go back to bed."

"I'm fine."

"I don't need sleep."

"I don't either."

"I never need sleep."

"Neither do I."

"I only wanted to talk — without all of them — always —"

"I know."

"They're always —"

"Yes."

"Will you tell them?"

"No."

"Not Pohamba?"

"No."

"He has a mouth. They all have mouths." She looked at me, looked away, looked at me. "I only wanted to talk without them," she said. "Why is that so difficult?"

"Where's the kid?" I asked.

"Behind us. Asleep in his car seat. I hope asleep. I bribed him with Twix."

"His car seat?"

"Now I need a car. Sit?"

"Here?"

"Why not? These dead Boers are comfortable chairs."

66

APOSTLE JOHN

Apostle John at the Mobil station in Karibib will always God bless you even if you don't give him any money. There's John in his wheelchair without tires, his slow rumble across the oily pavement, one hand out, the other doing his best to steer. His shoes are tied to his knees to remind you he'll never need them again. Some days Apostle John is blind. Other days he isn't. He says he got blown to Christ up north in the struggle. You try not to look at him. Apostle John rolling toward you, palm up — and still it doesn't matter, even if you don't give him a single rand. Still, it's God bless you. Apostle John's not a miser with the Almighty's love. You ignorer. You of the undeserving horde. Yes, you. You. I'm speaking to you. God bless you.

67

ANNUAL LIBRARY LECTURE (EXCERPTED)

Honorable Obadiah Horaseb
Chief Librarian

. . . while the Hindus, for instance, say that behind every book is a set of hands. Now in the context of a library, *a lending institution* (a lovely idea, no?), we may carry this golden idea further. The more a book is borrowed, the more hands have held it, cradled it. Would you have the imprint of a human soul go untouched? And yet what of those books that go years, nay, decades, unread, their words silent, waiting? Contemplate this a moment. Do unread words continue speaking? If so to whom? Is it not the lonely, unheard chattering of the dead? Is a closed book not a tomb? Oh, mourn the unborrowed books. Here's one. A fine copy of *Bleak House* published in 1957 by Black International, Hudson, New York. Last borrowed from this library in 1973. 1973! Would it were a crime, citizens. This book, these words, dormant? A book with the boldest first sentence ever composed! "London." That's all. "London." Amazing conjurement. Imagine you hold a book in your hands. Open it. "Goas." One of you boys might very well be the future crafter of such an evocation. A feeble example from a man of little poetic gifts might go something like this:

> Goas. Second term finally over and His Highness, the majordomo, is sitting on his patch of grass outside his princely office. Unflinching drought. As much sand in the air as if the wind had but newly

broomed up the desert itself, and it would not be fantastical to meet a sun-crazed grampus-like woman hulumphing down the road from her fence line . . .

Thus, I propose a moment of silence, not only for stories unread, but for stories untold. Was it not Cioran who said a book should both cure old wounds and inflict new ones? Thus, an unread book is what? A festering sore? A cancer? What then, I ask, is an *unwritten* book? I believe a silent prayer is called for. Yes, for dead authors and their fleshless hands, only bones and silence now. But also for ourselves, my boys, for all the stories you have yet to tell.

Amen.

Now concerning this copy of *Bleak House:* I will extend the due date ten days. Standard Sevens have increased privileges, so you may have it for up to two weeks provided you write a book report. Rubrecht? Petrus Matunda? Petrus Goraoab? Skinny Hilunda? Jeremiah? Members of the esteemed faculty? Anybody? Theofilus?

68

GRAVES

He pants at my door."

"Who?"

"Von Swine."

"The principal? When?"

"Call him von Swine."

"Okay. When does von Swine pant?"

"In the middle of the night."

"What does he want?"

"At three in the morning? To give me a new box of chalk."

"Is the door locked?"

"The door has no lock."

"Miss Tuyeni?"

"She sleeps heavy. Since we were girls. One morning my father hit her with a bottle."

"So he pants?"

"Yes."

"Why doesn't he just walk in? It isn't like he's shy."

"He's being polite. He's waiting for an invitation."

"So what are you going to do?"

"Do?"

"Can't you call the school inspector? Report him."

"The inspector? What would I say? My brother-in-law stands outside my door and breathes heavy?"

"Why not?"

"Like a dog out there, aching. I listen to him. I'll give this to him:

The man's a revulsion, but he has rhythm. I sleep to him — huh, huh, huh."

"Huh, huh, huh?"

"Huh, huh, huh, huh, huh."

69

SPIES

Pohamba had a sign on the wall opposite his bed. It said: COME AS A FRIEND NOT A SPY. I think of him now at dusk on those rare cooler days when for once the sky was more blue than white. Some weeks we were so berated by the heat that when it did seep away we missed it, because now our laziness had no excuses. A good time to plan our lessons, so we slept. Or tried to sleep. Pohamba lying on his bed rereading that sign, because his eyes are restless and he's out of magazines. A learner made it for him. In addition to math, Pohamba taught the only two electives offered at Goas, physical training and woodworking/mechanical arts. PT consisted of a few sets of jumping jacks and laps around the soccer field. Woodworking was once a week, on Wednesdays, in the mimeograph-machine shack, which was also the tool shack, which was also the place where boys on severe punishment were taken to be flogged. In math, Pohamba would assign problems, and then the boys would take their copy books up to his desk. If they got it wrong, Pohamba would feel betrayed. *I teach you and I teach you and I teach you and this is the thanks? Zero is nothing but a tool for coping with reality. Haven't I told you this x times? Nullify the value and then divide into negation. There is no end to our negative subparts.* But on Wednesdays, in the mimeograph shack, amid his tools and his wood, he talked to the boys, told them even more practical things about life. One of the things he had told them had ended up on that sign. He was proud of it. The day the boy gave it to him, he called me into his room. The sign was painted blue, red, and green, SWAPO colors.

He was just lying there, his hands folded across his chest, his feet hanging off the bed, admiring it.

"Nice," I said. "Who made it?"

"Eiseb's brother."

We both looked at the sign for a while. Then I went back to my own bed and thought about spies, about seeming to be one person and being another. Or were you both? Neither? At Goas, Pohamba was so completely *Pohamba*. What he wanted, what we all wanted, at times, was to be not only somewhere else but someone else. A friend, what was the challenge in that?

I mostly remember him in motion. Even when he was still, much about him was in motion. His eyes, his mouth, his jiggling knees. But the times I need to return to now are the rare moments he's at peace. Him on that saggy mattress that's too big for him. His head on his extorted pillows. His wardrobe door is open and his shirts hang neatly in plastic. His walls are bone-colored. Plaster crumbles in spots. On the same wall as the sign there's a long, jagged crack that runs from the ceiling to the floor. (Sometimes we pour hot water in our cracks to kill the ants.) He's there, reading his sign. A secret history of Pohamba? What of the horror of not having one, of being the person people think you are?

70

PRINSLOO

Sampie Prinsloo sells us vegetables. A jovial old-time Boer farmer who dresses the part. Veldskoens and no socks, khaki shorts, skinny legs holding up a belly like a small hillock. A cucumber dangling lazy out of his mouth like a cigar. No hat, just an exuberant bush of dusty hair. He's also the Republic of Namibia's most vocal local cheerleader. ("I'm a tough old bastard," he'd say. "If I can survive forty years in this forsaken place, I can live through President Nujoma.") Prinsloo was the first white in Karibib to line up for a new driver's license. His bakkie is festooned with patriotic bumper stickers.

GLORY TO OUR PLAN HEROES.
TO EVERY BIRTH ITS BLOOD.
ONE NATION, ONE NAMIBIA, SOUND YOUR HOOTER.

Once or twice a month, he and his wife pull up to the cattle gate and Prinsloo jams that hooter. Then he gets out and waits. His wife stays in the car. Apparently she doesn't share his enthusiasm for getting to know the neighbors now that things have changed so much. The boys come running out of the hostel or off the soccer field, springing over to him, and Prinsloo shouts, "Go back and get your money, boys!"

And the boys say, "We're poor, meneer, very poor boys. We have nothing, meneer, nothing."

"You think this fruit of the earth is free? You think I'm Communistic?"

And the boys in chorus say: *"Not Communistic. Meneer is very generous."*

Prinsloo sighs and cackles and takes his cucumber out of his mouth and spits and shows his golden teeth and then yanks out a box of small carrots and starts tossing them in the air. The boys leap for the carrots. High in the air for those runt carrots. Not because they're hungry, but because they're free and this is a game they still enjoy.

Dankie my baas! Dankie my baas!

Eventually, we the teachers walk down the road. We take our time. We are dignified teachers and we will not jump for carrots. No Boer's monkeys are the teachers. Antoinette carries down her knives. (Prinsloo is also the local knife sharpener.) And we look over the merchandise like discriminating shoppers. Prinsloo watches me put back a pumpkin. *What? The United States doesn't appreciate my vegetables? How about a nice squash for the U S of A?* How about green peppers, Brussels sprouts, oranges, corn, spinach, kumquats, lemons, pawpaws, okra, pears, pomegranates, eggplant (aubergine, Obadiah corrects)? Because there is nothing Prinsloo can't grow. The man grows cotton on the edge of the Namib. We pay our money to his wife, who watches us with small, suspicious eyes behind the dirty windshield. Then we head toward our rooms, our arms now piled high with the bounty of a suddenly miraculously generous earth. It helps that Prinsloo has the only irrigable standing water of any farm along the C-32. Still, he pretends it has less to do with his groundwater levels than his magic hands. Prinsloo's hands, gnarled, fattish, beet-red.

71

GOAS

Quiet out here during most of the bad years leading to independence. The eighties were years of calm, when Goas settled into its mission of churning out farm boys with sufficient arithmetic, Afrikaans, and Fear of the Lord. The shooting at the Old Location in this country, Soweto, Sharpeville, Steven Biko in South Africa — all that happened on some other planet. Yet it is true that one boy did burn down a classroom here in 1985, an event that now stands as Goas's proudest antiapartheid moment. At the time it was considered pure terrorism. The boy, Lucas Nambela, was sent down south to the juvenile prison in Mariental. That it was our current principal who whipped Lucas Nambela is an unspoken truth and one of the contradictions by which Goas runs. The principal does not discuss the particulars of back then. The revised truth is that everyone who was here believed in the cause of righteousness, all are survivors of apartheid's unmitigated evil and oppression. Lucas Nambela was a freedom fighter. The classroom he burned down was the school science lab. Four years later, on the eve of independence, the diocese in Windhoek sent Goas new equipment. Men came out with state-of-the-art everything: lab tables, sinks with running water, microscopes. There are beakers and flasks. Safety goggles. Hazardous chemicals. Bunsen burners! To this day no boy has touched any of it. The principal keeps the place locked up like a gleaming shrine. The Lucas Nambela Memorial Classroom. Even Festus, who's the science teacher, can't use it.

The principal Scotch-taped his edict to the door:

The equipment inside this room is very expensive. It took many years after the patriotic incident of 1985 for this equipment to arrive. There is too much risk involved in the use of this equipment at the present time. An inventory is being conducted. Following this inventory, the lab will be opened in limited circumstances. The public shall be apprised of any progress in this matter.

Meanwhile, we all peek in and look at the shiny hardware. Our own museum of the future, right there, two classes down from the principal's office. A form of worship to look at all that new stuff through the glass.

Across the courtyard, Festus teaches photosynthesis. Sometimes he points to the shackled class and says, "Behind that door, all that I'm telling you may be proved before your eyes." A sort of heaven waiting. There were times we wondered if it wasn't for the best. Bunsen burners get clogged. Beakers shatter. Crucibles rust. Theories go to hell. Let all remarkable things remain in the realm of perfection, of order . . .

72

GRAVES

There are no nights to remember, because we never had any. Out there by the graves after lunch. Only those stark early afternoons when the day died a little and everybody else wilted on their beds. Could we have snuck some nights? Probably, but first of all there was Tomo, and second, there was something about the lunacy of anybody being out in the veld during siesta. Weekdays only. (Weekends were too risky; Saturday and Sunday were like all-day random siestas, and you never knew who'd wander out in the veld.) We bucked the schedule of life at Goas, and this was some-how a small thrill, the best we could muster. We'd come from different directions and be shocked to see each other.

What a surprise —
Couldn't sleep. The heat.
And how is Grieta today?
Still dead, I'm afraid.

Her hands always smelled of the lotion she was continually rub-bing on the backs of Tomo's dry arms. In the bleak light, the two of us leaning against the graves. Her making small piles of gravel with her fingers, then smoothing them. Her fingers were always busy. Tomo on the other side of the graves, drunk off chocolate in his car seat, strapped in, an umbrella propped over him. I was more ex-hausted after lunch than at night. I lied. Mavala lied. We said we didn't need sleep. Sometimes we couldn't help it, and in that light it was like falling asleep under interrogation.

Even then she was restless, talking to herself and fisting and un-fisting her hands.

73

KRIEGER

Obadiah said: All our whites are demented in one way or another. It would indeed be interesting to come to America for the sole purpose of observing normal whites. This is not to say that our blacks are lacking in idiosyncrasies. Do you think it's the sun?

Our closest neighbor, Krieger, we saw only behind the wheel of a speeding bakkie. When he drove across Goas, he scattered anything in his path; boys, goats, teachers. It happened twice a day. Krieger on his way to and from the dorp. Krieger's truck wings around the church, rumbling across the ruts in the sandy road, then careens across the soccer field in the middle of a game. A fluffy-white-haired honking murderous Santa bellowing, Halloo! Halloo!

According to the principal, Krieger had a binding legal right to drive straight across the soccer field. Once, I spoke up about it during morning meeting. I usually kept quiet, but I felt the behavior of a white was something within my purview to comment on.

"Seems a little dangerous," I said.

"He holds an easement," the principal said. "I've seen the document, which was duly notarized in Windhoek."

"He can't drive around the field?"

"Why should he drive around when the document gives him the right?"

"To spare life and limb."

"Did I not say the document was duly notarized?"

*   *   *

165

Soccer. A round-robin tournament. We're holding a set of Pohamba's betting forms. That wet mimeograph ink, that deep indigo
you couldn't wash off. It dyed your hands purple for weeks. Made
you high if you sniffed it and we sniff it. The pool is set at fifteen
rand with a double on the last match. It's been nil-nil for as long as
anybody can remember. We're wilting in our seats like unwatered
geraniums.

"Watched high soccer is a lot more interesting," I say.

Pohamba shouts, "Can't you get it right? *Football*. It's an offense
on our culture."

I wave him away. I've discovered something else. If you watch the
ones without the ball it's even better. Their feet. How every move is
a beautiful anticipation. The ball is only incidental to the dance.
Which is the answer to the mystery. Not only isn't it about scoring,
it isn't even about the ball. I sniff the betting forms, understanding soccer, proud, loving it, between being bored and sleepy, when
suddenly from around the church comes Krieger, roaring, barreling,
honking, hallooing. His white arm banging the outside of the door,
his fury of white hair waving in the wind. "Run for your lives, boys!"
And the boys do. They dive, they tumble. They think it's hilarious.
They think everything's hilarious. Krieger drives on toward the C-32.
Play resumes.

"One of these days that Nazi is going to kill an innocent," I say.

Obadiah raises a Sherlockian brow. "Nazi?"

"Why not? He's the right age."

"Which doesn't necessarily mean —"

"The Nazis here never even had to learn Spanish."

"Is not a central tenet of your justice system the transcendent
concept of innocent before proven guilty?"

"This isn't a court. This is Goas."

"That's true," Pohamba says. "No justice here."

Mavala stands. "You're all ridiculous." She slaps twenty rand on
Pohamba's desk. "Put it on United Africa in the next round."

We watch her walk up the road. Tomo remains. He's digging a
tunnel beneath Vilho's chair.

I turn to Obadiah. "Look, I'm simply asking for a little empathy for another marginalized people." (Residual phrase fortuitously recalled from Prof E. L. Cloyd's Sociology 202, Bowling Green State, Larry Kaplanski's final grade: C+)

"A little empathy?" Obadiah says. "If empathy was money —"

Score! Kanhala with the header.

Krieger's other claim to fame is that he shoots zebra in the Erongos and donates the meat to the school. Zebra meat has a distinctive stink. It's acrid and gamey at the same time. Only the most meat-hungry boys eat it. But it does make for good biltong. When it's dried out, you can't smell it as much. Very chewy. So chewy you could chew it like gum, for hours. My own Standard Six Jeremiah Puleni walks around in the late afternoons and hawks zebra biltong to us for small change or old eraserless pencils.

GRAVES

Speak, quiet one."

"About what?"

"About where you're from."

"You want to hear about Cincinnati?"

"Yes."

"Not much to tell."

"Try."

I tell her about Cincinnati.

"That's all?"

"Oh yeah. And at Christmas they put these white lights up at the zoo. It's very beautiful. And there's Taft."

"Who?"

"William Howard Taft. Obesest president. Once he got stuck in a bathtub. They had to come chop him out with hammers. And Christ, Davey Concepcion. How could I forget Davey Concepcion? It must be the heat."

"Who's he?"

"You see the thing about Davey was that he wasn't the superstar. I mean, we're talking about a team with Johnny Bench, Caesar Geronimo, Tony Pérez, Joe Morgan. And Pete Rose. Hail, Pete Rose. In Cincinnati, he's lord of earth and sky and hell. Fuck the Hall of Fame. Yes, but it was Davey who had something you couldn't really name. Davey was the one with the intangibles. No ego, a little bat, just that great glove, but it was his spirit, his loyalty —"

"Like Kaplansk. He's vice president."

"Listen: I'd burn down this farm to be Davey Concepcion."

"Tell me more."

"He was a humanitarian. He'd send half his salary back to the poor people of the Dominican —"

"About you."

"Me?"

"Yes."

"There's nothing to tell."

"Anything."

"I once loved a girl named Rainy Pinkus."

"Her name was Rainy?"

"Yes. Rainy Pinkus."

"Why not Snowy?"

"It was Rainy."

"Did she love you back?"

"Not really."

"Tell me another thing."

"What?"

"About your childhood."

"I herded goats at dawn."

"Lies!"

INTOXICATIONISTS IN A DATSUN

Bottle of Zorba on the dash, long since emptied. Obadiah and Kaplansk. All that's left are their voices, their bodies are gone, floated up, evaporated, poofed.

OBADIAH: I understand that many Talmudic blessings require repetition as a way of ritualizing one's contact with God.

KAPLANSK: Really?

OBADIAH: In other words, God not as a bolt of thunder but there in the simple everyday moments, in the tying and retying of one's shoes. In a belch, if you will.

KAPLANSK: Interesting. I hadn't —

OBADIAH: I myself believe in absolutely nothing. At least not today. This of course is the paradox. One never knows when faith — like love — will wander back like an old dog you thought was dead. It would all be easier if it stayed away for good. Don't you think?

KAPLANSK: Probably, but —

OBADIAH: Would you like a mint?

KAPLANSK: Please.

ANTOINETTE

For her, it's nearly a love story. She tells it as she beats a carpet she's hung off the mapone in her garden. She beats the carpet with a wooden spoon the size of a small child's head. At her feet the wash towels are boiling. Her apron is tight around her chest like body armor.

Thump. Dust waffles up.

There was once a man who stuck his wife's hand with a fork to prove he loved her, and she walked around with this scar, proudly showing it to people. Then one morning she hacked off his legs with a panga and he bled to death in bed.

Thump. Dust waffles up.

But even after that, she showed her hand with pride. Four little valleys pronged in the flesh. Thy will be done. On earth as it is in heaven.

Thump. Thump. Dust waffles up.

MAGNUS AXAHOES

He runs barefoot in the limp sand of the riverbed. He loves the feel of it between his toes. That sound, that shish shish, of sand being thrown behind him. There are days it is the sound alone that keeps his feet moving. That beautiful grinding. One day he'll run as fast as Rubrecht Kanhala. To run with a pucker thorn in your foot is better, because then you feel no fatigue in the muscles, only the wound in your foot. The pain builds more than endurance. It creates forgetting — and if you can forget, that's all that matters. He's read this in a runners' magazine. A Kenyan said it and it's the truth.

78

POHAMBA

And the goats snoofing each other's asses and us sprawled, dunking buttermilk rusks in cold tea, and Pohamba's got another brother.

"God have mercy," Festus howls. "Spread-leg woman gave birth to an army."

Pohamba's on his stomach. A Standard Two he's hired to do some chiropractic work walks up and down on his back as he talks.

"Abner, my fourth brother. He worked at the Budget on Peter Mueller Strasse. My other Windhoek brother. He cleaned the cars when the tourists brought them back from a week of chasing elephants at Etosha. Dirty dirty cars, and my brother Abner washed them like babies' arses. The thick dust of Etosha made him sneeze and sneeze, but he washed and wiped and scrubbed and hosed. But this isn't what I want to tell you. What I want to tell you is, the baas wouldn't let him use the toilet to shit. The man was enlightened. He said my brother could piss in the toilet, but not shit in it. For that he had to go across the street to the takeaway."

"How would the baas know he was shitting?"

"Easy, if it was too quiet, he'd start pounding on the door."

(Obadiah, offstage left, from behind the mapone, where he's been dozing: "What the baas of course didn't know is that one's posterior is eighty percent cleaner on average than one's hands. Thus —")

"Thus what?" Pohamba says. He stands up. The Standard Two drops off his body like a free-falling Lilliputian. "Thus what?"

We wait. His brother could piss, but not shit. Thus what?

Obadiah comes out from behind the tree and, as if this were some proper debate in some proper debating place, concedes defeat, bows to Pohamba, his left arm swooping through the dust.

79

A VISIT FROM COMRADE GENERAL KANGULOHI

Antoinette enthroned on a plastic chair amid her wilted tomato plants and rock-hard radishes. The rest of us are frantic. On her sun-ravished face is the serenity of absolute truth. Not only wasn't she going to kiss the ring of any general, she wasn't going to grace him with a single wash of her eyes. Two of her nephews went north to fight the Boers. One came back in a plastic bag; the other didn't come back at all.

But that wasn't it. She said she didn't blame any general for what had happened to those boys. They were heading for it, even before they got the ridiculous idea they were men. This is the way of boys. They go off to war and come back dead, or not at all. She wasn't blaming the general for those boys, she was blaming the general for being a general.

Antoinette said we were so ignorant we didn't know the difference between Jesus and the devil's houseboy. "And make no mistake, your general is in Lucifer's pay," she said. Antoinette, radical pacifist, pontificating lazily, shockingly. As I swung around her house with a loaded wheelbarrow, I paused to ask, "So how do soldiers come home from war if they happen to still be alive?"

"Where are you taking that garbage?"

"Behind the toilet houses."

"Go farther."

"All right."

"What did you ask?"

"You think fighting the South Africans was righteous?"

She shook her head.

"If not righteous, then justifiable?"

"Acceptable under the circumstances."

"So then how does a soldier return?" I stood there with my garbage. Antoinette, calm in her plastic chair, began to soar, her eyes fanatical. "ON HIS KNEES!"

The door of their house flapped open and Obadiah stepped out in an aviator hat with earmuff flaps. "Bravo, wife! Oratory! But it's only pomp, and pomp never hurt a soul. Now, come, puss-puss, go slip on your green dress. It goes so well with the venom in your eyes."

No one had ever heard him call her puss-puss before. Maybe she hadn't either. She didn't blink. "In holy hell, my green dress."

Thus, Antoinette refused to lift a finger during the most comprehensive clean-up operation in the history of the farm. We buried random scrap metal. We skoffled the weeds. We picked up goat shit pellet by pellet. The principal had even ordered some boys to rake the veld, the *entire* veld, which is a bit like trying to siphon off the Atlantic, and they were doing it. The sand rippled out in crests in every direction. It was difficult to know where to walk, the scalloped veld looked so good. I thought of sand traps at the country club I used to caddy at before I got fired for being more interested in the cabana girls.

General Zacharias Kangulohi (combat alias Ho Chi Minh) was our famous alumnus. He rose from farm-boy dust to a great man in SWAPO. He'd lived in exile in London, Dar es Salaam, New York, Lusaka, Stockholm. We stood by the newly painted mural of Hendrik Witbooi with Namibian flags for his eyes and a scroll of the constitution in his hand. We waited. Each boy wore something around his neck that resembled a tie. Ribbons, scarves, cowhide, socks, braided plastic bags. One boy used a piece of biltong, which he nibbled on as morning wasted into noon. We waited. Mavala stood at attention in full camouflage, her green shirt buttoned to her neck, her pants tucked into her boots and blooming out. Her right fist clenched.

Her short short hair and bullet head. Her ears stuck out from under the edge of her cap. God, I wanted to bite them. Whatever bitterness she had over the way she was decommissioned (one last paycheck and so long, comrade) was at least temporarily displaced by her sense of ceremony. She was back in the sweat of it — if not of war, something.

Our guest of honor was hours late, and the principal held us there at gunpoint with his bullhorn. He couldn't get enough of the sound of his amplified voice. The flesh-gnawing horseflies couldn't get enough of us. They descended en masse. *Move in for the chew, boys!* We didn't want cold water anymore, or shade. We prayed only that the sun kill us faster. I've heard the same is true of freezing. After a certain point, it's blissful. We stood; we waited. When the general's motorcade did arrive, it was like an alien landing — a battalion of motorcycles, land cruisers, jeeps, a limousine, even a mobile home. We stood there as the parade rushed across the soccer field and formed a horseshoe in front of us. When the kicked-up dust settled on our slickened faces, we stood up straighter. The lines of the new anthem quivered on our lips, ready to burst:

> *Na-mib-ia*
> *Our country*
> *Na-mib-ia, motherland, we love . . . (Thee!)*

Nothing happened. Two minutes, five minutes. We waited on the edge of shrieking at the first sight of the great man. Sirens whirled. The cops on motorcycles spoke furtively into walkie-talkies. The noise of their engines revving, idling, revving. The windows of the limousine were tinted. We thought he was in there having a late lunch. Or maybe he was in the motor home having a nap after the long trip out to Goas from the capital. Sweat was beginning to show through the back of the principal's suit jacket. Pretty soon he would need to be wrung out. This a man who prided himself on never working hard enough to perspire. He was supposedly an old school chum of the general's. Our knees had buckled already (but we were packed so close together, we didn't fall), when we heard the gate clank. Our eyes moved as one, and we saw, at the cattle gate, a tiny man, his body weighed down by a jacket full of medals. He was carrying his shoes.

"I walked," he shouted. "I walked to my beloved Goas like the farm boy I used to be!"

The principal started toward him, breasts juggling under his lapels, panting into his bullhorn. "Oh, my dear Zacharias, welcome back! Your kindness to visit us here is really beyond the call of any —"

The general didn't take the principal's hand. Instead, we all watched him raise a tiny foot and show the bottom of it to the principal. "Fetch me a thorn, Charles."

Into the bullhorn, the principal continued to burble: "That you created time for these children, to help us, to inspire, to enlighten —"

"A thorn, Charles."

"Humble place such as this our school, that you should return —"

"If you don't put that thing down, I'll have you shot."

And we watched in amazement as the principal himself, not a minion, dashed off into the closeveld and stooped beneath an acacia and picked up a thorn. It was long, nail-like, and the principal carried it back to the general in the palm of his hand, gently, like a wounded bird.

"Inject it."

"Zacharias!"

"Now!"

We watched this also. The principal stuck a thorn in Comrade General's Kangulohi's foot, and the general cried, "See? Still rock-hard! Myself in cushiony exile! My bemedaled chest!"

He hopped toward us on one leg, ostrich-like, the thorn still sticking out of his foot. Now came the speech. The general said he'd learned everything he ever needed to know right here at Goas, that they were the happiest days of his life, but that the Boers ended that happiness for him, for everybody. He stood on one leg and espoused.

"But I'm not going to stand before you today and tell you about war," he said. He raised his thin arms and tossed his shoes into the sand.

"No, I will not speak of the long night of exile, of what it was to not see my mother or my mother's land for more than fourteen years. I will not discourse on such pain. Nor will I tell you of the hell of the South African prisons, or of Cassinga. Of the bombs that rained that bloody day. No, I will not stand before you and talk of the blood of your brothers and sisters, your mothers and your fathers."

The general paused, looked out at us, and grinned. This threw us off. You did not mention the massacre at Cassinga and grin.

The principal launched into a fit of clapping and we did the same.

The general ordered a cease-fire. "No applause. No, my children, I wish to speak of today, of now. My children, you have freedom. So much freedom. Lord, you even have the freedom to hate."

He hopped around in an angry circle to show us what hate looked like.

"Yet, I say, do not exercise this right. Hold it, even cherish it, but don't use it. *Why?*" He did that circle dance again. "Because it's too easy!" He hopped over and snatched up the principal's bullhorn and shrieked: "What's hard is loving! That's why I say to you, children of Namibia, saplings of a newly watered nation, I love you. You think a big man, a comrade such as myself, doesn't say such a thing. Well, I say it! And I will shock your little ears and say it again. Tell your mamas what Kangulohi said: I LOVE YOU!"

He hopped closer to us.

"All we must do now to build this nation, this beautiful country, is work. Work. Work and learn. Learn. Learn. Learn. Forget hate, hate, hate and love, love, love."

We clapped more frantically. The general again waved us away. "'Tis you," he roared. "I'm no one. 'Tis you!"

We felt light-headed, patriotic, and, yes, loved . . .

He spotted Mavala. "And who, may an old general ask, are you, comrade?"

"Shikongo, sir. Chetequera Camp, Angola. 1986 to 1989."

"Commanding officer?"

"Elias Haulyondjaba, sir."

"Elias. Bless his soul. I commend you for your commitment to the struggle in the past, and your commitment to the struggle in the future, Comrade Shikongo, from the bottom of my heart as well as from my sore foot."

Laughter, applause, applause.

Obadiah stepped forward. "May our distinguished guest allow a humble teacher to quote the great murdered poet Archilochus?"

"Permission granted, Humble Teacher."

And Obadiah took off his aviator hat and raised his mouth toward the sky and recited: *"I love not a tall general, not a straddling, nor one proud of his hair nor —"*

That she chose her husband's shining moment to water the hedge of the bush in front of their house should not, in the larger scheme of Goas, have been surprising. She wasn't a person to remain invisible any more than Obadiah was.

The nozzle of her hose rose slowly, very slowly, over the fence. One of the soldiers caught sight of it and raised his rifle.

"Wait," Obadiah shouted. "Don't fire! That's my hag. Wife!" The general motioned for the man to lower his gun and looked curiously at the head that was now peering over the bushes, as if daring him to shoot her face off in the name of love.

If you imagine Goas as a village, which it wasn't — it was a school on a farm in the otherwise empty veld — but even so, if you were to think of all of us living in a sort of idyll, the soccer field was our village square, our sacred ground.

It took him a while to hop across it.

We were too far away to hear any of it, but after speaking to her through the fence for five minutes, the general knelt down and kissed the ground. Then we watched her reach and lug him up by the armpits. Antoinette was a giant compared to that little general. Then — and you may dismiss this as just another of the daily lies of Goas, but I saw it happen — she clutched his head and kissed him. Hard and long and slobbery. It was not the kiss of a hag. She talked about it for days after. How he begged her pardon for his guns and even his cursed uniform. How he said in the future, in the glorious future, we wouldn't need armies anymore and that he was only holding on to his for a while longer because there were still people who didn't believe in love. She said the man lied so much his lips fell off. What choice did she have but to glue them back on? I'm not a woman without compassion. Shouldn't a doomed man, she said, have at least one good memory?

80

GRAVES

My grandfather?"
"Yes."
"He was a pants jobber. His name was Leo."
"A what?"
"An apprentice tailor. He also boxed hats and treffed coats. What about yours?"
"He was Tshaanika, eighteenth Onganjera king."
"Oh."
Mavala stretched her arms and yawned. On the underside of her right breast, a birthmark in the shape of a bean.

81

OBADIAH (HATS)

Porkpie, boater, homburg, fore and aft, bombardier, Panama, betty tilt, Ascot, chimney pot, cockade, tiara, bucket, ten-gallon, beanie, turban, bowler, Montecristi, Stetson, Borsalino . . . The very notion of haberdashery is fantastical. Hail the helmet of Mambrino! It's why their names are so picaresque. That a mere piece of felt or wool or, yes, even metal, could provide protection from God's ultimate wrath — yet we don these illusions daily. We cover our heads. As a sign of defiance? Of faith? Of respect? Of fear? Yes. But above all, my friends, above all — hats are love. No helmet in the universe more powerful than the belief that covering one's head will make a difference to God . . . Consider the case of Kaplansk's Jews: skullcaps? A thin layer, a mere chimera, and yet don them they do. As do we all.

"Hey, Kaplansk, you heathen, where's your yarmulke? . . . Kaplansk?"
  "He's asleep."
  "Again? At six o'clock in the evening?"

82

AUTIE

Late Monday afternoon, and Obadiah and I are contemplating each other's existences in the plastic chairs in front of his house. Soccer goes on. The thud of the ball like the irregular heartbeat of Goas. Pohamba's curtains are pulled. Weekend sinners sleep away Monday. Beneath the acacia, Festus is barbering boys with his battery-powered razor. One desk chair beneath the tree, a plastic bag for a bib shoved up under each customer's chin. Festus is not a subtle barber. He balds the boys, and one after another they walk away, shiny eggs.

Obadiah groans. "The mouth arriveth," he says. Moments later we watch her approach. She gets larger and larger, and yet Auntie doesn't move exactly; she oozes. She manifests. She heads toward us, calls out to Obadiah, "All men who have said I am beautiful have died. Except one. I see a shroud over your face, Head Teacher."

"But, my dear," Obadiah says, "never once have I ever said that a hirsute woman such as yourself was —"

"Happy death, Head Teacher," she says, and without stopping veers toward the field and begins to cross through the middle of the game. She picks up speed as she gets closer to her prey, which is clearly the fuzzless tennis ball the boys have been using since the latest soccer ball got punctured. *Ignore, ignore, ignore, but how can you when she's after the ball?* When she reaches it, Auntie savors the moment. Before she swipes anything, she always licks each of her fingers. She does this right now, agonizingly slowly, before swooping, reaching, snatching. She shoves the tennis ball down the front of her dress.

"Come, boys, come and get it."

For the first time in recorded history, the boys rush toward the hostel an hour before wash call. Auntie turns her sights next on the singles quarters. Obadiah and I watch. She reaches Pohamba's door. She knocks. He doesn't answer. She knocks more. Then Auntie begins to pound on Pohamba's door with both fists. Still no answer. She thrusts her wide corpus delicti against the door. Whap. Whap. We're surprised she doesn't break it down. Auntie insults easy. She knows he's in there. I recall the double-ply toilet paper we brought from the dorp on Wednesday, after weeks of forgetting to buy it. (We'd been using pages from old Afrikaans paperback novels.) Pohamba keeps the stash in his wardrobe. The door cracks open. Pohamba — in his lucky lilac undershirt — exhausted, slumped, bows, greets her. We watch from across the field. Then Pohamba stands straighter and crosses his arms over his chest as if he's barring the door. A mere boast. We know he'll give way. That he'll let her in, let her take what she wants. *Take the Charmin, woman.* But it doesn't happen, the giving way you do for Auntie when she comes a-calling. He — we can see this plain as day — is *listening* to her. The time to dodge the monologue has passed, and still Pohamba stands before her. It's an emergency — and us two cowards, we don't twitch. There is no hue and cry from the plastic chairs. Festus's buzzing razor clicks off, and we know he's hypnotized as well.

There's an unusual stillness in Pohamba, a tranquilizing of his spirit. His body, in the door frame, now limp. He's enchanted. It's here I make an obvious link, but still one I've never made before — between stealing and monologing. When she monologued us, she robbed us of our life's time, and maybe this is why she never quite aged like a normal person. Our time fattened her. We watch Pohamba grin. He backs into his room. This is a different sort of giving way. He does it willfully, joyfully, meltingly. Goodbye, friend, so long. It's been good to —

At the same time, I can't help but wonder, as Obadiah gags, what if it works? What if she could filch them? Our tormented desires. Our desires tormented. The door closes behind Auntie's enormous ass, like the gate of a bakkie on a load of mealie sacks. A few moments later a hand — not Pohamba's, a thick, soft, braceleted hand — appears out Pohamba's window. The hand holds a tennis ball. Then the hand's fingers spread open — all five fingers wide, ecstatic — and the ball, like a tiny skull, drops into the dust.

83

GRAVES

She hounded me about my cold feet, my literally cold feet, and she thought it hilarious that the desert didn't make any difference, that I could be sweating all over and my feet were still like ice water, and she asked once if I wanted her to blow on them, and I said, No, please, just stay away from them, don't call attention to them. And she asked how such a thing could happen. I said, I'm from North America, basically I'm an Eskimo. That, and the fact that my feet sweat and then they cool off too quickly. She didn't accept this explanation.

"Are they ugly? Ugly albino rabbits? Why are white people so afraid of their feet? Please, just a look —"

"Never."

In socks, nothing but socks, half off, bunched.

84

THE ASSISTANT PRINCIPAL

News off the farm line that Obadiah's old friend Ganaseb has died in town. I've been summoned by a boy to the Datsun. Normally Obadiah savors, today he palms the bottom of the bottle and drinks as if he's trying to shove it down his throat. "Naturally," he says, taking a break, "you will attend the funeral."

"But I never knew Ganaseb."

"Not important. The man was a teacher here. You and he are of the same family now, whether you choose to accept this onus or not, our families being nothing if not onuses. Follow me? By the way, have you written your father to forgive him his trespasses?"

"When's the funeral?"

"You see, Ganaseb was blessed. That was the difference. He escaped and enjoyed Goas only in his memory, the only true way to live here. You should have heard Ganaseb talk. The long veld nights, the clean air, the russet sunsets."

"I've got to go open the library."

"You're the librarian?"

"Sub-deputy chief."

"Who's chief?"

"You."

"In that case, I declare a day of mourning. All public institutions must be closed out of respect."

"I've got reading group."

"What are you reading?"

"Mowgli." I start to climb up and over the door.

"That tripe? Wait," he says. "Ganaseb was a big man, an important man, an assistant principal. Not once since he left did he return

to visit us. I always met him in town." He seizes my arm. "And do you want to know the vicious truth of it?"

"What?"

"The man had a Volvo."

The priest drove us into Karibib in the back of the bakkie. The women wore black dresses they looked too comfortable in, as if death were a uniform waiting in the closet. Antoinette gripped Tomo by the neck, like a puppet under arrest. Mavala held the tarts Antoinette had baked for Ganaseb's widow. Pohamba tried to sneak his hand under the foil and grab some crust off a tart. Mavala tucked the tarts under her dress, which didn't stop Pohamba's mission. As we pulled away, some boys chased us, shouting, "Teachers, buy us Lion Chips!" Antoinette commanded they desist with a flick of her wrist, and the boys fell away one by one, laughing and throwing their arms around one another.

Ganaseb had got so free of Goas, he deserted the Catholic Church. The Lutheran parish in the location was packed. People swelled out the doors. Old women wailed on the steps outside. Boys dangled from the windows. The air was thick with competing perfumes. Obadiah led our entourage down the aisle, saying, "Pardon us, old friends, pardon us." We made it to the third pew and squeezed in. I tried not to look at Mavala, who was wedged between Vilho and Dikeledi. She tried not to look at me. At that time everything about us — to us — was thrilling. I loved being close enough to touch her and to pretend I didn't want to. I tried to differentiate the smell of her sweat from everybody else's.

At last, the pastor began. Obadiah translated bits of the Afrikaans. "He says Ganaseb has only changed homes. From his modest house in Karibib to the Kingdom of Heaven. Yet he remains in our hearts."

A woman in the pew in front of us hunched over and sobbed wildly. Obadiah made a fucking motion with his hips. "One of Ganaseb's girlfriends," he whispered. "He was into more than her heart." He reached into his inside coat pocket for his flask. Antoinette's crabbed hand whapped across me and seized Obadiah's wrist like a talon. It remained there — welded to him — for the entire service.

Prayers, hymns, speeches, testimonials, weeping, more testimonials. When Ganaseb was justly honored, we shuffled slowly out into the sun and followed the casket. The dead man was sticking out of the trunk of his Volvo. The road to the cemetery was strewn with withered lettuce.

After the burial, we went to the Dolphin. Pohamba bought beers for the men and Cokes for the women (out of deference to Antoinette) and hard-boiled eggs for everybody. The women sat at a separate table (Tomo under it). The three of them, all beautiful in their way, sat there like a kind of cabal, a war council. Antoinette lording, trying not to judge everyone around her too harshly, trying to be a good Christian and love, love . . . Dikeledi so silent, taking everything in. She rarely came to town. I never knew she wore glasses. Mavala pops a whole egg in her mouth.

"It's funny," Vilho said. "A man dies and we all eat eggs."

Pohamba took the salt and shook it over Vilho's head. Then he got down to business. "With Ganaseb gone," he said, "won't Karibib hire a new teacher?"

"Faulty analysis, Teacher," Festus said. "They'll double up one classroom. And Kapapu will be the new assistant. Either Kapapu or Tjaherami."

"How many learners can fit in one room?"

"As many as they want."

"What about Hangula for assistant?"

"He's Ovambo. Hereros control the district. Also, they say Hangula voted DTA."

Mavala reached across the table and covered Antoinette's hand with her own. Then she looked my way, found me watching her, and mouthed, *Where's O.?*

I shrugged. *Don't know.*

"Wait — Kapapu's not Herero. Isn't he Damara?"

"Yes, but his wife's Herero."

"Ah. And Ngavirue?"

"Ngavirue's Herero, but nobody likes Ngavirue."

Outside, Father began to honk for us. Impatient little priestly beeps. When we'd all gathered back in the bakkie, it became clear we were still missing one of us. Antoinette groaned. This foray into decadence was enough for her without further humiliation. Festus and Pohamba checked the other bottle stores. Vilho checked the reeking public toilet. Then Antoinette sat bolt upright against the spare tire, her dress gathered up in her arms, and pointed to the cemetery with a long, unequivocal finger.

Together, Mavala and I ran down the rutted road. It was good to run with her. I wanted us to keep going. Near Ganaseb's grave, I spotted a single battered loafer. He wasn't far from his stray shoe, passed out, his face in the gnarled dirt. Mavala shook him. No movement. She shook him again. A limp hand waved her away.

"Don't disturb the dead."

"It's time."

"Time? Time for what?"

"Let's go." Mavala said. "The priest is snorting."

He sat up and brushed a dusty sleeve on his forehead. His eyes were past bloodshot now. They were a kind of viscous brown, murked by tears and sweat. For a moment he sat there and stared at the fresh mound.

"I did it," he said.

"Did what?" Mavala asked.

"Pissed on him."

"Why?"

"A long piss. I'd show you, but it's gone, evaporated. That too dries up." He laughed, asthmatic, parched. "Didn't I love him? Didn't I?"

We pulled him up by the armpits. He felt light, too light for a man so tall. He looked around at the cemetery, at the rows of cardboard markers, plastic sunflowers, and sleeping dogs. We walked slowly

191

back. It was late afternoon. Jazz was already playing in the living room of one of the houses closest to the cemetery road. Dust clouds from the taxis that roamed the location wafted above us. An old woman passed by wheezing loudly, holding a loaf of bread to her chest. When we reached the bottle store, the priest was revving the engine. Festus hooted at Obadiah's dusty suit as the three of us piled into the back with the others.

85

POHAMBA

Same place as always. In front of our doors. Mosquito carcass—bloody morning. Pohamba sitting on a rock and brushing his teeth, talks like he's been smoking dagga, but we're at least a month out of dagga. He spits out the side of his mouth, doesn't look at me.

"Sooooooooo."

"What?"

"Been good, *ja bassie?*"

"What?"

"Good afternoons, *ja?* Siesta. No sleepy-peepy time for *bassie.*"

"Why are you talking like that?"

"Veld? Thorny but good, *ja?* No need sleep. Oh, *bassie* got juicy thing, happy!"

He brushes his teeth some more, sticks his tongue out, wiggles it, brushes it.

"What do you want me to say?"

"Say?"

And then him looking at me as if he's only seeing me now for the first time. He points his toothbrush at me. "Don't say anything." Then in a low, officious growl: "*Sir, I'm afraid that's highly classified, confidential information.*" He sticks his brush back in his mouth.

A hen struts by and Pohamba stands, toothbrush-mouthed, tries to wallop it, misses. His flip-flop airborne into the acacia. The hen flutters, then begins to mosey around again like nobody just tried to murder her. Pohamba goes inside his room to rinse his mouth.

86

A PIANO FOR GOAS

Let us now blame Kaplansk's mother, Sylvia. At the League of Women Voters of Greater Cincinnati, Avendale Chapter, she mentioned it offhandedly to Ruthie Goldblatt, who mentioned it to Kitty Levine, who mentioned it to Bebe Pomerantz. Which was all it took. Sylvia's son is teaching at an adorable little school somewhere in deepest Africa. I forget where. *New Bubia?* Anyway, they're in direful need of donations. Simply in direful need. What sort of donations? Oh, any donation! A donation is a donation is a donation! And besides, Bebe, Kitty says, Sylvia says these children have nothing, *nothing.* Well, I do seem to remember an old piano in my basement, Bebe Pomerantz says. I think it was Miles's mother's sister's. Died young, poor thing. They say she won contests.

Tremendous idea! Send Chopin! Send Debussy!

Four weeks later a wooden box weighing upward of two tons landed at the postkantoor in Karibib with the fanfare of a meteor. It had been delivered from Walvis Bay in its own lorry, and the postmaster called the principal personally to announce the arrival of a "mighty crate."

Mavala proclaimed the creation of a Goas music department. She had some boys on punishment clear out the storage room. The piano was the lead story in the first edition of *The Goas Harbinger.* Obadiah wrote:

What is significant, friends, brethren, Goasonians, about music and our impending new piano is that it is the physical embodiment of God's infinite varieties. Eighty keys! Give me eighty keys and I give you the miracle of creation itself. On behalf of Goas, I wish to extend our heartfelt gratitude to Kaplansk's long-suffering mother, Saint-in-waiting Sylvia Kaplansk, for this remarkable bestowal upon our humble institute of learning . . .

Festus, Pohamba, and I rode out in the priest's lorry, Theofilus driving, to fetch it. And, returning, we were like triumphant combatants. Pohamba stood on the crate and gyrated, drunkenly fingering "Tea for Two" on Festus's head. So many boys wanted to help lift the box that two Standard Fours got trampled. Even the priest and the principal stood side by side at a small ceremony in the piano's honor, the crate at their powerful feet. The two of them stood there with their pregnant-looking stomachs and refused to look at each other. Church versus state in the battle of the chubbies. The principal announced music, the great equalizer, the future of African democracy. The priest offered that music was the most direct path to salvation of our corrupted souls. Mavala wept with joy for music. Tomo waddled over and took a chomp of the crate.

So. All night. All night we tried. Maybe because at heart we were optimists, even Pohamba. Maybe at our cores we adhered to Vilho's benevolent view of mankind. All night we hammered. We sawed. We nailed. We glued. We prayed. We schemed. We didn't leave the new music room until eight o'clock the next morning, when we held a press conference in the courtyard to announce that the random shit in the box could no more be made into a piano than the feathers of a slaughtered dinner rooster could be pushed back together to make a live bird. Mavala wept again, this time with rage.

"Who are you people to send that across the ocean?"

I found myself defending Bebe Pomerantz and the good people of Cincinnati, Ohio. It was possible, wasn't it, that the stuff in the box — some wood planks, a multitude of keys, some wires, brass pedals — could have had a prior career as an actual piano?

"Rough passage?" I suggested.

That night we went out to Goas Stonehenge — an assortment of large granite boulders lacking in mystery — and roasted a goat on the remains of that piano. Festus slit its throat, I held it down with my knees as if it were Bebe Pomerantz and reveled in its childlike screams. And we drank to that piano's second and final destruction. Mavala stood up in her heels on one of the boulders and, with a fist of meat in one hand, said, "Tonight, I curse Cincinnati, curse it beyond —"

"It's already cursed," I said.

And Mavala, drunk and furious, ignoring me and the rest of us, twisting and wiggling in the windblown smoke, in the hectic light of the fire. I wanted to stand up there and let her rail in my ear, but I stayed in the shadows in my Ohio shame and composed:

Dear Kaplansk's Long-Suffering Mother,

I'm sorry, Mother. I'm sorry for so many things, and so please understand that I am even more sorry than usual to say that I will never, as long as live, and may this apply also to my corpse, set one cold toenail again in Cincinnati, Ohio. Rest assured, I'm in good hands. Her name is Mavala Shikongo. You always said you were the first person to admire spunk. I think of your passion for Geraldine Ferraro. I'd like you to meet my destiny, my destination, my disintegration. A former guerrilla fighter. She can take apart an AK-47 in seventeen seconds. Now she teaches kindergarten. Please tell Bebe thanks so much for the piano.

All my love,
Kaplansk

Other days it was less that the sun rose than that the veld seemed to pull itself up out of the darkness on its own volition. I woke up drowsy to the horizon's slow bleed. In my left hand was a high heel. Everybody else had somehow managed to get back to their beds. Only Obadiah and I were still out there. The piano was no longer, except some keys hadn't burned. They were scarred and blackened but intact, as if mocking our attempts to incinerate them.

I shook Obadiah awake and we started back. I carried Mavala's shoe stuffed in my pants. A rare dawn wind lifted the veld, and we moved slowly against the gusting sand, our bodies weighing nothing.

87

GRAVES

She's gnawing a pear, and pauses in chewing to accuse me of not having any money. Since Americans are supposed to have money, I must have thought coming here was an easy way to make a fortune — typical colonialist model, I'm out here only to loot.

"What's here to loot?"

"That's what I can't understand."

"Anyway, I've got money."

"How much?"

"A little."

"Where is it?"

"Stocks."

"Stocks! Capitalist carnivore, *It's in stocks* . . . You could, though, have a bigger enogo. Isn't that what they say in America, that the blacks have these monster penises? Do people believe such things?"

"My grandfather was a pants jobber. I'm the proletariat."

"So you have no comment on this penis issue?"

Words dissolving, muffled so as not to wake Tomo — rolling across the tablecloth we hid in the rocks. It was an old checkered one. Antoinette had given it to us so that Pohamba and I would eat less like jackals. Every time we went out there, we had to shake the sand out of it. Gradually we began to smuggle other stuff and hide it behind the graves. A pillow, a mattress cover, an umbrella (which we used to protect us from the sun, but that made us too hot), a can of Doom for the ants, library books. Afternoons of flung clothes. You couldn't call it an escape, because we didn't go far and we didn't go long. Mavala unbuttons slow. One button at a time, and then she stands and yanks off her dress. And I have to think it again, remember it again. Unbuttoning slow, pushing plastic through penny slits. Not looking at me, looking at the veld. Then she stands and yanks her dress over her head. She yawns. No claims about the sex we had, only the sex we didn't have. The sex we imagined was superior. The sex we had was hurried, diminished by the heat, sand-irritated. She rips open a condom with her teeth. And then only us and the sand crickets we try not to roll over and kill.

"Davey?"

"Yeah?"

"Davey Concepcion?"

"Yeah."

"Touch me."

"Where?"

"Here."

"Here?"

"And a little lower."

"And here. Wait, Davey, slow, Davey, too fast, Davey —"

88

MAJESTY OF THE LAW

The court decrees that the porter who ate his bread by the smoke of the roast has duly and civilly paid the cook by the jingle of his money . . . Case dismissed.

RABELAIS

Progress, Obadiah would often espouse, is having an efficient legal system based solely on principles of fairness and blind justice. One day he received a certified letter from the law firm of Tuhadeleni, Enkono, Sheehama & Partners, Windhoek.

Dear Sir,

We beg forthwith to inform you that herein described vehicle, Datsun 180 B, 1979, VIN # 3972268377AC12, currently in your possession and under your control, is the subject of an ex parte application filed at the magistrate's court, Windhoek, under a rule *nisi* attaching said vehicle. *Cur avd vult.* (Dated May 31, 1991.) Duly filed by S. Vivier on behalf of legal practitioners, Tuhadeleni, Enkono, Sheehama & Partners, Windhoek. Note that said action being duly filed resulting therein from an outstanding balance under a repair lien in the sum of rand 32,185.11. (Dated April 11, 1977.) Please see standard established under Rule 59 (a) in support thereof, providing that attachment be made on a vehicle alienated without balance duly forthwithed in full. Please also see Amalgamated Engineering *v.* Minister of Labor (1949) (3) SA (A) 337 at 661, as the person claiming to be lien holder will have direct and substantive interest in the subject of said lien. Further see *In re:* Tokien Butchery (1974) (4) SA (T) 893.

We sat in the Datsun and read it, reread it.

"I think they want money," I said.

Obadiah took his glasses off. He blew on one lens, stuck it half in his mouth and huffed, wiped it off. Did the same with the other one. Then he called a boy over — a Standard Five on punishment named Nashikoto. He'd been hosing out the chicken coop and, alternately, trying to drown the chickens.

"Go get some help."

A few minutes later, Nashikoto came back with more boys. We got out of the car and Obadiah stood on the hood in his bathrobe and read the letter, the entire letter.

When it was over, he said:

Bless this nation, its magistrates, its Minister of Justice, its constitution. But above all, a prayer for the Messers Tuhadeleni, Enkono, Sheehama & Partners and the poetry they send to Obadiah Horaseb via certified mail. Amen.

He stepped off the rostrum of the hood of the Datsun, his Datsun, and stared at it awhile. "Now bury it," he said.

It took the rest of the afternoon, but even then the pile still looked like an oafish mound in the shape of a Datsun. Observe the majesty of the law's corpus, Obadiah says, arms outstretched, his palms up like the balanced scales of justice.

89

POHAMBA

Months since Dikeledi's rain. The few clumps of green that hung on into summer are now a memory. The only thing that grows in the veld are those bizarre spiderwebs that seem to have no hold anywhere. They seem to float. They greet us in the morning, wet with slight dew, across our faces. Other than this, the days are long and dry. The cows have gotten thin again. And everybody says it's too hot even for this season.

Pohamba paces back and forth, from the fire pit to his door, from the acacia to his door, his hands behind his back. He looks me over. I'm sitting against a tire trying to read. He paces more. Undrunk Saturday and no transport to Karibib, his boredom rising to anger. Fucking Boers, he says. Fucking, *focking* Boers. That it's the Boers' fault that we have no transport to town is of course true if you follow the chain of causation to the beginning, starting with colonialism moving through apartheid all the way to what this school is doing way the hell out here to begin with, but today, forgive me, I'm only trying to read a little. I toss my teabag to the chickens.

"Listen," he says. "This happened to a friend of my Uncle Johannes. Late at night, there's a pound on the door. Like a hammer to your skull in your dreams. This friend of my Uncle Johannes gets up and answers the door. Military police on a late-night visit. 'What can I do for you, gentlemen?' 'Kaffir, we have intelligence that your son's SWAPO. Now we're going to punish the womb that birthed a terrorist.' And so they drag the old guy out of his house, this friend of my Uncle Johannes. They tie him to a goat who's tethered to a tree. They go back inside. His wife of forty-eight years. Why don't you go and write this down, Kaplansk? Why don't you go and get a pen and write it? They stuff a doek in her mouth. Her husband's in the yard married to a nanny goat."

Pohamba sucks his teeth, looks at me. I'm slumped against the door. We sit there awhile. I reread the same sentence: *I wanted to buy three passable horses for my britzka. I wanted to buy three passable horses for my britzka. I wanted to buy three*

"You don't want to go to the dorp?" he says finally. "If we start now we could have a good night."

"No thanks."

"What are you reading?"

"Still this Turgenev book."

"Russian?"

"Yeah."

"Communist?"

"I don't think so. Maybe socialist."

"Rich?"

"I don't know. Probably."

"All socialists are rich. That's why they're socialist."

"He supported the serfs."

"You don't like my story? You have better stories to listen to now?"

"I like your story fine."

Pohamba steps over to me and raises a flip-flopped foot to my face. He holds it there, quivering. I drop the book in the sand.

"Why don't you do it? Smash my head?"

He waggles his foot in my face. "He supported the serfs," Pohamba says. "Good for him."

90

THE ILLEGALS

They emerged one morning out of the veld during those days of ruthless heat. It was a Friday and we were in morning meeting. That morning's tale concerned, if I remember, the importance of proper dental hygiene in an emerging democracy. The principal was reading to us from a *Namibian* article about the alarmingly high incidence of tooth decay in Ombalantu. "Citizens must floss. A nation must maintain its oral health. I prefer waxed. Watch me now."

We hardly had our eyes open. Caffeine never did much for us on Fridays. Then there was a knock on the door, which was strange, because the boys knew better than to disturb this ritual. The principal was working on a trouble spot in the back of his mouth. He pointed to Mavala: "Open it." He loved to give her orders in public. And Mavala, more out of curiosity than the command, did it. When she saw them, she dropped to her knees, still holding her cup of coffee. After, she said she didn't know why, only that there was something so heavy about them. They weren't bedraggled. The most alarming thing was how scrubbed clean they looked. But they ignored Mavala's outstretched arms. They seemed to understand immediately that the one in the tie flossing his teeth was boss. Of the two boys, one was tall and gangly, with extremely thin arms and long hands. The other was squat, with roving eyes that seemed to troll over us, summing us up. We were pampered. We knew nothing of suffering. All we cared about in the world was our coffee and egg-and-tomato sandwiches at mid-morning break. You never see yourself as plainly as through the eyes of children who aren't children anymore.

The girl never looked up. She only gazed at her feet, which were sun-cracked and blistered, but somehow too clean. Her not looking up didn't seem to be out of fear exactly. She appeared past any notion of being scared of anything. She wore a light blue dress with delicately embroidered frills around the edges. Mavala said it looked like a communion dress she once wore. The tall one was probably her brother. They had similar eyes, smallish, worried. He stood next to her, the edge of his bare feet touching hers. The squat one spoke to the principal.

"We greet Teacher."

"Greetings, child. Where are you coming from?"

"North, Teacher."

"How far north?"

The boy hesitated. "The border."

"The other side of it?"

"Yes."

"Running?"

"Yes."

"From what?"

The boy hesitated again. "The fighting, Teacher."

"Savimbi?"

The boy knew better than to take sides, even in another country, even as far south as Goas. "Only from the fighting, Teacher."

"Parents?"

"None."

"How did you come here? Who brought you?"

"We walked, Teacher."

"Walked! From Angola!"

"Yes."

"Impossible!" the principal cried. "It's eight hundred kilometers!"

The squat boy's expression didn't change. He seemed to be sizing the principal up, seeing he wasn't a fool, only bombastic.

Quietly he repeated it: "We walked, Teacher."

The principal looked down at their feet, the first time he had. "You're hungry?"

"No, Teacher."

"You need a place to sleep?"

"No."

"What do you want, then?"

This time the boy didn't hesitate. "School."

"What?"

"We want to go to school, Teacher."

The simple truth of it. Not food, not a place to sleep, only school. The principal shrugged, pleased they'd come to him instead of the priest. Had it been Father who sheltered these lambs, the principal would have been on the farm line to the police barracks in Karibib and those three might have been deported within a day, shipped back to more civil war, to Dr. Savimbi, in the back of a cattle lorry.

"There is room, children," he said, "in our inn."

For a week or so, they sat quietly in our classrooms. When there weren't enough chairs, they sat on the floor. We gave them pencils and paper, but they rarely wrote anything down. They rotated from class to class like benevolent versions of the dreaded school inspectors who descended on Goas once a term with their checklists, rating us on the old Bantu education scale from *Goed* to *Swak*. They often started their days in Mavala's class of sub b's and ended them in Pohamba's Standard Sevens, each day an entire trajectory of whatever we had (or didn't have) to offer, which was probably more school than they'd had in mind. They didn't talk to the boys or even among themselves. Even the squat one, after his initial boldness, settled down to the life of just another silent learner. Once, Mavala tried to talk to him, to ask him what happened to them. She said she might understand, but he only turned away without a word.

Out at the graves she said, "He only talks when he needs to. I forgot the virtue of that."

"You don't tell anything."

She shrugged. It was a lying-down shrug, and the sand made a dull rasp.

"I've nothing to tell."

"I don't believe you."

We never learned their names, or anything about what they'd been through. Of course, we had Obadiah's radio and week-old newspapers. We had an idea. We could have imagined things if we were up to it. Soldiers tossing babies in the air and shooting them in front of their mothers. But who can truly see this?

They never lingered. The three of them arrived at school in the morning after the second triangle and left promptly after last class. At break, they went out into the veld by themselves.

In class, silent or not, the girl was the only lesson. You could smell the boys sweating over her. Her eyes had a kind of sad vagueness as she looked straight ahead at the board. She seemed unaware of the boys' agitation. The only time she showed any real expression was when she looked at her brother. Sometimes, in class, she touched the side of his face, and the boys swooned. The squat one could obviously take care of himself. But of her timid brother — always next to her, his feet touching hers — she seemed to wonder, What will become of you when I leave you?

When they were gone from us, a boy discovered they'd been living out by the road. Theofilus must have known this. We figured he also gave them food, and they may well have accepted it from someone as unobtrusive as Theofilus. He never mentioned it either way. But when they were among us, nobody, not even the most lawless of the Standard Sevens, followed them back to where they slept. The only way I can explain this is to suggest that for some reason all of Goas recognized — without it being decreed from on high — that a part of the veld out toward the road was, for a time, theirs, in a place where they were like stowaways.

They left us as abruptly as they'd come. Nobody chased them.

SNAKE PARK

We rented a bakkie from Felix Desconde. According to Pohamba, Desconde was the richest man in Karibib, and he had a fleet of Toyotas he rented out at usurious prices. Desconde owned the grocery, the hardware, and the marble works on the edge of town. He was also a man of the people, and wanted to live among them, so he built the only two-story house in the location, a mock castle with a four-car garage, a razor-wire security fence, and eight roaming dogs.

All of us were going. Just as we were pulling away from Goas, Auntie ran — the first time anybody had seen this happen — and lunged at us. Her breasts caught on the open back gate of the bakkie, and we had no choice but to haul her up. As we rattled down the Goas road toward the C-32, we saw Miss Tuyeni out walking in the veld. She was becoming more ignored than Auntie. Alone, she looked more like Mavala than when they were near each other. They had the same shoulders. Vilho suggested we invite her along, but Pohamba didn't hear him over the noise of the radio. As we passed her, Miss Tuyeni didn't look at us. She stooped, took off a shoe, and jiggled a rock out of it.

The Erongo Snake Park was down the C-32 toward Otjimbingwe and run by an ancient Polish couple. Who knows how they got marooned at a tourist attraction on a road where not a single tourist ever strayed, but they'd been there since long before independence. A decrepit Mercedes was parked in front of a small flat house with the windows boarded up. The Poles were incredibly tiny, sun-shrunk people. The Mercedes was apparently their ticket office, as well as, perhaps, their house. They were both sitting in it when we pulled up. The snake park consisted of seven or eight glass boxes. The glass hadn't been cleaned in years. It was hard to see the snakes. Inside the boxes were rocks and sand that looked very much like the rocks and sand outside the boxes. In one of them we could see, past the green slime of the glass, the outlines of two Neilson vipers looped together in a pretzeled twist.

"Do you think they are more bored with the box or with each other?" someone said.

"Each other."

"The box."

"Each other."

We moved on to the next box, a lone giant python thick and sedentary as a car tire.

I remember very little else except for the heat and the overall wobbly drunkenness of the day and how the sun glinted against the glass of the boxes.

On the way back, Mavala put on Obadiah's touring hat, an argyle pot lid–looking thing he said was most appropriate for motoring in Scotland. It blew off and sailed like a frisbee into the veld, but Pohamba wouldn't stop for it. This was his trip. He'd rented the truck. He'd organized us. Now we were all exhausted and wilted and letting him down because we weren't whooping it up anymore, and so he wasn't stopping for any fucking Scottish hats.

OBADIAH

Another Sunday. Obadiah on his back under the mapone, his upper body in the shade, his lower in the full sun. His shoes are off and they are facing in opposite directions. He reads out loud from a week-old *Namibian* that he is holding over his head to block the sun:

> February 12. Epako Location, Gobabis: An as yet unidentified twelve-year-old boy was found in the cemetery adjoining the playground of the Gobabis-Epako Primary School at Epako Location yesterday evening. Police estimate the time of death to have been between twenty-one hundred and twenty-three hundred hours Tuesday night. The boy was found disemboweled.

Then, speaking not to us, not to anyone listening anyway, he says, "A reporter wrote that. Byline: Oswald Kambabi. *The boy was found* — First Oswald scribbled the word down on a pad at a police briefing. Then, later, back at the office, he typed out his copy."

A lone finger rises and begins to peck, slowly hunting the air for letters.

T-H-E-B-O-Y-W-A-S-F-O-U-N-D-D-I-S-E-M-B-O-W-E-L-E-D.

"Oswald, did your hand tremble to type those letters? Or is such sentiment entirely vanished from the earth? Have we lost even the right to be surprised, much less indignant? Antoinette prays to God. I pray to God. But there are new Gods now. Oswald Kambabi who types such things without trembling."

And Obadiah begins to rock slowly from side to side under the mapone. He lets go of the paper. It drifts slowly down and covers his face. Chanting: *The boy was found, the boy was found, the boy was found . . .*

He sits up, talks to the bark of the tree. "Twelve years old. Only the shit beetles who crawled all over what was left of him weren't indifferent to that child."

WALLS

H ey, Truelove, how's she tasting?"
    "I'm not answering that."
"Come now, is she satisfying your meatful needs?"
"Kill yourself."
"Suicide? What about my learners?"
"I'll cover your classes."
"What about the Pope?"
"He won't care, one less pagan."
"You think I've never been in true love, Truelove?"

It's not a question, it's a proclamation. I let it hang in the dark.
Let him nail it to his forehead. Night is a hole I fall into, with papery
walls and his voice is like a camera eye with a loudspeaker, as if I'm
in some low-tech *1984*. I wait for him to say something else. Maybe
he's gone to sleep. All bedsprings silent. No noise of his breathing.
Nothing.

GRAVES

Us lying on Grieta backward. Mavala's head is hanging off the front of the grave. There's a scratch on her left cheek from a thorn. She's eating cheese. She holds it out to me.

"No, thanks."

"You don't like Cheddar?"

"I do. I ate."

"What did you eat?"

"Tuna and cabbage soup."

"Who made the soup?"

"Dikeledi sent it over."

"*Dikeledi, Dikeledi, Dikeledi.* You men like them silent. Why am I so hungry all the time? These condoms. If I'm pregnant, I don't want a kid that looks like old butter."

"I look like old butter?"

She kisses my chin.

"Sorry, but in certain light, yes."

"I don't need to listen to this shit. I could be in a real bed. Alone. Unharassed."

"Why *did* you come here?"

"It seemed like a good idea at the time."

"What?"

"To come and save all the dark babies."

"Come here, Teacher."

"You come here, Teacher."

"Tell me more about Snowy Pinkus."

"Rainy."

"Snowy's a bitch."

Our legs are twined up. She's still holding the hunk of cheese.

95

GRAVES

I want to spit on her," she says.

"On who?"

"Grieta."

"Why?"

"You're asking me why?"

"I'm asking you why."

"Listen. I heard this story about them once. A train of ox wagons are crossing the Kalahari from the Free State. The great trek to unknown parts. It's their second day without water. They're wandering trackless. A baby dies. There's no time to stop, and so the father of the baby tosses it out in the veld — not because he's cruel, but because he wants to save his other children and there's no time. But the mother won't have this. She leaps out for her dead child. So they stop, outspan long enough to dig a small hole and say *Our Father*. But before they can move on, another child dies, and so they do it again. *Our Father*. This land beat the Boers into natives, didn't it?"

"Sounds like it."

"But when they saw us, they didn't see themselves."

"So spit, or not?"

"I say spit."

"What about us?"

"Us what?"

"Us this. Here. This isn't desecration?"

"This is nothing, darling."

And she rolled away from me into the grooves of hot sand, her body wearing it.

GRAVES

L ook at me. Tell me what you see."

"Can you flare your nostrils like that on demand? I've always —"

"You mean you can't ? It's easy, just —"

"I'm trying, I'm trying."

"Shhh. Be quiet and look at me."

Her nails dig into my arm, painted pink death — "Look."

Instead I go closer to her and she blurs, closer until our faces crash.

And Mavala stands and marches away: marching, swinging her arms, her knees like levers, heading farther into the veld, shedding everything, blouse, necklace, strap-tangled bra, skirt — all in puddled clumps off the goat path, into the trackless veld, heading for the C-32, across a river of sand, not stopping, me chasing and picking up clothes, her not looking back, shouting, "Leper! Make way! Leper!"

DR. SAVIMBI

Namibia never made the BBC. What would they have said? *Nothing much raged again today across newly indepen-dent . . .* So we had to be content with Angola or South Africa news, both of which were consistently bloody enough to make the radio.

One night, I dreamed I heard on the BBC that Jonas Savimbi was assassinated, blown up by a hand grenade. The next morning, I trumpeted it around school: "Savimbi's dead!"

"How do you know?"

"I heard it last night on the BBC."

Hallelujah, the BBC. The BBC! Could the sun rise without the BBC? The earth rotate? The tides roll in? The tides recede?

Mavala shouted from her classroom: "Finally, that Bantustan got what he deserved!"

"The war will be over up there," Pohamba said.

"And now our illegal nomads will go home," Vilho said.

That night we gathered at Antoinette and Obadiah's and waited. Obadiah was soaking his feet in water and salt. He said his feet had the hardness. *Beep, beep, beep. BBC News. Thirteen hours Green-wich mean time. The main points read by Wynford Vaughn-Thomas: In the Slovenian capital, Ljubljana, federal troops clashed with demonstrators demanding an independent Slovenian state for a sec-ond straight day . . . In Angola, UNITA rebel leader Dr. Jonas Sav-imbi has again failed to honor the cease-fire, and his men are reportedly on the march toward Huambo. The Zairian president, Mr. Mobutu Sese Seko, has renewed his role as mediator in the con-flict . . . A reprieve for Galileo. The Vatican announced today that*

Galileo Galilei has been formally absolved of charges of heresy and that the earth is in fact round.

Obadiah clicked it off.

"Fine work, Kaplansk," Pohamba said.

"You're going to blame me for dreaming?"

"I've been punished my whole life for it," Pohamba said.

"Let's have a drink," Obadiah said and poured a little zorba for each of us. "Now I have a question for us to ponder. What in God's name is that Mephistopheles a doctor of?"

We pondered.

Gastrology?

Demonology?

Scientology?

"Aaaaaaaaha!" Obadiah raised his feet and showed them to us. Then he put them back and stood up and began to march in place, splashing water all over. "All that marching. Imagine what such raping and pillaging can do to a man's arches. The man's a podiatrist! 'Halt, men, show the good doctor your soles. Not your souls, fools! I have no use for your souls!'"

98

ANTOINETTE AND OBADIAH

Those times when a real catastrophe reached us at Goas, Antoinette would accuse the dead of gossiping. Sister Ursula at the clinic in Usakos called the principal to say that one of our boys, a Standard Four named Nicholas Kombumbi — coming back from a weekend with his parents in Windhoek — was killed when the bakkie he was riding in the back of flipped over on the C-32.

Antoinette dropped to the sand, held her hands to her ears, and begged them to stop. Enough, mongers! Enough!

There was a great sense of order in her world of scouring, of washing, of lining the boys up, of feeding them, of punishing them. Any threat to this universe caused her temporarily to abdicate, to leave us. Obadiah and I helped her up. He tried to be kind to her when she broke down on account of other people's misfortunes. It took the focus away from her own misfortunes, for which he, Obadiah, was responsible. When she was calm again, the three of us sat on the bench by the garden fence and watched the commotion in front of the principal's office. The principal was standing in his doorway holding the phone. He was now publicly — with great ceremony, but not without genuine sorrow — calling the parents of the dead boy. At one point, however, for all his love of ritual and formality, the principal sat down heavily on the step that led up into his office and slumped against the door frame. He took the receiver away from his ear. Seeing this sent Antoinette back to cursing the dead and all their cheap, nasty, behind-the-back talk. Obadiah got angry then, tired of it.

"We are doomed," he said. "Superstition will be death of this country. Something went wrong. Perhaps the driver was drunk. Or perhaps he was from Windhoek, unaccustomed to driving on our treacherous gravel roads. There is a rational explanation why that boy is dead. A peace officer will investigate the true cause and create a public report."

Antoinette, still looking at the principal, who had not yet responded to the wailing we could practically hear, stooped and picked up a rock at her feet. Without saying anything, she caressed it for a while. I wondered if she was going to smash Obadiah's face with it. Instead, she went down to her knees again and began to beat the ground with the rock. Slowly, methodically, one thud after another. Obadiah just sat there, stiff, not watching her, only hearing her, as he stared helplessly at the now completely silent crowd in front of the principal's office.

99

GOAS

Our fences, unlike Krieger's gleaming razor wire (talk that he went out there and barbed it himself when he wasn't busy running down children), were mostly patchworks made up of hub-caps, sheet metal, plywood, car parts, bedsprings, hammered barrel lids, plastic crates, bricks, goatskins, crushed cans, assorted broken furniture, and in spite of Theofilus's constant repairs, they didn't do much but lean away from the wind. Although the cows mostly stayed on the farm, any and all predators — jackals, baboons, hyenas, Kala-hari foxes, our friends the dwarfed hedgehogs, leopards, carnivo-rous bush rabbits, warthogs, neighboring thieving farmhands — all were absolutely welcome at Goas. Our saddest fences, though, were the ones that didn't even try. Those sections of fence line where the land dipped into dry tributaries and the fence couldn't follow suit were called "flying fences," the most useless man-made things in the universe. A bit of cordoned-off void, winging across nothing, the only true mascot of Goas.

100

VILHO

Outside Goas church. After the funeral for Nicholas Kombumbi, Vilho and I sit across from each other on the benches that used to be part of the stolen picnic table. The table must have been a monster to lift. It was a solid slab of concrete. We imagine it is out in the veld somewhere, although nobody has come up with a satisfactory motive for taking it, other than to prove that if it's stealable, Pohamba's Standard Sevens will light the way. Vilho and I shuffle our best shoes in the sand. We've stopped trying to talk about it. The boy Nicholas was his. Not his best learner, but not his worst either, so he didn't know him very well. Now he feels he failed the boy. The boy's mediocrity was a mask that prevented Vilho from seeing an individual soul. Now he goes to his final reward unknown by the people entrusted to remember him. I have given up trying to talk him out of this. So here we sit. We watch the priest lock the door of the church. He greets us with a slow, solemn nod and disappears behind the tall rectory gate. A pair of goats wander by, their ribs protruding. Vilho is trying to remember a single thing about this boy. His body has already left for Karibib, followed by cars and bakkies loaded with relatives and friends. There's a whistle in the late-afternoon wind. Vilho stops shuffling his feet and looks as though something has occurred to him. I watch his face tighten. Grief is useless without memory, yet he might be making progress. Everybody else has gone to sleep, or to Obadiah's for a nip, then sleep.

101

GOAS CHRISTMAS

Hot gray light, Christmas afternoon. Those who could have gone somewhere have. Antoinette and Obadiah to their kids in Windhoek. Festus and Dikeledi to her family in Gobabis. The principal and Miss Tuyeni to the north. By car, by lorry, by bakkie, by donkey cart — foot — people have fled. The farm is beyond quiet without the stampede. At night, with the boys asleep, all their breathing still made the place feel alive. Now we are walking around listening to the churn of our own feet in the sand. The wind's relented. There's no service. The priest has gone to say Mass at Otjimbingwe. We who've been left behind go on our own to church and sit in the silence, listening to the echoes of our own respectful coughs. Mavala chants softly: *I am the resurrection and the life, saith the Lord; he that believeth in me, though he were dead, yet shall he live. Whosoever liveth and believeth in me shall never die.*

I whisper, "Isn't that what you say when someone dies? It's Christmas."

"Someone didn't die?" She whispers back. "What about Vilho's learner? What was his name?"

"Kombumbi."

"Yes, Kombumbi. And others, so many others." She leans forward and sinks her face in her hands.

And that was it, just Mavala, Tomo, me, Auntie, and Pohamba, who only went to church because the priest wasn't there, and some boys who for whatever reason couldn't make it home.

*   *   *

The church cool in the shadows in spite of the heat outside. A cement cavern with a roof that is also used to store feed and diesel-engine parts. A dusty gold cloth draped over the altar. There was no vestry, just that one room. A velvet robe hung on a nail. Nothing on the walls but a one-legged crucifixion dangling precariously above the altar. Occasionally Christ fell and Theofilus had to nail him back up. The strange thing was that it had been built to be a church. It wasn't converted from something else, which would have given it some excuse. A piece of plastic covering a broken window flapped now and then in the feeble breeze.

Mavala didn't play the organ. She only sang a little. Then she left early. Stood up, crossed herself, and walked out. She had to go to the dining hall to cook for the few boys who remained.

Pohamba and I made some spaghetti and sauce. Pohamba talked into the night about Christmas in Otavi, with his enormous family. He said there was sometimes so much family they had to rent a hall. Cold spaghetti is Christmas? How is it possible? I wondered why he hadn't gone this year. The house up the road empty of the principal. I could feel my not going to her in my stomach, and his not wanting to be alone, practically demanding it, talking on about Christmas in Otavi, how this could not be Christmas. Music, dancing, roasted pigs, and beer.

"And liver, we always have liver on Christmas in Otavi."

"Liver?"

"Why don't you go to her?"

"It's fine."

"She's alone on Christmas."

"No, she's got Tomo. It's fine."

Us by the fire late, until the heat gave out and the chill woke us up.

Part Three

AN
ORDINARY
DROUGHT

102

GRAVES

I'm a diversion," I said.
    "Did I say that?"

"A weigh station."

"No."

"A break in your action."

"I said no."

"An oasis."

"Fine — you're an oasis."

"A pillow to lay your weary head."

"Yes."

"No, I'm a grave."

"Grieta's?"

"Yes, Grieta's."

"What did she die of?"

"Living here."

"Yes!"

"And she starved."

"Whites don't starve."

"That's bullshit."

"Name a white that's starved."

"The Irish. Jews. Russians. Poles when they weren't killing Jews. Some Mormons. I am pretty sure some Mormons starved."

"A round for Kaplansk! Whites suffer too! What else did she die of?"

"Spinsterhood."

"She died of not having a man? That's stupid."

"There's been documented cases. Look at your sister."

225

"*Having* a man is her problem."

"Right, that's true. But all he does is sweat over you."

"What man doesn't sweat over me?"

"Vilho."

"Vilho doesn't count."

"Festus."

"You think Festus would refuse me?"

"You'd sleep with Festus?"

"For ten thousand rand."

"For ten thousand rand, I'd sleep with both of them."

"Both who?"

"Dikeledi and Festus."

"That's because all you want is Dikeledi. To get her, you'd take Festus."

"Festus would take up the whole bed. Anyway, forget Dikeledi. There's only you. You."

"Only me."

103

WALLS

Morning meeting slowly rising, and Pohamba pounds.

"I remembered something in my sleep," he says.

"Can't you tell it tomorrow?"

I listen to him turn over. I can see him cupping his head in his hands, talking to the ceiling, happily wrecking other people's sleep.

"You asked me to tell you about independence. I was at the Dolphin the day of the election. The radio was on. You know the matron? Tangeni's wife?"

"The drunk one?"

"Yes, except it was strange. That day she wasn't drunk. It was noisy outside in the street, everybody was already celebrating, but in the bar it was quiet, only myself and the matron. A report came on and gave the lead to DTA. It was only in the south, because the polls closed down earlier there. Fewer people, fewer votes to count. But the only thing anybody heard was DTA wins, SWAPO loses. *DTA wins, SWAPO loses.* And do you know what happened? I saw it all from my stool in the Dolphin. People didn't shout or curse. Not a word. They sat down in the road. Taxis stopped, and the men who were driving them and the women who were passengers got out and did the same thing. They all sat down in the road. And Tangeni's wife laughed so hard at them she gagged. I can still hear her."

Of course, it all turned out to be wrong. The hundreds of thousands of votes in the north got counted. SWAPO won in a landslide. And since it was wrong, and since it ended up not meaning anything, Pohamba wants to know, demands to know, through the wall at five in the morning, "Why am I seeing those people in the road right now? In my pig bed at pig Goas? Tell me —"

I don't answer.

From his silent room, Vilho doesn't either.

104

DROUGHT STORIES

he Namibian had already been at it for months, quoting experts, statistics. The isohyets for mean annual rainfall have been falling dangerously . . . atmospheric and ocean circulation patterns consistent with . . . climatic change and variability remain constant . . . water surface catchment areas are shrinking throughout the central . . .

But drought being a negation, an unhappening, it doesn't make for interesting copy.

We skipped those articles. It came every year. It was only a question of which region would get it worse. No drought was news. Extreme drought was news. Anything else was page 6, after sports. What emergency on earth is duller?

105

CLASSROOM

I, the great general of the German troops, send this letter to the
Herero people. The Herero are no longer German subjects. They
have murdered and stolen; they have cut off the noses, ears, and
other bodily parts of wounded soldiers. And now, because of
cowardice, they will fight no more . . . All Herero must leave the
land. If people do not do this, I will force them to do it with the
great guns. Any Herero found within German borders, with or
without a gun, with or without cattle, will be shot. I shall no
longer receive any women or children, I will drive them back to
their people or I will shoot them. This is my decision for the
Herero people.

THE GREAT GENERAL OF THE MIGHTY EMPEROR,
LOTHAR VON TROTHA, 1904

I await the arrival of the new history text from the Ministry of
Education. There's been a delay. The word is, they're still re-
writing.

Among other things I have taught my learners, out of the old
text, is that the Roman Empire brought civilized society to the coun-
tries of western Europe — to Britain, Holland, Germany, and so on.
So, when the fathers of South Africa settled at the Cape, they
brought all these beautiful elements of civilization with them.

Even the feeblest teacher has to draw a line in the sand with his
toe. Despite my general ineptitude, I somehow hit upon what I now
know to be a time-honored way of killing an hour in the classroom.

Strategic use of a guest lecturer. I bring in the big gun to teach Waterberg.

"Scholars, I introduce you to a man who needs no introduction. This man doesn't teach history, he endures it. When history has a question, it comes to this man to find out what happened, who massacred whom, who cheated whom out of what . . . Boys, I give you your former Standard Three master, Head Teacher Obadiah Horaseb." Cheers for Obadiah, who struts in a pith helmet.

"Please, I'm only a man, corrupt blood in my veins. Sit. Sit. Now, boys, I understand you are to learn about Waterberg. Let me first say that prior to colonialism this was not a land of angels. This was as brutal a place as any other. And yet when the white devils came — pardon, Teacher Kaplansk — things did become, in a number of ways, worse. This is especially true, given that these adventurers, merchants, missionaries, claimed to come to us in the name of God. Now, skipping ahead to today's lesson, if I may. May I?"

"Yes, Head Teacher."

"It's 1901, and the Herero people — how many Hereros here today? — seven, no eight, good. Yes, the Herero people, after decades of brutality, slavery, impoverishment, one day rose up to challenge the greatest military force known to man. The German army. What made them do it that day? This is a question not answerable by a man with such poor faculties as myself. It is a questions for scholars. Suffice it to say that there always comes a day when a flogged man accepts the last lash. And when, after fighting bravely for years, the Hereros found themselves trapped atop Waterberg Mountain — not only soldiers, but thousands of women and children and cattle as well — surrounded on all sides but one, what did they do? I ask you, sons of the sons of the sons of those valiants, what did they do?"

A hand slowly rises. It's Magnus Axahoes.

"Child, you aren't a Herero, are you?"

"No, Teacher."

"A Damara?"

"Yes, Teacher."

"A Damara knows the answer! No tribalism here at Goas. Prime Minister Geingob would be proud. We know each other's histories on this farm. What's the answer, child?"

"They went to the desert, Teacher."

And Obadiah goes to Magnus and kneels and whispers something no one can hear.

Then he stands before the boys, lanky in his tweed coat. His arms at his sides, his hands limp. Obadiah once told me he did not believe in the power of hands to convey meaning. If your voice can't do it, don't think you can overcome its defects with your sorry hands.

"Yes, they went to the desert. The sea does not part for the Hereros. There is no sea. Only Kalahari sand. Welcome to the Twentieth Century of Apocalypse. And the people die, by the thousands, by the tens of thousands, the people die. But understand, my futures, my hopes, understand that they knew it. The moment the Hereros began to head for the desert, they knew the only answer was death. And so might we consider their choice a heroic one?"

106

GRAVES

She's bored, and she's got one of those little school scissors, the kind with the rubber handles. She thinks it's absurd they make them for lefties.

"Why wouldn't they?"

She looks at me the way she does. Mavala's eyebrows. Even when her face does nothing to make them, they have a way of seeming arched. Then she points the little scissors at my head. "Talk."

"About what?"

"Anything. Speak."

"I have nothing, zero."

"What sort of name is Larry?"

"French, I think."

"You're French?"

"No."

"Say something else."

"School?"

"Even that."

"Obadiah came to my fifth hour and taught about Waterberg."

"What did the guru say?"

"That it was heroic."

"What was?"

"For the Hereros to go to the desert rather than get shot by Germans."

"Heroic?"

"Yes. Biblically heroic."

"What would you do?"

"I don't know."

"You'd walk."

"To not get shot by Germans? Yeah, I'd probably walk."

"Is that heroic?"

"Slightly."

"You see, he's always making things into a poem. Seventy years later, the Boers took a kid and shoved his mouth into the exhaust pipe of a helicopter. What happened?"

"What?"

"It blew him apart. They found pieces of him ten K's away. Was the boy a hero?"

"Is this an argument?"

"Was the boy a hero or not?"

"That wasn't a choice. There's a difference, that's all I'm saying."

"And I'm saying it's a part of a continuum. Which will keep on happening as long as old stupid men tell stories of how heroic it is to be murdered."

She stands up, brushes herself off like she's leaving early. She never leaves early. Neither of us ever leaves early.

"You're leaving?"

"Is having your mouth shoved into an exhaust pipe biblically heroic or not?"

"Are you asking me if there are any helicopters in the Bible?"

"There are chariots."

"So how would you tell Waterberg?"

"I would say it was a military strategy. That the Hereros meant to live to fight another day."

"With no ammunition and no water? With women and children? Isn't that as much of a fantasy as that they were heroes?"

"Yes — but at least then the guru can't cry for them. The way I see it, they still had it in their minds to murder back the Germans."

"Will you guest-lecture?"

"No."

"Will you come here?"

"No."

107

GRAVES

I see them now. I get it."

She's picking at the skin between her toes. She won't look at me. "Feeling sorry isn't seeing them," she says.

"Not feeling sorry. I'm only saying there's something to be said for letting the land kill you rather than the Germans."

"Listen. The myth is a lie. As soon as you tell it, you can't see it anymore. For it to be — I don't say *mean,* I say *be* — you don't talk it, you just see it. Try, try and imagine it."

"I'm trying."

"See them?" Mavala whispers. "They're so delirious they can no longer remember where the secret boreholes are, and the ones that are known to the Germans are patrolled by soldiers with orders to kill. So they start to dig — anywhere. No divining rod, no intuition. They aren't even thirsty anymore. There's only something in their throats that feels like a scream. And so they dig, the people dig. And what happens?"

I sit up and grab her arm, pull her hand away from her feet.

"They dug their own graves. I get it."

"No. You're going too fast. When they started to claw that ground, they were looking for the water that might be down there. I'm talking about the moment they understood what they'd built — not when they got down into it. I'm talking about when they looked down into the hole. What did they see?"

108

ABRAM

He lived for a few months up near Auntie and her whelps. His toes poked out of his shoes. One side of his face was caved in. It could have been from a rifle butt or a bullet, but he made no claims to either. He arrived like other castaways before him. He said he was a farmhand, that he'd lived all his life on a farm near Khorixas. After the elections, his baas sold out and left him with nothing and nowhere to live. It was another familiar story. He'd trekked south to Goas. The priest gave him a job helping Theofilus with the goats.

Nobody believed him. His command of languages made us suspicious. There wasn't a language in the country he couldn't speak. He could talk to every boy at Goas in his mother tongue, and for this he was soon famous. Some days he'd lead the goats to the courtyard, careful to keep them off Ireland, and stand and talk, ringed by a group of boys begging him to speak to them personally.

He also spoke Portuguese.

What choice did we have but to gossip? A farmhand as far south as Khorixas speaking Portuguese? It was all anybody needed. It put him on the border during the war. And if he was on the border during the struggle — and he didn't want to boast about it — there was only one answer to the question of what he'd been doing up there. He'd been a stooge.

At first, nobody made anything of it. The war was still too close. He wasn't the only one at Goas hiding something. And the man seemed to know his place now. He was doing his penance, like any honest traitor would. To the Church, to God, to whomever. His toes poked out of his shoes. Someone had caved his face in. Now he watched goats look for something to swallow during a drought. How much lower can a man descend?

The principal didn't see it this way. But whether Abram had sold out freedom fighters during the struggle didn't matter to him. What bothered the principal was the possibility that the new shepherd might be smarter than he was. He couldn't have some farmhand wearing his head so high. Obadiah could very well be brilliant — if that's what being brilliant is like — so long as he remained a foolish drunk. This new Abram only drank cooldrink. The problem, though, was that as an employee of the Church, Abram wasn't his to banish.

"Teacher Festus?"

"Yes, Master Sir?"

"Would you step into my office a moment?"

"With pleasure."

It didn't take our lovable henchman long. We were drinking by the fire. It was a Saturday night. After a few lagers, Festus said, "Abram?"

"Teacher?"

"I have a curiosity."

"Yes?"

"We live in a new nation, am I correct?"

"Yes, Teacher."

"One in which it is possible for a man to rise?"

"I suppose so, Teacher."

"Then I must ask you this: Why do you remain a slave? You don't want to do more than tend goats? Comrade Nujoma says we must all do our share. Brother, why are you still asleep?"

Someone stoked the fire by nudging it with a shoe. Abram didn't make a sound with his mouth. He seemed to be laughing from somewhere deep down in his stomach. It was unsettling. We hadn't heard him laugh before. He took a long gulp of his Pepsi. Then he laughed with his mouth. He wasn't a big man, but his laugh in the dark made him seem like one. We took a step back from the fire. Finally, I thought, someone's going to murder Festus.

"It's interesting to be asked such a question by a black man such as you seem to be, Teacher," Abram said.

Someone murmured, *Amen*.

Then Abram tossed his Pepsi on the fire (half full, it sizzled) and stepped away into the night. We listened to his slow steps across the rocks. When he was out of earshot, Festus was bold again.

"See the way he threatens? Isn't it obvious?" Festus paused and sucked his teeth. "The man's an assassin."

"Who's he here to kill?"

"I place my vote for Master Sir."

"No, better the priest. Better to keep the devil we know —"

"No, let them live. Auntie."

"Yes, Auntie!"

"All in favor say aye?" Pohamba said.

Chorus of ayes, with one mouth silent.

"Vilho?"

"All right. Auntie," Vilho said. "In certain circumstances, even the Lord would condone —"

Obadiah squeezed my elbow. "Who wasted an honest beer?"

"It's Pepsi. Abram's."

"Ai, die Pepsi."

Even so. *Assassin?* Doesn't the word itself carry its own hiss of truth? And don't rumors have a way of overcoming the artlessness of their spreader? So it was born. Abram, the new farmhand, had been in the pay of the Boers, a member of a hit squad during the war. Ferreting out traitors never gets dull. And didn't they train him well? Who better than a champion linguist? What part of the country couldn't the man infiltrate? And why else would someone have caved his face in like that? There he is in the courtyard. The murderer. Look at the man now. Goats, he tends goats. Safe in the doorways of our classrooms, the boys are silently laughing, their mouths opening and closing like mocking fish.

I wonder now if fear would have been easier for him to take. That man standing there in those raggy shoes, bewildered. He seemed to like Pohamba and me. He used to come by the quarters with some of his home brew and share it with us. But in the end we weren't any more helpful to him than Festus.

Even Mavala said it was probably true about Abram, and if not that, something else. She was writing a lesson plan, a notepad propped on her knees. Sometimes she was practical with our time. I groped her. She fended me off.

"What do you mean?"

"Oh, anything. Maybe he hit his wife. Maybe he kicked a dog."

"So he pays for it this way?"

She didn't look up from her writing.

"There's been worse injustice, no?"

Thursday, and the skeletal goats wander into the grassless courtyard alone. The last we hear of Abram, he's working day labor at the gravel pit near Pawkwas.

109

GRAVES

Antoinette would say that we'd been cavorting in the stench of sin. She wouldn't be surprised, or blame us. She expected it. She expected it of everybody. What else do people do but ultimately degrade themselves? She'd say we have as much control over our sinning as we do against the wind, because we are born to it — unless every day, every hour, every minute, we are vigilant. She made no claims to being any better. She was only a humble servant of the Lord and of boys. Because defeating the devil is merely work. And since we were lazy, since we wanted only to enjoy, it was only a matter of time before we would cave in to his desires. Afternoons of shut-up rooms and Mavala and me out there. You couldn't call it an escape, because we didn't go far and we didn't go long and we didn't close our eyes and we didn't care about our knees in the sand or the rocks in our backs, or even the sun-dried goat shit, nothing.

"Like a couple of baboons in the veld."

"As if this farm didn't have any beds!"

"The girl who fought in the struggle, the one with the baby and —"

"Yesssss! I remember. And the volunteer. From where was that volunteer?"

Us becoming a story, then, if not much of one — we were only an hour a day on weekdays, an hour and fifteen minutes if we were bold. Still, something people might tell years from now just because it was something to tell. It made us feel slightly famous.

What did the kid see when he saw us fucked-out, sweat-glazed, the sun lashing us and we're too tired to move? The last thing I remember before we slept was that Mavala splayed her toes and grasped some sand and threw it with her foot at Grieta — and then we both were out. We had it down. Eight minutes of sleep before Tomo air-raided us. And then the footfall, and I wake up and see the kid running backward, the face of my Standard Six Magnus Axahoes — disgusted? sad? — and then him whirling around, his untucked shirt flapping like a cape.

"It doesn't matter," she says.

"No. Why would it matter?"

110

POHAMBA

Dead center of a Sunday, Pohamba singing in the shower, door-less shower, trickly spigot. Hot water rare. It spouts forth now only in the middle of the day, when it's the last thing you want, but since it's so rare, you've got to love it. The rapture of wasting water in a drought. Pohamba slathered up and screeching *Please, please, please, please.*

On a rock near the spigot, a Standard Four waits, a bored valet. Over his arm, a towel; in his hand, a cup of cold tea.

111

GRAVES

Lonely hot afternoon and our shoes, all four of them, in a line on the grave. Us shoulder to shoulder on the tablecloth.

She tries to scratch her back.

"Will you?"

I shift around and scratch her.

"Harder," she says.

"You go," I say.

"What?"

"Tell something. Anything. What about your mother?"

"I haven't seen her in five years."

"Tell me —"

"She loves handbags. Or at least she used to."

"Handbags."

"Yes, my mother always said a lady should never be seen in public without a handbag. Even at the market at Ondangwa, where there weren't any of the ladies she was talking about. What ladies was she talking about? My sister and I walked around like queens because my father was an assistant headman, because he worked in an office. A sell-out, my father. But I *loved* the market. Bream fish, barbell fish, sour milk. Dry beans, cassava, cabbage. The fat koeks in the bubbling oil. All I wanted on earth was a fat koek in greasy paper. That first bite was like eating a peach, only better. And one was never enough. Sometimes Tuyeni gave me half of hers."

"Tell me more."

"Don't stop. Keep scratching."

"Go on."

"She never let go of our wrists. Always so many men around. And

243

they letched the assistant headman's daughters. Men. There are always, everywhere, so many men. Have you noticed?"

"I notice here."

"And there was a war, and still my mother walked around as if she never heard of it. Four years later I was gone. Tuyeni says after I left, my mother wouldn't be seen in the market. *Went off where? To fight for whom? An assistant headman's daughter?*"

"And Tuyeni?"

"What about her?"

"Your sister."

"Wife now, not sister."

112

GRAVES

Sharing a bag of crisps. I'm trying to share. Mavala's munching most of them, in between repainting her toenails. I'm loving the smell of the polish.

"Nothing else?" she says. "Your entire life?"

"All right. I remember running through an airport once. I was about to miss a plane. There was a woman in front of me, young, she had a kid with her. Maybe he was five. She was late for the same plane and was trying to run with the kid, but it wasn't working. I came up behind them and took the kid's other hand, and we held him up in the air as we ran. The kid was loving it, him flying and he hasn't even gotten on the plane yet. The whole time we didn't say a word."

"This is what you remember of your life?"

"Basically."

"Did you make it to the plane?"

"Yes."

"Then what happened?"

"That was it. She thanked me. I think I bowed. I never saw her again."

"You bowed?"

"Why not? Why not bow?"

"Daddy, husband, alone — how long did that take?"

"About four minutes. Come back with me."

"Where?"

"I'll get a job, go to graduate school. I've got to do something."

"Me? What will I do?"

"You could go to school. You said you wanted to go back to school. You could study accounting again."

"Tomo?"

"Of course."

"Our volunteer has gone amuck."

"Why?"

"Start with the visa problem. The other thing is, well, the kid does hate you."

"I knew it. The whole time —"

"A joke, Davey! He bites what he loves."

"So we get married. Goas could use a wedding."

She nearly hyperventilates, gulps air and holds her stomach, writhes around in the sand. And Tomo — as if he hasn't been asleep, as if he's heard every word — starts right then to rev up the siren on the other side of the tombs.

"Hand me the polish."

"Why?" she says.

"I want to smell it harder."

"Don't be jealous."

"Of who?"

She looks away. Then, with her eyes half-closed, kisses me.

"Tell me."

"Isn't it time?"

113

GRAVES

The dry yellow veld is moving. It takes a long stare to see that it's a herd of springbok leaping, as one. No one can take this away from me. Because it's real. It's grace. The Green Hills of Africa. There isn't a green hill in this entire country. Who needs green anything? The springbok are leaping toward the long shadows of the Erongos.

"Look," I say.

She watches for a while. We're out of the dagga I stole from Pohamba's new stash. We're sharing her last van Ryn. Her knees under the tablecloth are like small bumps. Tomo's on the edge of awake. I can hear him, his pre-wake snorfle. He's onto us now. Mavala's bribes have become less effective. Yesterday, after she topped his pap with cinnamon and brown sugar, he knocked it over.

She hands me the last nub of cigarette.

"What? You want to go on safari? They have these tours out of Windhoek, why don't you —"

"Fuck off."

She lifts her neck a little and holds it toward the sun with her eyes closed.

"Three yet?"

She doesn't answer.

The sun belligerent, slackless. She rolls over on her back and talks. "Up at the camp we used to hunt springbok in the jeep, drunk off peach schnapps. We wouldn't shoot. It was part of the game not to shoot. You had to separate one from the herd and ram it down. Someone in the unit learned it from a Boer farmer. A good thing about the Boers. You can always blame your sins on them. Springbok have the tenderest meat. They say it tastes better when it's bloody, but that's a lie."

"Did you get this from Pohamba?"

I watch her. She digs the nail of her thumb into her cheek.

"It wasn't easy. You know, buck zigzag. You had to be careful not to hit trees. Harder because we did it at night, without lights, because the planes patrolled —"

"You did it at night?"

"Yes."

"A few things I'd like to do at night."

She holds her hand over her mouth. Maybe she winces, it's hard to tell in the glare.

"You think I'm on vacation?"

She doesn't raise her head.

"You think I don't know I'm on vacation?"

She doesn't answer. She looks back at the place where the buck had been leaping.

"Once, I drove. When I hit her, I didn't hit her hard enough, only wounded her. She staggered away. I chased her again, rammed her down again. She was so quiet. I remember wanting her to scream, whimper, something, anything, but she didn't. Like this was natural — as if all her life she expected to be crushed to death by a jeep full of Marxists drunk off peach schnapps."

She holds her face to the sun again, holds it there for a while. I'm drowsy. I reach for her. She winces.

OBADIAH (3 A.M.)

Words in a small moon of light. History, at night, by torch, is the guiltiest of pleasures. Turn the page and there's always more mayhem. In 1827, at Moordkoopie, south of Okahandja, an Orlam chief ordered the hands and feet of two hundred women captives lopped off so he could have their silver bangles. They were the wives, daughters, and concubines of his enemy. Couldn't he have simply shouted: All right, ladies, take off those beautiful bangles or I'll kill you? Do I repeat myself? How much is too much when there's always another page? Why is the only rule that innocents pay?

Theophrastus said throwing a stone is less fatiguing than throwing emptiness. Don't I know it. I talk in my head, and even I don't listen. And my wife? While I mutter she sleeps, and even then she grasps the blankets as if they contain work she could get done in a dead hour. How do you say that even when she's asleep your wife's hands crave creation?

Speak to me, won't you speak to me? I want to know of the pain in your hands. You carry a potato in your pocket. You think I haven't seen you rub it? Is being born alone our transgression? My wife has hands and feet. She wears a thin gown that hangs loosely off her thinning body. Talk to me. Tell me about the pain in your hands.

115

ANTOINETTE

You want it in words, everything in words. All right, then, here are words:

My hands are His hands, and I don't call it pain. Now come to bed.

DROUGHT STORIES

MAGISTRATE McHUGH: I have come to see how you people live. I have heard you have had a very hard time during the latest drought, but hope you will soon recover.

FREDERICH MUKAUAMBI: We greet the magistrate. We are glad to see the magistrate here today. We have no rain and there is nothing left for the stock to eat. The people are shouting for water. The dams are dry. May we not trek to the east?

MAGISTRATE McHUGH: No. All the ground you are thinking about has now been occupied and there is no further land available. Both the Europeans and the natives are in the same position and must depend on Providence — it is all we can do.

LOT OPPOSEMAB: We have nothing more to say.

At this stage permission was given to smoke.

— From the minutes of the quarterly meeting at the Otjimb-ingwe Native Reserve, presided by Magistrate M. J. McHugh, Esq., 16 February 1949.

117

GRAVES

Line going around Goas: How do you know Mavala Shikongo's war stories are true?

Because she never tells any.

"War," I say. "Now."

"All right." She pauses. She runs her tongue around her lips twice. "War. Yes. I remember. You are woman, they said. Woman! The men gave many speeches saying we were the soul and the strength of the movement. A commander would say, 'Ladies, your Kalashnikov is an extension of your arm. Now, go do the wash. Go teach the little ones school. Wait, before you go, my darling, bring me a tea. Three sugars!'"

"That's not a war story."

"Isn't it? What about this? I'd been sent to scout the food lorry. A good job for a woman. It was days late. We were living off refried pap and chocolate bars. Sometimes UNITA ambushed the lorries, so we never knew when, or if, the food would come. I walked about three kilometers from camp to wait. I was leaning against a tree when a man, one of ours, came out of the bush. He wasn't a commander. He was only a new recruit. He'd just come up from the Kavango. I outranked him three levels. He raised a pistol at me and told me to drop my Kalashnikov. I told him he didn't need a gun. Comrade, I said, we're all here together. Long camp days, long camp nights. I think I insulted him by the suggestion. He wanted it by force or not at all. So he went away."

"He did?"

"Yes."

"Were you serious?"

"About what?"

"You know, giving yourself."

"I don't know."

"You believed in it? That you were all comrades?"

"Listen, I'm tired."

"Of what?"

"Of talk."

"I'm only asking."

"All right, I shot him. When he was turned away, I picked up my gun and shot him. Do you like that story better? Or should I try another? I have other versions."

She rolls away from me. I watch the drought for a while. I look at the trails the cows have made across the veld, the way they loop and crisscross and join and separate again. I shake her.

"Was that guy Tomo's father?"

Only her face turns back toward me. "Where did you — no — God, no." And out of nowhere she smiles in a way I hadn't seen. The way people do. When they're remembering a face, another face?

"Why don't you tell me anything?"

"I just did."

"Tell me more."

"No."

DROUGHT STORIES

Morning, cusp of the first ring of the triangle. I groggle over to the tap and nothing happens. I knock on Pohamba's wall. "There's no water."

"None?"

"Check your tap."

He checks his tap. "There's no water."

Through the wall, Vilho calls, "There's no water."

"We're a chorus," Pohamba says. "Let's all sing. *There's no* —"

"It's the drought," Vilho says. "The water levels in the dams —"

Pohamba groans. "How are we going to have coffee?"

"I'll eat it dry out of the can," I say.

"Theofilus!" Pohamba shouts. "Theofilus!"

It came out later in the day that Theofilus had diverted our drinking water to try to save the cows. It was such a brazen act of love, he wasn't even called to task for it by either the principal or the priest (who was gone to Swakop during the crisis). The principal finally had to call the municipality in Karibib, and the town council arranged for a water truck to come out to the farm. We had a holiday drinking water and spraying each other with the hose attached to the truck. For a week, nobody bathed. The classrooms got a little rank, but it was all right. You got to know other people better. You got to know yourself better. Being from Ohio, I have always thought of death as something cold. The bones of my grandfather in the cemetery in Walnut Hills in February, the snow falling lightly on his chiseled name. No longer.

*   *   *

It made for days of stink by the graves. Together we were festering. Not only the sand and pebbles that clung to us, but everything. Naked, we wore loose change, buttons, peanut shells, toenail clippings.

"Teacher, you smell malodorous."

"I smell malodorous?"

WHELPS

There was cause for minor celebration. Auntie collapsed in the heat while trying to pry a hubcap off the principal's car. It was three in the afternoon. Festus saw her flop over face-first in the sand. He waited for her to twitch. When she didn't, he ran around the farm telling everybody she was dead. She wasn't. Theofilus drove her to the clinic at Usakos to be examined. Why hadn't she thought of this before? Clean sheets and pills and male orderlies? Why live anywhere else?

Her whelps suffered for it. They started roaming like the pack of wolves they almost were, living off our garbage — emptied pilchard cans, the last bit of dust at the bottom of a box of dried milk. Antoinette began leaving them scraps at the back of the hostel dining hall. They had mottled, thorn-bitten fur and sorrowful eyes. They no longer came close enough to allow us to pet them, as if the absence of Auntie had ended their official association with human hands. At night they'd yowl for their lost mother, who'd stolen them and pampered them, who'd shampooed them and fed them rotten hamburger. The whelps looked so much alike, they were always nameless to us — Antoinette called them her starvelings — but somebody remembered they did have names, names like Shaka and Beethoven and Rasputin. The too-well-endowed one with his eye gouged out she called Houdini. They didn't live up to their names. They weren't nearly so bold as their benefactor, and they didn't steal, which surprised us. They'd only creep slowly, reticently, as if they didn't want to bother anybody with their hunger.

"If that woman doesn't come back," Antoinette said, "we'll have to drown them."

"In what water?" Obadiah said.

120

GRAVES

She unbuttons and rebuttons her shirt as she talks. She's been talking since the beginning of our hour.

"I wasn't the only young mother in the camp. There were others. I remember thinking how calm they seemed. Nursing and cooing. I never gained it. I could teach myself so many other things. But that beautiful mothering. So I told myself they were cows."

"Cows," I repeat.

She sits up and looks at me. What was I doing in the sand with her? Goas is still asleep, but it's that time when you can feel the silence about to be trampled.

"Are you calm now?"

"No," she says.

I listen to her breathing, to her hand piling and smoothing the gravel. Leaning against Grieta's grave, we don't face the mountains, only the scorched plain, the rocks, the dry tufts bent to the wind. I reach for her. She uncoils slowly toward me.

POHAMBA

He leans against the wall outside his room. He's marking homework assignments. Long division. His red pen flinging. He had little tolerance for messy papers and would sometimes mark off for it even if they got the answer right. His shadow plump and flattened next to him, squashed by the angle of the early-afternoon sun. His door is held open by a brick, but in this glare you can see nothing of his room but a hole in the dark. He stops his pen for a moment and stares out at the veld. As if it isn't distance but time he's looking at. His shoulder blades tense. Not his, this parch. His place is Otavi, where it always rains at least twice after the fifteenth of February. He takes up the pen again and continues to slash.

122

COMRADE YANAYEV

And still nothing happens here. We walk the veld and the dry puckerthorns explode beneath our feet. Where the dead grass has gusted away, there are deep fissures in the dirt. The sun squashes and the weeks pass flat. And then an occurrence: Obadiah loses his TransNamib hat. A farmwide search has yielded no suspects. Standard Sevens, under heavy questioning, deny any involvement. Then, off the radio, still more news. Gorbachev's been murdered. An hour later he's resurrected, but now imprisoned on treason charges, in his dacha, in the Crimea. The BBC intones: *All seven phone lines leading into the vacation house are reported to have been cut.*

And somebody named Gennady Yanayev declares a renewal of Soviet proletarian fortunes.

"Sounds like a putsch."

"Tasty putsch?" Pohamba says.

"Yanayev? Who the hell's Yanayev?"

And Obadiah sermonizes, hatless, during mid-morning break: "Wherefore I ask: Who will deliver our Daniel from the ferocity of the lions?"

Empires keel. And still the goats come in from the veld on wobbly legs, and still they don't know they're starving.

123

DROUGHT STORIES

It is said that goats eventually go mad. When this happens, they refuse to obey their shepherd and flee to the open desert, where they roam like the great wild horses of the Namib until they die alone, proud, and free of the shackles of bondage and unforgiving husbandry . . .

Our goats never got the chance. When they stopped recognizing Theofilus, he loaded them on the lorry and trucked them north to a farm near Tsumeb. But Father refused to send the cows. He told Theofilus the grazing fee per head for cattle was more than our poor church could afford.

So the cows go it on their own now. They starve more gently. Poor fat-witted things. They do not go mad. They do not roam. They simply graze where there's nothing to graze. When they're thirsty, they simply plunk their noses in the empty dams and huff around.

GRAVES

There are afternoons now when to so much as touch is the last thing either of us wants. An hour we stay apart. Her up on the grave, me down on the tablecloth. What little grass is left is so dry it pokes through the tablecloth like freshly sharpened pencils. I'm spraying a beetle with Doom to see how much it can take before it dies.

"I don't know why," she says.

"Why what?"

"Sometimes in the morning I'm lying in bed and all I want to do is lie in bed. How can you want something you're already doing?"

"My grandfather used to say when you're dead you spend your time wishing you could pay taxes."

The beetle's not dead yet. "It isn't the work. That beyond this bed there's work I have to do. All those little boys. Tomo. Soon he'll be awake and pulling on the edge of my sheets. He might be already awake and doing that. Because times like this I only know what I'm thinking, not what's happening."

"I understand. Tomo. It's difficult."

"I said, it isn't Tomo. It's the wanting —"

"But wanting what?"

"Didn't I just explain it to you?"

THE PHARAOH'S DREAM

To give them hope, Antoinette read Genesis to the cows. She brought her Bible out to the veld and read to them.

"And Pharaoh said unto Joseph, In my dream, behold, I stood upon the bank of a river:

"And, behold, there came up out of the river seven kine, fat fleshed and well favored; and they fed in a meadow."

(Kine, Antoinette explained to them, means you.)

"And, behold, seven other kine came up after them, poor and very ill favored, such as I never saw in all the land of Egypt for sadness:

"And the lean and ill favored kine did eat up the first seven fat kine."

The cows stood there and listened to her. Their eyes were hardly visible through the dust that coated them. They had dug their faces into the earth till the earth blinded them.

What she left out, she told me later as she fiddled with the nozzle of the paraffin can in order to stoke the Primus — the swoop of the paraffin catching, its muted steady roar — was what happened after the ill favored kine ate the fat ones. Her Bible on the counter, a pen holding the spot, her hand reaching for it.

She reads, "And when they had eaten them up, it could not be known that they had eaten them; but they were still ill favored, as at the beginning. So I awoke."

The stove, a perfect circle of blue flame. The tiny black flecks in the flame. Antoinette closes the book.

That night we listened to their raspy lows from our beds. Night being the only time they expressed their displeasure toward God at being ill favored.

126

GOAS THEATER

A new Goas tradition. In honor of independence, Obadiah would write a play for Cassinga Day, May 4. And so weekends he sequestered himself in the mimeograph shack with the big crank machine, the chemicals, and the spiders. He had some boys carry over his personal library. He'd refuse to eat anything other than rusks and cold tea. Through the grimy window we watched him, surrounded by all those tented books. Occasionally he'd emerge lost in thought. We knew this because if you happened to be passing by when he was standing outside the door, he'd say, "Yes, well, I'm lost in thought." Then, if you laughed he stared at you, not at your face, at your heart, as if something was missing there. We did not understand the tribulations.

A knock on the door. "Head Teacher?"

"Come in."

A boy, a Standard Two named Tonderai, famous around Goas as the one who loves to run messages back and forth for teachers, enters the writer's chamber shyly.

"Ah, Muse, I thought you'd forsaken me. I must say I was expecting someone taller."

"Auntie will be back to tomorrow, Teacher. Sister Ursula phoned."

Obadiah uncaps a pen and hands it to the boy.

"Slay me."

"Excuse, Teacher?"

"With this lance — do it."

UP ON THE HILL BY THE CROSS

I climb up the hill to the cross and find Vilho up there by himself. He's reading and doesn't say anything to me, and I don't say anything to him.

When Vilho read, he had a strange way of squinching his eyes. It occurs to me now that this might have been because he was rereading sentences. He would hold the book close to his face and remain on the same page for a long time. On a farm full of readers, he might have been the only one who read with pure delight.

I sit bookless and read the names of boys left on the rocks near the base of the cross: Absalom Shipanga '81, Phillemon Silvanus '77, Nestor Nashongo '74, Titus Mueshihua '86, Matundu Kapute '77, Erwin Mbando '70, Rodney Goaseb '87, Adonis Gowab '84, Abraham Haifiku '73, Petrus Van Weyk '73, Johannes Isack '77, Rueben Holongo '79, Ihepa Enkono '82, Stephanus Nami '81, Andreas Kati '75, Joseph Manasse '77, David Visser '74, Phineas Shivute '82.

After a while, Vilho peers over the rim of his book. "Do you know what today is?"

"Thursday."

"Maundy Thursday."

"What's that?"

"The day in John when the supplicants wash the feet of the poorest."

"Whose poorest?"

"How much do you have?" Vilho says.

We empty our pockets of rands, toss the money in the sand. Four rand, sixty total. The light retreats like another traitor. Neither of us washes the other's feet. We sit in the gray silence, our socks off.

Absalom Shipanga. Phillemon Silvanus. Nestor Nashongo. Titus Mueshihua. Matundu Kapute. Erwin Mbando. Rodney Goaseb. Adonis Gowab. Abraham Haifiku. Petrus Van Weyk. Johannes Isack. Rueben Holongo . . .

128

MORNING MEETING

Nothing like this has ever happened to us before. Precipitation is more common. Obadiah's place is empty at morning meeting. The principal sends a boy and the boy returns, stands, waiting to be told to speak. He's a Standard Three, one of Obadiah's, and his uniform's in good order. Gray wool shorts, clean shirt buttoned to the neck. I don't know his name. He is nervous, and his lips are trembling. He stands on one bare foot. With the other he scratches the back of his leg.

"Well?"

"Teacher says he is sick, Master Sir."

"Sick?"

"Yes."

"He's in bed?"

"No, Master Sir."

"Where is he, then?"

"On his car, Master Sir."

"The pile of sand?"

"Yes."

"Sick with what?"

"I don't know, Master Sir."

"Go find out."

And so we wait in silence, the principal clearing and reclearing his throat. It was unthinkable to pontificate in the morning without Obadiah. The principal fancied himself not only Obadiah's boss but also his rhetorical better. Every day he declared victory in this battle.

The boy comes back.

"Speak."

The boy hesitates.

"Out with it!"

"Teacher says he is sick with creation, Master Sir."

At break we went out there to check on him. Above our heads, a cloud, pallid and lazy, floated by, promising nothing. I watched it scatter and break apart above the Erongos. He was sitting at the top of the mound, on a chair he'd brought from his kitchen. Under one of the legs of the chair, as if driven through by a stake, was his play.

"How's it, Teacher?"

"Disgusting."

"So you've finished?"

He hid his face with his hands. "Finished?" he whispered. "Finished?"

"Yes, are you —"

"There is no finished. There's only surrender."

He took his hands away and gazed for a long time at each of us, but it looked, somehow, as if he were only remembering us. As if we were gone and he was lonely already.

Then he said, "They lie. It's nothing at all like giving birth. Giving death? Yes. They lived in my head and they came out in the world shriveled, blue." He thumbed himself in the chest. "I'm a murderer."

"Who'd you kill?"

"Ignatius and the others."

"*Who?*"

He shook his head. We joined him on the mound until the triangle called us back to work.

129

GOAS THEATER

The Most Excellent and Lamentable Tragedy
of Ignatius Mumbeli
or,
The Suitcase
by
Mimnermus

Ignatius Mumbeli, an unknown soldier	*Erastus Pohamba*
Kosmos Indongo, a famous elder statesman	*Obadiah Horaseb*
Izelda Indongo, Indongo's wife	*Antoinette Horaseb*
Paradise Gowab, a seamstress	*Mavala Shikongo*
Boer Policeman Number 1, bearded	*Larry Kaplansk*
Boer Policeman Number 2, beardless	*Larry Kaplansk*
Boer Policeman Number 3, bald	*Larry Kaplansk*
Auntie Wilhelmina	*Auntie Wilhelmina*
Festus Festus Galli, U.N. Secretary General	*Festus Uises*
Suitcase	*Courtesy of Mavala Shikongo*
Platoon of Blue Helmets	*Boys of Standard Seven*
Gunfire Sound Effects	*Boys of Standard Six*
Refreshment Specialist/Spiritual Advisor	*Vilho Kakuritjire*
Set Design	*Theofilus !Nowases*
Lighting	*Theofilus !Nowases*
Box Office	*Theofilus !Nowases*
Costumes	*Theofilus !Nowases*
First Grip	*Theofilus !Nowases*
Second Grip	*Theofilus !Nowases*
Dramaturge	*Theofilus !Nowases*

The Players would like to thank the following sponsors:

Desconde Motors, Schmidsdorf Meats and Poultry, and the Kingdom of Sweden

SCENE 1: *The bedsheet rises on the cramped kitchen of a typical location house in the Ovambo section of Katatura location, Windhoek. A battered kitchen table, a battered cupboard, a battered kettle on the stove. If possible, a cockroach should scramble back and forth across the table during the scene. If no cockroaches are available (when are they around when you need them?), a drawing of a cockroach in motion will suffice.* KOSMOS INDONGO *in an elegant white suit and Panama hat. His beautiful wife, in a simple frock, tends to the kettle. Throughout the scene she gazes lovingly at her husband. There is a sharp rap on the door.*

INDONGO: *Entrez.*

MUMBELI (*offstage*): Sir?

INDONGO: I said, *Entrez*. It's French for entrez. *Entrez!*

The door opens hesitantly.

MUMBELI (*dressed in the simple blue jumper of a railway worker*): Good evening, sir. (*He nods to* IZELDA, *who is gazing lovingly at her husband.*)

INDONGO (*a man of action bored by pleasantries*): So, my man, you wish to join the struggle?

MUMBELI: I do, sir.

INDONGO: Very dangerous.

MUMBELI: I accept the dangers. Every night I dream —

INDONGO (*whaps the cockroach*): In dreams begin lies, my son.

MUMBELI: Excuse?

INDONGO: I have dreamed away decades. Not the years, but the dreams that age us. It's odd. They seem so harmless in the morning. (IZELDA *gazes lovingly at her husband*.) Who are you, my son?

MUMBELI: I am Ignatius Mumbeli.

INDONGO: May your name be remembered.

MUMBELI: It is not my name that's important. It is my country.

INDONGO (*smiles*): Well spoken. I too have waited long enough. Across two world wars. Two colonial powers. Two international organizations. Countless useless toothless resolutions. The rulings of the World Court. Whose court is the World Court? Are we not part of the world? I misplaced my faith. (*He takes a gun from his pocket and sets it on the table*.) And yet you think I am in love with the gun of this, the first act?

MUMBELI (*taking up the gun*): No, sir.

INDONGO: My son, I grant you this valise of high quality. Fill it with many things, including ammunition, but most of all with courage.

MUMBELI: I thank you for this case, sir. I pledge to fill it not only with the necessary items, such as socks, undershirts, sweaters, small keepsakes, but also with —

BOER POLICEMAN NUMBER 1 (*shouting*): Ah! Is this a meeting in violation of the Non-Assembly Act, SA 771, Section 10, as applicable to the mandated territory? Am I late? Passes, var are your passes? Vostek! Bliksem! (INDONGO *and* MUMBELI *run around the table, followed by* BOER POLICEMAN NUMBER 1, *waving his sjambok. Eventually who is chasing whom becomes confused after* MUMBELI *seizes the sjambok and he and* INDONGO *chase the* POLICEMAN. IZELDA *holds the kettle, watches*.)

Bulb dims.

SCENE 2: *The living room of a typical location house in the Damara section of Katatura location. Two blue chairs.*

PARADISE (*sewing a scarf*): So you have come, my gallant, to say farewell? (*She begins to cry.*)

MUMBELI (*placing his suitcase center stage*): Don't weep, baby.

PARADISE: Would you I show more mirth than I am mistress of?

MUMBELI: Oh, in a better world than this . . .

PARADISE: Alas. (*They clasp hands.*)

MUMBELI: Alas.

PARADISE: My pride in you is a mansion bitter built. My heart, however, is torn asunder. Go, my lovely! But know this: I will wait for you. (*Pause. Quietly*) That's a very nice case.

MUMBELI: Always judge the man by the caliber of his luggage.

PARADISE (*holds up scarf*): I knit you this. Carry it well.

MUMBELI: Baby, it's beautiful. (*Pause.*) But I'm not sure I've got room.

PARADISE: Your case is full?

MUMBELI: Yes, I have filled it with the necessary items, such as under-garments and sweaters, but also with — (*The door swings open.*)

BOER POLICEMAN NUMBER 2: What here? A Damara and an Ovambo cavorting? A clear violation of the Division of Races Act, SA 193, Section 18, Clause 15 (2) (C), as such is applicable to man-dated territories. Passes! Var are your passes! Ah! Beautiful knitting! I never cease to be amazed by the craftiness of you native wenches. Such innate talent! May I? (*MUMBELI refuses and begins to chase* BOER POLICEMAN NUMBER 2, *with the scarf, as if it were a sjambok. . . .*)

Bulb dims.

SCENE 3: *On the border. A barbed-wire fence strewn across the stage. On the other side of the fence, a sign:* ANGOLA. MUMBELI *looks at Angola, then turns around slowly — a great weight on his shoul-*

ders and a gun in his hand — to look lovingly at the audience, as at a much-loved country.

MUMBELI: My story? You should like to know my story? *Now* you ask? I have none. I was killed on the border, by a fence. Once, I had one. I was called Ignatius Mumbeli. I had a mother also. You too? Funny how we all — Mine was a charwoman for a white family in the dorp. I remember waiting on the stoep while she folded sheets. Sheets were washed on Wednesdays. They were aired out all other days. She mopped the floor before dinner and after dinner. On her hands and knees, she mopped the floor. Before dinner and after dinner. She shined their shoes. She raised four of them and five of us. Once, one of them died. I remember. His name was Jan. She came home and wept over him. Now, may I ask, whose mother will weep over me? I had a girl. If I had more time, I would tell you about my beautiful. Her name was Paradise. Her parents, you see, were optimists —

AUNTIE (*having climbed in through a stage-left window*): Come to my boozalum, angel.

MUMBELI: Are you a ghost, Mother?

AUNTIE: No ghost, boy, I'm your fantasy.

OBADIAH: [Cut! Cut! Cut! Get her out of here!]

BOER POLICEMAN NUMBER 3 (*gun drawn, plastic bag wrapped tight on his head to simulate baldness*): Aha! Terrorist! Dummkopf! Var do you think you're going? Who gave you a pass to leave the mandated territory, eh? Eh? (*BOER POLICEMAN NUMBER 3 and MUM-BELI [and AUNTIE] fight. BOER POLICEMAN NUMBER 3 shoots MUMBELI. MUMBELI shoots BOER POLICEMAN NUMBER 3. MUMBELI dies. BOER POLICEMAN NUMBER 3 dies.*)

AUNTIE (*noticing the suitcase*): Hmmmm. (*Snatches it, creeps off.*)

FESTUS FESTUS GALLI (*trailed by a platoon of blue helmets, stops at the bodies*): Ah, tut tut tut. Clean this mess up, boys. Oh, this quarry cries havoc. (*Consults script.*) Or is it this havoc cries quarry?

Bulb out.

130

NOTES FROM THE LAST
AND FIRST REHEARSAL

Hostel dining hall. Night.

MAVALA: I don't mind being a seamstress, but I'm definitely too tall to play a Damara.

POHAMBA: Herr Director, do you not think there ought to be a kiss in Scene 2? When both of them say, "Alas." Right there would be an excellent moment —

KAPLANSK: Do I really have to say "native wenches"? I'll say anything in any language I don't understand, but I draw the line at saying native wenches.

POHAMBA: That doesn't mean you don't think it.

KAPLANSK: Think what? What are you insinuating?

POHAMBA: Insinuating your arse.

ANTOINETTE (*Scowls. Leaves.*)

FESTUS: Maybe that's a long speech for Mumbeli at the end?

OBADIAH (*wit's end, end of the rope, last hurrah, goodbye to all that, things don't fall apart, they implode*): Even Festus is a critic. All we ever do is make speeches. Don't you even understand that? You think anybody talks to each other? Ever? Talks to each other?

131

GRAVES

I have something to tell you."

"Is it shocking?"

"Von Swine is aware."

"Of what?"

"This."

"That's not shocking."

"Listen. Last night after rehearsal, he didn't pant, he knocked. So I was curious. He'd never knocked before. I got up and opened it. He only smiled. Then he turned around and walked away. It was the first time I ever closed the door on him."

"So the kid told. Or maybe it was Festus. Anyway, he's the last to —"

"Who told Festus?"

"Nobody. I'm just saying we're not a well-kept — do you think he'll tell the priest?"

"Why not? Father, there's fornication going on in the veld and it isn't only the goats."

"The goats are gone."

"Yes."

"He didn't say anything?"

"No, only that smile."

"Smiled like how?"

"Like he was taking joy in it."

"In what?"

"In my success. In proving, once again — so I called him back."

"What?"

"I invited him in."

"What?"

"Yes. And he comes back. He sighs, rubs his fat face. 'I couldn't sleep,' he says. 'I thought perhaps you couldn't either.' It was all very formal and dignified. Then he starts sliding off his belt. When he's down to his shorts, I start shouting for my sister. Oh, did I shout. You didn't hear me down there?"

"No."

"Tuyeni! And the man is so confused. Tomo starts bawling. And Tuyeni, heavy sleeper always, but this time she comes running."

Mavala rolls over, runs her finger from the ditch in the hinge of my arm to my wrist.

"Wait."

"There isn't much time."

"Just tell it."

"Well, she came into my room, and what do you think?"

"He's in your room, with his pants down, in the middle of the night? I think she freaked."

"No. She looked at me like she used to look at me when we were sisters. Like she loved me, but there was also nothing to be done with me. Then she took him by the hand and led him away like he was a child. It was very beautiful. And man and wife left the slut with her crying kid."

GRAVES

The light slants, the sun nonexistent behind a wall of sky. The graves rise like hulks. The wind is so constant you don't know you're hearing it until it falls. She drapes her arm across my neck.

"Hold me."

"All right."

Then: "Will you go?"

"Now? We've got twenty minutes at least. Why?"

"Don't ask. Will you? Here, take your sock."

WUNDERBUSCH

"*Myrothamnas flabellifolia:* A small, woody, aromatically fragrant shrub. It endures droughts by putting itself into a state of dormancy wherein its leaves shrivel, turn brown as the chlorophyll becomes inactive, and eventually become so dry that they can be crumpled into dust between one's fingers. At the same time, its branches bend upward into a vertically bunched position. Yet at first rain the plant suddenly becomes 'alive' once more. The branches descend into more normal positions, the leaves become soft and pliable, and the chlorophyll becomes green and active. This transformation takes only an hour at most, and can be brought about artificially by spraying the plants with water or by immersing them in a tub of water for only a few minutes. Because of this ability to return to life after apparent death, the species is called the 'resurrection plant' (in German, *Wunderbusch*). The natives use the plants for the brewing of a pleasantly scented tea, hence there is a name for the species in each of the native tongues. For instance, in Herero it is *Ongandulwaze* and in Nama it is *!godogib.*"

FARM LINE

Just after the second triangle, the farm line will ring. It will sound, as it always does, like a chain being dragged across asphalt. The principal will pick it up from his office. Miss Tuyeni will pick it up from the kitchen of their house. The priest from his office. Krieger from his house. There will be a chorus of *Hellos* and *Who is calling? Who is calling? Asking for whom? The headmaster, please. Speaking!* It will be Prinsloo, and he will tell the principal (and everyone else listening) that he saw the girl teacher, the one with the bitty skirts, walking down the C-32 at what odd in the morning. The sky still bloody. Strange for a Wednesday. Is today another one of these new holidays? I thought we just had one. A suitcase too. She didn't put her hand out, so I didn't stop. I thought you might like to know.

135

GOAS MORNING

Not yet dawn, that strange light before the light, and Antoinette's in the dining-hall kitchen slicing morning bread for the boys, thick slices of brown bread with an ungenerous slap of butter that the boys will try to make go further by spreading it around with their tongues. They eat their morning bread slowly. Mavala knocks on the glass window of the door. Antoinette looks up, not surprised, because to her there is no such thing as a surprise. She opens the door and Mavala carries Tomo inside. He's sleeping in his car seat. She sets him down in the corner of the kitchen where the gray hasn't reached. She leaves his stuffed horse, a few of his cars. A plastic bag full of clothes and diapers. He'll be saying more words soon. After that will come sentences. So beautiful when he's helpless with sleep, she'd like to sink down with him in the corner. Her body arcing toward him. She drags her fingers down his face. Then she stands and whispers things to Antoinette that Antoinette listens to — but as always with the two of them, their understanding goes beyond words, and now, past the promises Mavala's making, promises she insists on repeating.

Antoinette scrapes out the last of the butter from the tub, and nods. "I'll heat some milk," she says.

COFFEE FIRE

S he can act, that one."
    "Quite an exit."
"Oh, she'll be back."
"Of course, she'll be back."
"Where'd she go?"
"Windhoek. Where else is there to go?"
"No! Jo'burg. City of Gold! That's where the real money is. She'll be a real actress in Jo'burg. Forget Windhoek."
"She'll be back, I say."
"It's true, that girl can act."
"I thought she wanted to be an accountant."
"Still, it exhausts."
"What?"
"Leaving. Any leaving."
"Coming back's tiring also."
"That's true. But the boy."
"Yes, the boy."

MORNING MEETING

In morning meeting, the principal doesn't mention her. Moral tales come and go, and he doesn't once look at her empty space. She normally stands between Obadiah and Vilho. They leave a gap for her, whether as a reminder or a tribute, I don't know. The principal doesn't seem interested in taking anything out on me. One, because he knows I'd never say a word, and two, because if it is a game, which it is to him, then we've both lost.

Finally, after she's been gone eight school days — apparently some official level of delinquency — he distributes mimeograph copies of a typed letter. We stand there and sniff it. There's no moral tale this day. He's all bluster and business. He reads the letter to us.

Dear Deputy Minister Tjoruzumo:

I regret to inform you, Sir, of a vacancy effective immediately at the Don Bosco Primary School (Goas Farm RC), District Erongo.

Grade: Sub B

Reason for Vacancy: Teacher Mavala Shikongo abandoned her post May 5 of the current calendar year, without notice and without explanation. In addition, she left her son, Tomo (surname unknown), 2, at the mercy of the charity of the state.

Request: Please send a replacement teacher as soon as convenient.

If you have any further questions, please feel free to contact me at the below address.

Obediently yours,
Charles Komesho, Principal
Goas Primary School, RC
Private Bag 79
Karibib

Tuyeni stared straight ahead as he read it. Not a word. Although we believed she was the power behind him, she never tipped her hand either way. She was almost godlike in that way. And so, finally, difficult to hate. To hate Tuyeni took more imagination than any of us had. Maybe she got what she wanted. Maybe there can never be enough disgrace. The woman was impenetrable, hollow-eyed. Mavala's leaving left her no more numb than she'd always seemed. Morning meeting, staring at nothing.

"My wife is not the charity of the state," Obadiah says.

The principal swallows. Then he gently rubs his hands together, as if preparing to eat. "Her food is. Her house is. And now that I consider it, Head Teacher, her man is also."

"The boy's name is Shikongo, Master Sir."

"You're informing me, Head Teacher, of the name of my own bastard nephew?"

WALLS

He liked to think his love for her was a thing he kept pure. I was the degrader in this respect. He was proud of what he considered his refusal, how he didn't give chase. How he loved her from a distance. He was the untainted one.

Wall thumped by foot.

"Are you awake?"

"No."

"You should have left her alone."

"I should have left her alone? You're lecturing me on women? I can't even think of a good analogy. I should have left her alone. I'm asleep. We all should have left her alone. Everybody should have left her alone."

"There's no we in this instance."

"All right. I. I."

"What is she running from? That fat harmless?"

"I don't know."

"You never asked her?"

"Asked her what? I didn't know she was leaving."

"You think you're harmless?"

"I'm asleep."

"When are *you* leaving?"

"I don't know."

"Back to O-hi-o. Must be good. Blink your eyes and fly away. Whee!"

"You want to come to Ohio?"

"I want to go to Dallas."

"There's only one choice. Ohio."

"What did she want?"

"She said she didn't know."

"She didn't know?"

"That's what she said."

"Not you?"

"No."

"And why don't you chase her?"

"Chase her where?"

This seems to satisfy him. He farts as if to signal an end, a long, sad sigh of a fart, and I roll over to try to sleep. Moments later, he bops the wall again.

"What did you do out there in the veld?"

"Talked."

"That kind of talk's where she found Tomo. You're not harmless, comrade. None of us is."

139

TOMO

I found myself needing to be around him. I'd sit in Antoinette's garden and watch him destroy things. Wasn't he beautiful in that way?

One night during Sunday dinner at Antoinette's, over chicken, rice, and radishes from the garden, the subject of his presence in their house as opposed to the principal's was finally breeched. Antoinette and Obadiah usually waited until Sunday dinner to argue, and sometimes they invited spectators.

"Whatever else Tuyeni may be," Obadiah said, "the woman is the boy's aunt."

"Aunt," Antoinette piffed. "Aunt!"

"Under the law, she's next of kin. Lord knows, those two might accuse us of kidnapping."

"Kidnapping? They live up the road."

"The law says —"

"The law! Whose law? I will not give them the satisfaction of granting me permission."

"The fact of the matter is that we're not relatives. Now, in the old days, yes, this sort of thing happened all the time, but today we have . . ." He ran down of his own accord. We ate on in silence, to the noise of crunching radishes. I wondered: How can it be so loud in your own ears and the room so quiet?

140

WALLS

Well, son."
         "What?"
"I fucked her too."
"Go to hell."
"One night the man went a-knocking."
"Don't you get tired?"
"Of what, son?
"Lying like an asshole."
"Asshole or arsehole. Which is the correct pronunciation?"
"I'm through."
"It's a geographic variation," Vilho interjects. "The British say it one way, the Americans —"
"Through?"
"Listening to you."
"In any case, I believe 'anus' would be most correct."
"It was hot. Very hot. I couldn't sleep. She couldn't sleep. The woman said she wanted a real man, not a —"
"Not a what?"
"Notta notta notta. Sleep, son, sleep —"

141

ACROSS THE ROAD

We're walking the open veld on the other side of the C-32, south of Prinsloo's. A man named Schwicker used to farm here. A sun-faded, bullet-holed sign FARM SALE 18,000 HECTARES leans out of the ditch by the side of the road like an arm reaching up out of the grave. Obadiah said we needed new ground to cover, that we hadn't yet seen everything. The veld is just as flat out this way.

"What people don't know," Obadiah says, "but the cows do, is that so long as there's grass, something like grass, it's all right. This parch has more nutrients than the green stuff. But water — without water —"

"She's not coming back," I say.

"Funny. I've always thought of water as woman. You too?"

Then he stops and I stop. He places a mournful hand on my shoulder and says solemnly, "Jimmy Carter."

"What about him?"

"Blame him."

"For what?"

"Optimism."

"Can we just walk? Not say anything, just walk?"

He sniffs. He takes off his glasses, pinches his nose, puts his glasses back on, gazes east, west.

"You see, Carter was the only one of your presidents who had a nimble enough mind to see we weren't Communists in the truest sense. There were some real ones. Joe Slovo, perhaps. Chris Hani. But for the most part, it was always a question of playing Commie because at that time it didn't quite matter."

"Please —"

"Because the fight was the only thing. And that takes money. Independence would come and it would all be solved. With Jimmy Carter, through the black man at the United Nations, Andrew Young — there was hope. But hope. One pays dear for it. Next came your movie star. The war went on another decade. Then, when the fighting was finally over, Sam Nujoma said, 'Commie? Who me?' Because by then the money was coming from somewhere else. See? Easy?"

"But —"

"Of course there were people who believed in it! Your Mavala being one — and it was, wasn't it, a beautiful thing? Houses, jobs. Food enough for all? How does one argue with this? Where's the dear man now?"

"Who?"

"Andrew Young!"

"I don't know."

"Faded away did he?"

"How should I know?"

"A man like Andrew Young and you don't know?"

I stop. He walks on ahead. An old man banging away and banging away and banging away. When I leave this place, this old man will still be banging away. I turn around and walk faster, head for the road. He starts hollering.

"You think there's honor in inconsolable? Over a girl in a skirt? You think that's devastation?"

I'm on the road. The gravel stretches across the veld like a long tongue. I shout back, "I didn't say. I only —"

He stands on a koppie, a lonely tree of a man against the sky. "And Andrew Young? You think it's a joke. How many people would be alive today if anybody listened to him? Families intact? Glorious futures? And that blameless girl would have stayed home in her village with her mother."

142

SIESTA

Siesta and my eyes feel like they've been torn open. I knock on the wall. I knock on it again, again. "Wake the fuck up."

"May I help you?"

"Fok jou mama se poes."

"Hey! That's not bad. But with *poes,* you want to drag it out, like this: *Pooooooes.*"

"She had a birthmark."

"Where?"

"Fuck off."

"Have you so little faith?"

"She once said, Don't be jealous."

"Of who?"

"She didn't say."

"Now, that is romantic. He's probably dead. Aren't all the heroes dead?" He calls to Vilho. "Pious one!"

"Yes?"

"We've found our martyr."

"Who?"

"Tomo's daddy."

"What about his mother?" I ask.

"It's too early to tell."

"Bless them both," Vilho says.

"And Kaplansk?" Pohamba says.

"Why not?"

143

OBADIAH (3 A.M.)

In 1897, rinderpest wiped out three quarters of the cattle in the country. The disease was followed by drought. Next came, for the human beings, hunger. Those who had been baptized gave up on God, but those who hadn't besieged the mission stations on their knees. *Give us food. Give us Christianity.* In such a year, when even the missions had so little, belief was easier to dollop than porridge. And so the missionaries said, Here's Christ.

In the morning, they counted saved souls in corpses.

Absolve me, Love. Do you think I enjoy repeating such things, even to myself? But can a man *un*read himself blind? Can he close these books and live? Don't answer this. I know you hear me. Don't answer.

144

ANTOINETTE

Less each word than the cumulative weight of them. At the sink holding the one true book in her hand. With her other hand, she digs crud out of the drain. The boy is out back, stalking a hungry whelp. Unnoticing now. Tonight he will remember and wail. He'll reject my arms.

It is not that I don't understand. If she had a Jerusalem, it was somewhere far from here, and she had to go alone. What cost to me to raise another? But forgive a woman a thought: Would she have left behind a daughter?

145

PRINSLOO'S WIFE

They shot Sampie Prinsloo. The papers said they raped his wife, but let her live. The Afrikaans paper, *The Republikein*, screamed that it was an epidemic, that this was what democracy was going to look like. Yet the truth was that, as Pohamba said, farmers had always been murdered. You lit your own death in the veld every time you turned on a lamp at night. The price of land bought so cheaply, so to speak. Dogs and the electric fences could do only so much. Farmers at the Rossman Hotel in Karibib would often laugh about their dates with destiny.

We wondered where we'd get our vegetables.

A week or so after it happened, Prinsloo's bakkie pulled up to the cattle gate. We were all in class. There was no horn, but no motorized vehicle could get within a half kilometer of Goas without making news. When we saw whose bakkie it was, nobody knew exactly what to do. The boys didn't run for it. They walked slowly, curious. So clever, those whites. A man dies and still his ghost has transport.

It was his wife. No one had known her. She was only that woman who never got out of the bakkie, who watched us from behind the glass. But now she had no choice. She got out of the bakkie and put the free box of withered carrots on the ground and motioned for the boys to take what they wanted. She wasn't going to toss them in the air. We looked over what she'd brought. Not much. A few peppers, an undersized pumpkin. Those bostostos must have had their fill of produce as well. She spoke a halting English. We didn't offer condolences. Standing up, she was taller than we expected, and her face was blanched too white, as if even the Erongo sun had given up trying to redden it. She didn't look stunned by grief. What would it have looked like if she had been? We watched her, lingered over her slim pickings. We gave her more than any of it was worth.

Then she stooped and picked up the free box, tossed it in the back, and nodded to us. She was about to drive away when Antoinette, who'd bought the single sad pumpkin and was now cradling it in her left arm like another child (Tomo was in her right), went up to the driver's side window and knocked on it. Prinsloo's wife didn't roll the window down. She was a Boer farmer's wife and wasn't used to taking orders from any native grootma. Antoinette in her plastic Pep Boy Shop sandals, her starchy clean dress, her head wrapped in a scarf, pumpkin in one arm, child in the other. And her face like a fist she'd smash the window with. She demanded so much from people. Buck up. Be better, be stronger. Rise above.

Had she still been on the farm then, Mavala might have said that nothing happened. That Prinsloo's wife was broken when she pulled up in the bakkie and broken when she drove away. That all she was doing was selling the last of her vegetables. Nothing happened when those two women looked at each other. Nothing.

But she wasn't there. She'd left us by then. So I'm going to see it, remember it, differently.

Antoinette knocked on the window and eyed that woman, and it wasn't strength she gave, but something smaller. Maybe it was only recognition. What happened to you, what happened to you.

MAGNUS AXAHOES

His desk is empty now. The only one besides Mavala who leaves and stays gone. I don't report him missing. Nobody notices other than the boys and me, because I am his teacher. Antoinette has her hands full these days with Tomo and with end-of-the-term cleaning. She hasn't done a roll call in weeks. One day Magnus's father comes up to the school asking for him.

No phone to call, so I came here to see him myself. You see, his mother passed this year and I worry over the boy.

The principal doesn't stand up. Magnus Axahoes's father standing there in his blue jumper isn't anybody he has to get up out of his chair for. "These farm boys run away all the time," the principal says. "What can I do? Alert the constable every time?"

DROUGHT STORIES

The oldest and weakest cattle began dying in the middle of June. Our only rain had been that single storm. Dikeledi in the rain, and now nothing. Everybody said it was never a surprise. How could it be a surprise? Still, it was odd how you went along, the days opening, the days closing, and then one afternoon it was as if the grass got a crack more brittle and you knew. You knew the worst wasn't coming tomorrow, it was here. Everybody knows when a drought ends, but when does it begin? The cows went from quietly starving to actually dying, and Theofilus had to go to Karibib for fodder to keep them alive another day. He couldn't water them fast enough.

We voyeurs wanted to watch their suffering up close. Their bulging eyes, their slowly whirling pupils. I had always thought cows have sad eyes. The one thing I know now is that this is conceit. That their eyes hold some sort of sorrow seems beside the point. They died with them open.

Out of mercy, Theofilus shoots a few of them that are no longer able to stand. Their meat's all gone, but still he wants to save them the indignity of having their carcasses picked clean by the already circling, murderously patient vultures. How do they smell death before it even happens? We go out there with some boys and watch. Small bonfires light the veld. Petrol and smoke line our nostrils. The cows burn down to bone.

SINGLES QUARTERS

Morning meeting in eight minutes. Vilho gongs a pot to make certain, because aren't there too many days now we sleep through the third triangle? Pohamba's waking coughs, his cursing the universe that made Vilho's mother, the foundry that made the pot, the God who gave us dreams and then wrenched them away from us for fucking morning meeting. Rarer times, I beat the first triangle. On my knees, in the chill, watching out my torn screen the blue as it rises above the shoulders of the mountains.

THE B-1 SOUTH

She was pretty, a little nasty-mouthed, but pretty. Tall, with a bullet-looking head. Standing west of Karibib with a suitcase. She didn't wing her arm out when I drove by. Waiting on something better. They're always waiting on something better while I work. But I stopped anyway, and she walked up, and I leaned over and opened the door. She didn't say anything and didn't get in. I didn't say anything either. What would I? I leaned over to close the door. You're getting in, you're not getting in. What difference does it make to me? She put her hand on the door, and my eyes said to her, In or out? Her hand on the door like I'm the one in the road begging a lift. Where are you going? she said. I pointed up the road. How far? she said. I have to answer questions? Upington, I said. Tonight. Her hand was still on the edge of the door. All right, she said. She hoisted her suitcase and expected me to take it. I let the thing stand there in the air above the seat. She put it down on the seat and climbed up. I jerked my thumb. There's room for it in the back, and she, with her knees on the seat, lifted it and put it back there. Then she sat with her hands folded like a nun. She wasn't a nun. She looked straight ahead out the windscreen. I don't play the radio. I like to think when I drive. Thirty, forty kilometers, she didn't say a word. Up and over the hills and straight up to the checkpoint before Windhoek. At the checkpoint she didn't take out her card and they didn't ask her to. That's how it is now. Six times in a route now I show my card. The other day they fined me two hundred rand for my tires. Cop measured my treads with a ruler and said I was in violation. Straight past Windhoek on the underway, and she's so still it doesn't look like she's breathing. Maybe she thought if she breathed she'd be giving me something. I got used to it. I feel her there and don't feel her, and listen for her breathing and don't hear it. I do the three hundred k's to Mariental, where I stop for petrol. When I get back in the cab, there's thirty rand on my seat. I look at it awhile and then get in and sit on it. She doesn't say anything, but I see her breathe. Outside Horncranz, I ask her if she has a name, and without taking her eyes off the glass or moving her nasty little mouth, she says she does. Outside Gibeon, I said, Do you ever tell people what it is? and then she did tilt her head and she did look straight at me. And all right, I want to touch her, not grab her, just touch her. And I look at her and she knows it. Stop, she says. Here? A flat stretch of tarmac south of Keetmans, at least two hundred more k to the border. Nothing, no dorp for sixty, seventy k in either direction. An hour to dark. You want to get out here?

Here.

The Russian loves recalling life,
but he does not love living.

— CHEKHOV

150

GOAS

Kaplansk,

Excuse a long silence. We haven't forsaken you. Your letters have not gone unread, only unanswered. Is there a word for letters like these? Not dead letters. Mutters on the wind? We've heard you, is what I'm trying to say. Don't fear. We do think it's high time for you to leave Cincinnati and see the world. Did you see so much of it the last time you ventured forth? Why don't you at least cross the river and visit Kentucky?

Of this plague you refer to, my Antoinette merely says, Who are we to question His will? Then, of course, she deliberately, and with all her remaining strength, tries to thwart that very will. Often she rides into town with the priest and feeds the sick. I myself read the newspapers and wring my hands, weep, but open a can of beans and feed the sick? Never. What sort of man does this make me?

Our Tomo continues to be a hellion, but a kind one. He even writes poetry now, though I confess it is not of the sort that moves me. Teacher Pohamba has taken it upon himself to be another father to him. This has yielded, as you might expect, mixed results. The boy no longer seems to remember his mother, which I suppose is natural.

Everyone greets you.

One of these days expect a treatise on the practical uses of lamentation. I am preparing an anthology you may find interesting.

Affectionately,
O. Horaseb

151

CINCINNATI PUBLIC

When I run out of remembering, I sit here and read. I read haphazardly, finish nothing, collect much. I like this library. There's a lot of light. It's mostly quiet, with the exception of the guy who snores the liquidy snores. I'm talking about the Cincinnati Public, downtown branch, second floor, near the periodicals, the room with the puffy chairs.

I've come across another story of walking. I've found it in a footnote. It's 1919 and the dawn of a new era. A group of men are hired to work in the diamond fields on the coast. They are not slaves; they are contract laborers. It's only that the contract says they're not free until their employer signs a paper. They work sixteen hours a day in the sand and wind. One night, one of the men makes a calculation that they can make it to a mining town called Rosh Pinah after only a day and a half of walking. All we have to do is follow the dry river. Who's with me?

Everybody was with him.

Mavala would laugh at this, if not with her mouth, at least with her shoulders. Her silent laugh like a tremor. You'd have to watch her closely to see it. Not laughing at the men as men, but at their notion of how easy it would be. All we have to do is . . .

No heroes. The men wander eight days. There was no Rosh Pinah, at least not at the end of that dry river. Those who survived were recaptured and sent back to the diamond fields in chains.

My snorer gently wakes. He rubs his forehead with the back of his hand and squints into the light.

152

MAVALA

Antoinette thinks of her. She thinks of her in a crowded room in a place unknown but familiar. She thinks of her wanting to speak and how difficult that must be because it isn't the kilometers or even the years that create distance, it's silence.

Antoinette, I want you to under stand that I
Antoinette, I only want to explain to you
Why are there so many words in my head and none on the page? There is only the noise outside this window, the shouting that never ends, all this clashing music. Do I need to tell you this is not a room for a child, my child?
May I still call him that?

It is not for me to say.

153

ON THE MOLE AT SWAKOPMUND

They watch the sun flatten into the Atlantic. Soon the light so powerful for so long will be nothing but a smear on the horizon. The white-capped southwest rollers wrinkle toward them and pound the rocks at their feet. Above swoon the terrible gulls. Obadiah spits happily into the water. He said they needed to show Tomo the ocean, *his* ocean. The two of them in topcoats over their best clothes, on the mole at Swakopmund. Behind them murmur tourists toasting the sunset.

"Before the Germans built this," Obadiah says, "they dropped horses off the sides of the ships."

"Why?"

"To swim in the chattel."

"Chattel?"

"The merchandize."

"Did the horses make it?"

"Sometimes."

"Some drowned."

"Of course."

She looks north, at the stretch of beach, at Tomo. Now that he's built his palace of sand, he stomps it. Then he calls out to them — his ouma and oupa — on the mole: "PAY ATTENTION PEOPLE!" He sprints into the water and dives into the waves. She waits for Tomo's head to bob up before she breathes.

Obadiah nudges her, points at the sun, at the last slit of light drawn across the edge of the water.

"Cold?"

"Not so much."

She leans against him as the wind flaps their topcoats.

GRAVES

I'm losing her face. I remember more her hands, which were not small, and how they once took my feet hostage and rubbed them while I swore at her. Her eyebrows were thorny. I think of her lips and how parched they were, and her voice that got huskier when she was thirsty. I'd try to keep the water away from her so she'd talk that way longer. Her voice alone, I tell you, could slow an afternoon.

HOSTEL (NIGHT)

The boys are flailing up and down on their beds. Some nights the pillow wars go on for hours. That long a battle can get bloody, especially with foam pillows hardened by years of sweaty heads. The lights stay on all night in the hall that separates the two dorms. Antoinette enters through the far door and walks the hall, peeks in the west dorm and then the east dorm. Her shadow reaches, reaches across the beds. The quiet is immediate. Only their heartbeats are loud. Tiny squeaks of the bedsprings, like dying mice, their bodies tense — waiting, praying for the shadow's retreat.

Other nights she prowls around outside, watches the chaos through the little windows, lets them carry on as if she's curious to see what a world without her looks like.

In memory of Anna Nugolo, Anna Kanjimbi, and Freddy Khairabeb.

Namibia:
Colonized by Germany in 1884 and known as *Deutsch-Südwest-afrika*. After the defeat of the Germans during World War I, the name was changed to South-West Africa and the country was governed by South Africa under a mandate issued by the League of Nations. The mandate was abolished by the United Nations General Assembly in 1966. South Africa remained in power, claiming that the UN had no authority to rescind the mandate, and continued to govern the territory as a virtual fifth province. Apartheid was officially implemented in 1977. In 1988, after two decades of war between SWAPO and South Africa, a UN-sponsored cease-fire ended the conflict. Namibia became independent in 1990.

SWAPO:
Southwest Africa People's Organization, liberation organization formed in 1960 to fight South African rule. After winning the 1989 elections, SWAPO became the governing party in independent Namibia.

PLAN:
People's Liberation Army of Namibia, military wing of SWAPO.

SADF:
South African Defense Force, name of the South African military force that fought SWAPO.

The Struggle:
Commonly used in Namibia to describe the long war between SWAPO and the SADF. Much of the war was fought along the more densely populated border Namibia shares with Angola. SWAPO had established bases in Angola. No accurate death toll numbers exist. Conservative estimates reach 25,000 combat casualties.

DTA:
Democratic Turnhalle Alliance, opposition party in independent Namibia. Prior to independence, DTA was associated with the ruling white regime.

Cassinga:
On May 4, 1978, South African planes bombed a SWAPO base deep in Angola, killing an estimated seven hundred people, among them hundreds of civilian refugees.

Angolan Civil War:
A chaotic civil war broke out in Angola after the Portuguese withdrawal in 1975. Among those fighting were the MPLA, supported by Cuba and the Soviet Union, and Jonas Savimbi's UNITA (National Union for the Total Independence of Angola), supported by South Africa and the United States. SWAPO was aligned with the MPLA and also received support from the Soviet Union as well as China. Hence, both wars, in Angola and Namibia, took on elements of a proxy Cold War. The war in Angola ended in 2002.

CDM:
Consolidated Diamond Mines, mining company located along the southern coast, a subsidiary of the DeBeers Corporation.

Zorba:
A fine whiskey with a smooth licorice finish.

ACKNOWLEDGMENTS

I would like to thank the following for their time and immeasurable support over the course of many years: In Namibia, the Khairabeb, Guidaooab, and Brandt families, and in the United States, Pat Strachan, Ellen Levine, Eric Orner, Robert Preskill, David Krause, Melissa Kirsch, and Rhoda Kaplan Pierce. Further, I would like to thank Giorgio Miescher and the staff at the Namibian Resource Center (of the Basler Afrika Bibliographien) in Basel, Switzerland. I am also grateful to the American Academy of Arts and Letters and the American Academy in Rome for a generous fellowship. Finally, thanks to Dantia Maur MacDonald, without whom this book and so much else would not exist.

ABOUT THE AUTHOR

Peter Orner's stories have appeared in many periodicals, including the *Atlantic Monthly, McSweeney's,* and *Bomb,* as well as in *The Best American Short Stories 2001* and *The Pushcart Prize XXV.* Some are collected in his first book, *Esther Stories,* which received the Rome Prize from the American Academy of Arts and Letters. *The Second Coming of Mavala Shikongo* received the Bard Fiction Prize for 2007 and was a finalist for the Mercantile Library's John Sargent Sr. First Novel Prize. Orner received 2006 Guggenheim and Lannan Foundation fellowships. He has lived in Namibia and currently teaches at San Francisco State University. *The Second Coming of Mavala Shikongo* is his first novel.

READING GROUP GUIDE

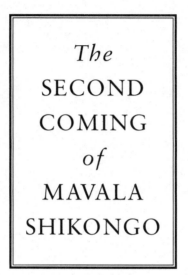

The
SECOND
COMING
of
MAVALA
SHIKONGO

A novel by
Peter Orner

A CONVERSATION WITH PETER ORNER

In The Second Coming of Mavala Shikongo, *Larry Kaplanski from Cincinnati has moved to Namibia to become a teacher. You, too, were raised in the Midwest and taught in Namibia. How much of the novel is based on your own experience?*

Kaplanski's life in Namibia was a lot more eventful than my own. But it is true that, like him, I'm a Jew from the Midwest who found himself confused in the desert veld of Namibia. And I'm definitely as much an awkward goofball in real life. I lived there in the early 1990s, just after the country became independent. It happened that Namibia got under my skin, way under my skin, and I carried memories of the place around with me for years until the desert farm where I lived (itself a strange thing) became more mythical than actual. I couldn't shake those days, and so I had to try and write about them. What came out, though, as so often happens, is experience totally reimagined.

While I identify with Kaplanski (or Kaplansk, as he comes to be called in the novel), I would say that the character I feel closest to in the book is Obadiah. He's someone who may be outgoing in public but broods when he's alone. Obadiah gives voice to the things I might actually think. His obsession with history is also a lot like my own. I'll also add here that the character of Mavala is roughly based on two women teachers I knew, both of whom were veterans of the war against South Africa. Both were reluctant to talk about it, unlike the men I knew, who always wanted to talk about it.

In terms of setting and character development, The Second Coming of Mavala Shikongo *is quite a departure from your first book, the story collection* Esther Stories. *On the other hand, the short, sharply focused chapters of the novel are not unlike short stories themselves. When you started to write* The Second Coming of Mavala Shikongo, *were you expecting to write a novel, a story cycle, or something else?*

My expectation was, God help me! I didn't know what the book was going to be. I only knew that there was something about Namibia and the people I encountered there that I wanted to say. I also knew I wanted it to be a kind of love story, an ultimately sad one. A story about memory and what gets lost. I showed a few pieces of the book early on to Andre Dubus, who liked them and sent them to *Epoch* magazine, which published them. That was in 1995. I kept working on the book, even while I was writing the stories in *Esther Stories*. I do like concision, and I think this is a characteristic of my work. I read a lot of poetry and envy the wallop poets can pack in a few words. I try to emulate this sometimes. And yet I love Dickens and Melville, so I'm not sure what this means.

Your career has been varied, and you've lived in many different parts of the world. What led you from a law degree at Northeastern University to an MFA at the Iowa Writers' Workshop?

I do like to wander around. I'm in Chiapas now, which is fascinating but very cold at the moment. I'm training to be a human-rights observer — which basically means when the army comes to harass people, you take notes and stand clear. They have problems down here with the Mexican army and their associates, the paramilitaries, comically named Peace and Justice.

I went to law school, originally, because I wanted to be a criminal defense attorney. During stints away from law school I worked in the prison system in North Carolina (investigating prisoner complaints) and also in the juvenile division of the public defender's office in Boston, representing juvenile defendants. Both jobs were great introductions to the criminal-justice system in the U.S., and I learned an incredible amount about how we treat our own people.

These experiences often crop up in various ways in my work. But after three years, it became pretty clear that writing was going to take precedence. I was starting to publish and spending more and more of my time working on fiction. Teaching law, though, as I've done in the past, has allowed me to remain working in the law without the pressure of day-to-day practice. It has also allowed me to live in various parts of the world, and I'm grateful for this.

Although you teach in the MFA program at San Francisco State, you haven't given up law. Discuss your work as a volunteer attorney for the Lawyers' Committee for Civil Rights.

As I say, although I don't practice law, I do remain very interested in it. We think of law as an abstraction sometimes, but I have always been fascinated (and often repulsed) by its impact on people, especially those who can't afford decent representation. In order to try and get more involved, I worked last year as a volunteer attorney at an organization in San Francisco that represents asylum seekers before the immigration court. Sorry to say I lost my first case — one involving a young man from Guatemala who'd been tortured. Unfortunately, the immigration judge didn't see his being tortured — for years — as rising to the level of persecution. The case is currently on appeal, and we are still waiting for the decision.

The characters in The Second Coming of Mavala Shikongo *narrate the novel through the stories they tell about life on the veld, with little additional narration or description. And yet, through this minimal structure, you are able to draw such a vivid picture. Why did the material demand this unusual style?*

I appreciate the question. As my beloved editor, Pat Strachan, knows well, it took me a long time to figure out what I was doing. I started working on the book around 1993. I don't like to write about a place unless I feel that I know it backward and forward. And though I spent nearly a year and a half in Namibia, it still wasn't my place. So I spent a lot of time reading everything I could get my hands on about Namibia. I read a ton of history as well as great African writers like Bessie Head, Dambudzo Marechera, Wole Soyinka, Camara Laye, Can Themba, Herman Charles Bosman, Ezekiel Mphahlele, and Richard Rive. I loathe novels and travel books that go out of their way to announce "I know this exotic place and you don't." You know what I mean? I wanted this book to feel familiar to readers, whether they were born in Des Moines or Usakos, Namibia. And I think this should always be the case. I've found that certain aspects of love, politics, gossip (especially gossip) don't change a lick when you cross borders. The same basic concerns prevail. Tip O'Neill's phrase "all politics is local" applies also to fiction — all literature is local. Love goes wrong. The government lets you down. You gossip about your neighbor — a lot. And are there any truly exotic places? I think you'd have to find a place that wasn't inhabited by actual people for it to be exotic. Maybe parts of the Arctic?

I did, though, feel a need to return to Namibia because I love it there. And over the course of years, I went back as much and as often as I could afford to. I needed to feel the place again to finish the book. I also wanted to observe firsthand how the country was changing as the euphoria of independence began to wear off. While back in Namibia, I interviewed old friends and war veterans, and spent much time in the extensive national archives to research the colonial years, as well as the long decades of South African occupation. As for the shape of the book — I came to it while thinking about those long desert days when I lived there. So often we passed the time through stories. Laughter helps a day go by faster. And so I eventually came to the point where the shape of the book took on the shape of those days, blending together, one after another after another.

How has Namibia changed in the years since independence?

The terrible story over the past decade has been AIDS. Like all of southern Africa, Namibia was hit hard and infection rates are incredibly high. Advanced drugs remain expensive and difficult to come by. When I lived there, AIDS existed but was nothing like it is now. The good news has been that the country has been at peace. The president, Sam Nujoma, voluntarily stepped down after fifteen years in power. But peace has come with a cost, I think, and this has to do with the fact that, unlike South Africa, Namibia never had a public accounting of its apartheid past. The country has been content with a policy of national reconciliation. In other words, silence. A good thing in some ways maybe, but this silence has also caused many stories and much pain to be swept under the rug. Although *The Second Coming of Mavala Shikongo* is about one small place and its people, I've also tried to tell some of the stories I collected over the years.

What works of art and what other writers have inspired you and shaped your journey as a novelist?

For a number of years, before his too-early death, I was close to Andre Dubus. Andre ran a workshop out of his house after a car accident left him without the use of his legs. It was four years of education — every Thursday night — with one of our great writers, and I feel lucky and privileged to have known him as long as I did. His work continues to sustain me. There's no end to what you can find in his stories. And it was Andre who gave me the courage to give up law and try to make a life this way. Not that he ever said it would be easy. It was never easy for him.

The same goes for Marilynne Robinson, with whom I worked at Iowa and who remains an important and constant source of inspiration. I could go on for days on this question, but I'll say that two writers I never stop rereading are Isaac Babel and Franz Kafka.

Kafka somewhere wrote something like: "In the bathroom mirror, I'm an orphan." I've never forgotten this. It's something of a guide for me. That in some senses, we're always alone. I confess that Obadiah says something like this in the book. I should have credited Kafka.

And the one book I always have close is Babel's *1920 Diary*, which he used to create his remarkable Red Cavalry stories. I've had to tape my copy back together a few times. In it he makes little notes to himself like, "Don't forget to remember Konstantinovich's red hair." Babel reminds me to pay attention to everything.

Can you share anything about your writing process, perhaps something you tell your students to inspire them?

I'm very slow. I write by hand, usually in the morning, and usually till my hand cramps up. This is another reason I tend to write short. I'm also, unfortunately, an obsessive rewriter and sometimes spend days on the same one or two lines. I wish I could cure myself of this and write something like *Shogun*. Just for fun.

What's your favorite part of the writing experience? How do you manage to balance your writing with your teaching career? Do the two conflict with or nourish each other?

There are rare mornings when I literally lose time — when I look up and see that I've been sitting there for hours without knowing it — those days are the best. I enjoy teaching. It keeps me honest. I have many wonderful students, who as a general rule are a lot smarter than I am. They inspire and push me. The rest of the time, I'm free to brood on my own.

QUESTIONS AND TOPICS FOR DISCUSSION

1. Larry Kaplanski introduces you to a community of Namibians in a remote region of the country. Were you comfortable with this? Did you think the gulf between cultures was narrowed by Kaplanski's (and Peter Orner's) powers of empathy? What other books about Africa by outsiders have you read, and how does *The Second Coming of Mavala Shikongo* differ from them?

2. Although Kaplanski is the principal narrator of the book, the shift often focuses to the points of views of other characters. As the *San Francisco Chronicle* put it, the novel becomes "a kind of living village." Assess the success or failure of the novel's shifting points of view.

3. *The Second Coming of Mavala Shikongo* has been called an unusually structured novel. Do you think the novel's disparate pieces come together successfully? Does the economy of Peter Orner's prose influence your opinion?

4. How is Antoinette, Obadiah's wife and the school's dorm mother, different in the eyes of the male teachers from Festus's wife, Dikeledi, or even Mavala herself? Do they see a caretaker as superior to a lover? How, in the end, is a world without its Antoinettes imagined?

5. How does Theofilus's beating the donkey that won't take him to his wife — who lives far away, on another farm — mirror the lonely frustration of his more well-educated colleagues? Did you forgive him his atypical burst of violence?

6. The local butcher and neighboring farmer are both of German, or Boer, extraction. How does their attitude toward the residents of Goas speak to a still-simmering racial divide? Consider that Namibia was a nation that endured decades of apartheid.

7. Were you surprised when Mavala made an overture to Kaplanski during morning meeting? Or did you think her boldness in character for a former warrior?

8. Mavala and Kaplanski conduct their affair on the graves of Boer settlers. How does this underline the history of the region and its previous racial divide? Does the location of their meetings signal a doomed relationship from the start, or do you think hope remains, in spite of the book's ultimate conclusion?

9. How does the school's hierarchy remind you of the hierarchies of groups you belong to? Does the powerful principal merit his position over the teachers? Note the scene on page 140, where the principal says of a drunk Obadiah, "This is the Head Teacher with whom I am to build a new nation out of the ashes of war?" Is the principal the sort of man to lead a newly independent Namibia?

10. Goas is a place that becomes an unlikely haven for characters in the novel, including three children who are fleeing violence in their home country of Angola (chapter 90). What is it about Goas that makes it such a strangely welcoming place?

11. Do you think spending significant time alone in an entirely unfamiliar place and culture would have a major, lasting effect on the way you think about your place in the world? What impact do you think Kaplanski's experiences in Namibia will have on his future?

PETER ORNER'S SUGGESTIONS
FOR FURTHER READING

Becoming Abigail by Chris Abani

A harrowing novella about a Nigerian teenager brought to London by relatives who then try to force her into prostitution. An honest look at what African women — and women the world over — so often must endure. Not for the fainthearted, this extremely painful book is ultimately redemptive.

The Purple Violet of Oshaantu by Neshani Andreas

A recent Namibian novel. The story of an unhappy marriage that results in the death of an abusive husband. More than this, however, the book is a chronicle of an enduring friendship against very strong odds. Andreas, a former teacher, is the first Namibian to be published in the African Writers Series.

Life and Times of Michael K. by J. M. Coetzee

Among Coetzee's most moving books. An aching and humane account of the wanderings of Michael K., a former gardener for the city of Cape Town, during a not-so-mythical civil war.

Blood Knot by Athol Fugard

A play about two brothers — one light-skinned, the other black — living together in a one-room shack in Port Elizabeth, South Africa. An early but great work of Fugard's. The humor of the play belies the grim prospects of the brothers under apartheid.

Scribbling the Cat by Alexandra Fuller

A brutal examination of the effects of war on the psyche. Ostensibly the book is a nonfiction account of a trip to Mozambique with a white former soldier, but it is more about one man's battle with memories that will always lurk, no matter how many times he reinvents himself.

My Son's Story by Nadine Gordimer

A novel about the personal costs of politics. The book revolves around the lives of a schoolteacher turned resistance movement leader, his son, and the white activist with whom the father has an intense affair.

Collector of Treasures by Bessie Head

A book about village life in Botswana. Head was born in South Africa but lived much of her life in exile in Botswana in a village similar to the one described — from so many angles — in this seminal story collection.

The Radiance of the King by Camara Laye

This odd and beautiful novel, published in 1954, is a masterpiece of French African literature. Laye, a Guinean, is often compared to Kafka. This book is about a shipwrecked white man who is sold — without his even realizing it — into slavery.

The House of Hunger by Dambudzo Marechera

A harrowing series of stories set in war-ravaged Zimbabwe. The violence of Marechera's essential book is not confined to the physical — the true terror here is the violence that is inflicted on one's mind by racism, war, and homelessness. Of the post-independence government of Zimbabwe, Marechera said, "It is the same old ox and wagon story with the rich getting richer and the poor getting poorer." He died, destitute, at thirty-five in 1987.

Down Second Avenue by Ezekiel Mphahlele

A memoir by the eminent South African man of letters. A journalist, essayist, short story writer, and novelist, Mphahlele has written some of the most important criticism of African literature. He lived in exile in both Nigeria and the U.S., where he taught English for many years at the University of Denver. This classic book about growing up under (and subsequently out of) apartheid in the 1940s is unsurpassed in its descriptions and moral power.

Buckingham Palace, District Six by Richard Rive

An often hilarious but ultimately devastating novel about the destruction via bulldozer of District Six, an area of Cape Town famous for the diversity (and colorful exploits) of its inhabitants. Sadly, Rive, one of South Africa's most talented story writers and novelists, was murdered in 1989.

Ìsarà: A Voyage Around "Essay" by Wole Soyinka

A sequel to Soyinka's *Aké: The Years of Childhood,* this memoir is a re-creation of the life of the author's schoolteacher father, Essay, and is set in Nigeria, under colonial rule. Essay — a voracious reader with an insatiable curiosity about all things philosophical — was an important inspiration for my character Obadiah Horaseb.